Arab Jazz

Arab Jazz

KARIM MISKÉ

Translated from the French by Sam Gordon

MacLehose Press
New York • London

MacLehose Press
An imprint of Quercus
New York • London

First published in the French language as *Arab Jazz* by Éditions Viviane Hamy in 2012

Copyright © Éditions Viviane Hamy, 2012
English translation copyright © 2015 by Sam Gordon
First published in the United States by Quercus in 2016

This book is supported by the Institut français (Royaume-Uni) as part of the Burgess program.

This book has been selected to receive financial assistance from English PEN's *PEN Promotes!* program. English PEN exists to promote literature and our understanding of it, to uphold writers' freedoms around the world, to campaign against the persecution and imprisonment of writers for stating their views, and to promote the friendly cooperation of writers and the free exchange of ideas. www.englishpen.org

ISBN 978-1-68144-614-1

Library of Congress Control Number: 2015956915

Distributed in the United States and Canada by
Hachette Book Group
1290 Avenue of the Americas
New York, NY 10104

Manufactured in the United States

10 9 8 7 6 5 4 3 2 1

www.quercus.com

Tu parl'ras moins avec un Glock dans la bouche.

Booba

(You'll talk less with a Glock in your mouth.)

1

Ahmed is looking at the clouds in the sky, the clouds, the wondrous clouds, floating up there.

Ahmed loves poetry, even if his memory of it consists of fleeting snippets that bubble occasionally to the surface of his soul. Lines often return of their own accord, without author or title. This one brings back Baudelaire: something about a stranger, freedom, something English. Baudelaire was his favorite writer back in the day, along with Van Gogh and Artaud. Debord followed later. And then he stopped reading. Well, almost. Nowadays—when he goes downstairs, at least—he buys *Le Parisien*. And stacks of translated English-language pulp thrillers: Connelly, Cornwell, Coben. The names swirl around his head so much he gets the feeling he is reading one and the same novel, with the odd exception. And that's what he wants. To lose himself by devouring the whole world in a single, uninterrupted story written by others.

He gets his fix from the second-hand bookshop on rue Petit, a tiny store from a different age that has miraculously survived between the Lubavitch school complex, the Salafist prayer room, and the evangelical church. Possibly because Monsieur Paul, the old Armenian anarchist who runs it, does not fall into any of the categories of luminary now holed up in the neighborhood. And because he sells his irreverent literature by the pound, which makes him seem more like a grocer than a dealer of Satanic texts. From time to time, the bookseller chucks in an extra copy without mentioning it. Ellroy, Tosches, an unpublished Manchette. Ahmed blinks very slightly. He is grateful to his dealer for not letting him go completely under. These authors he remembers.

He hasn't gone downstairs today. There are still a few bits in the fridge: a baguette; some ham tortellini; a salmon and spinach quiche; enough butter for three bread *tartines*; some leftover strawberry jam made by Laura, his neighbor upstairs, a girl he might have loved if he still knew how; a pack of Evian; a bar of hazelnut Ivoria dark chocolate; five Tsingtao beers (twenty-two ounces); a half-bottle of William Lawson (twenty-five ounces); three bottles of wine (red, rosé, sweet Monbazillac); and three cans of Almaza alcohol-free beer cowardly left behind by his cousin Mohamed before he took off for Bordeaux eight months earlier. Not forgetting a packet of Tuc crackers, the remains of a *saucisse sèche*, two thirds of a Valençay cheese, two cups of skim milk, and a few crumbs of Leader Price muesli. Plus, of course, the obligatory box of Gunpowder green tea and some Malongo filter coffee. Just enough to keep him going until he has polished off the eight pounds of books he bought from Monsieur Paul the day before.

Ahmed is dreaming right now. He is watching the wondrous midafternoon clouds and he is dreaming. His mind is drifting away from the neighborhood where his life has stood still for five years. The detachment he longs for is fast approaching. Watch the clouds, read, sleep, and drink once evening has fallen. Little by little he has managed to distance himself from television, from screens. He knows very well that books have colonized his thoughts, but still he needs them. It is too soon for Ahmed to face his demons alone. Other people's horrors, other people's sick imaginations allow him to live with the monsters crouching in the back of his head.

Slowly his mind takes off, soaring toward the far-off lands of his ancestors. The impossible source. The outbound journey is direct, free of obstacles. Six miles up and he strains to see fields, mountains, water, rocks, and finally sand. A hundred dunes into the desert, he begins his descent toward the great blue erg. All of a sudden he sees camel-skin tents, men, beasts, slaves. That biblical race, at once so coveted yet so horrifically cruel. That crazy world that is both him and the opposite of him. That contradiction. Ahmed keeps a sensible distance, content as with every journey to glide at a safe height above the encampment of his distant cousins. He hovers incognito, floating among the desert's keepers and the heavy-winged vultures who still recognize him as one of their own.

The man-vulture wheels in the cloudless sky and observes the changes since his last visit. The air is different, denser. Throughout this hazy territory populated by rebels, carved up into different states, men and vehicles appear ready for war: combat gear and Kalashnikovs. Nothing new there. What is new is the length of some of their beards, the sermon delivered after the communal prayer toward the rising sun, the eyes which flicker disconcertingly between fever, certainty, anxiety, elation, and unfathomable suffering. The tragic irony of the desert warrior has given way to an existential dismay that is as thick and heavy as tar, uniting them in a self-loathing which—depending on their disposition—either shrouds them in darkness or blinds them with light. This has replaced the air they breathe. Ahmed is already holding this invisible, noxious gas in his lungs, its effects beginning to register. But he refuses to surrender, to bid farewell to his secret garden, his little bit of sand, his inner purity. He delays; dawdling, loitering. And then, behind a tent, the final decisive image, the grotesque depiction he cannot bear to face. A black, bizarre shape is huddled down there, a shape with no start and no finish. A sort of phantom, maybe human, maybe feminine, its eyes, covered by the darkness of a veil, turned to the sky. The mask-woman's invisible eyes bore into his, a salvo of pure horror, perfect anguish. The man-vulture hesitates. Overcome by lethargy, he tears toward the ground at great speed, capable only of expressing the desire not to fall. His winged companions look on. They know those veiled eyes have shattered the traveler's fragile invulnerability. Reminded of their duty as gatekeepers of the frontier between the worlds, the celestial scavengers flock to him, forcing him back up into the sky.

HIGHER! HIGHER! HIGHER!
FORWARD! FORWARD! FORWARD!
DON'T TURN BACK!

Driven back at tremendous speed to the outer limits of the aerial realm by his former fellow kin, Ahmed knows that from now on he is banished. At liberty to explore Siberia or Patagonia, but no longer welcome in these parts.

Laghouat, Ain Ben Tili, Meroe, Tiris, Tassili, Goulimine, Cyrenaica, Sicily, Ibiza, Olbia, Bonifacio, Valletta. Each time the return takes many twists. This time more so than ever.

Ahmed needs to process it, to stagger the time between the crazy world of there and his presence here, now. High above Valletta, some turbulence brings him back to reality with brutal abruptness. Could be a line from a poem by Desnos: "High above Valletta, a tempted Templar let himself fall." Forget and carry on . . . In any event, he won't mention it in his testimony, his confession, not that there will be one. And anyway, who would understand?

And so it is in the Valletta of Paris 75019 that he feels the first drop on his upturned face, his half-closed eyes gazing up at the sky. The second comes crashing down onto the gleaming sleeve of his djellaba, a present from his cousin Mohamed. Ahmed looks down and watches the scarlet stain spread across the white cotton. It's not rain. A third tear strikes him on the end of his nose. He tastes it. It's blood. His eyes slowly move upward, as if they know the sight that awaits them. A motionless foot is hanging two yards above him. It sits at a peculiarly obtuse angle to the ankle, itself patterned with a kind of geometric henna tattoo. On the tip of the big toe, the next droplet is forming, waiting to fall on his forehead. He moves aside, letting it splash onto his white lily, the only thing to adorn his balcony. Laura's blood inscribes itself on the immaculate flower. And Ahmed comes back to Earth. He glances at the wall clock, round and green with a metal frame that only displays the number four. 9:15 p.m. That voyage lasted some time.

* * *

Well-thumbed books cover the walls of his studio apartment. In the absence of a bookcase, he just piles them up. His living space recedes as his reading progresses. He is keeping count: two tons and eleven pounds of paperbacks, all bought from Monsieur Paul. He'll stop when he hits five tons. According to his calculations, by that point he'll have just enough space to get from his mattress to his front door. When that day arrives, Ahmed will close the door, slide the key back under it, and leave, never to return.

He realizes immediately from the awkward angle of the foot that Laura is dead. Thanks to his books, he has picked up a few of the basic rules for such dire circumstances: don't leave a single trace; no fingerprints. And all the rest. A second thing is immediately clear to him: they want to pin the blame on him. This certainty wells up from somewhere in the outer reaches of his consciousness, a place where a whole host of tiny, almost imperceptible signals has built up . . . throwaway lines uttered in passing. Sam the barber's smile, which burns into the nape of his neck the second his back is turned. Or, in the corner of his eye, a complicit glance between two supposedly sworn enemies. Small, unsettling things like that, which he realizes take on some greater significance in light of Laura's death. But what significance? Reluctant to make himself the prime suspect, he decides he will not flee, but he does need to know more, to determine the nature of the conspiracy and work out why they want to implicate him. Laura is still bleeding—the murder is recent. He is sure the killer wants to incriminate him, the victim's neighbor, but no doubt he'll want to cover some ground before calling the police or the press. Ahmed has a key to the girl's one-bedroom apartment. He goes upstairs. The door is slightly ajar, creaking in the wind.

He pushes it open with his shoulder, making sure his skin doesn't come in contact with anything. He has to see for himself. To experience it. The window at the far end of the apartment is wide open, a terrible breeze working its way down the passage. The gray sky suddenly fills with the dark clouds gathering over parc de la Villette. A distant growl of thunder. He has to act fast. In the center of the main room, the table has been painstakingly laid for two people.

An open bottle of Bordeaux, glasses two-thirds full. An uncooked pork joint sits on a white porcelain platter, bathing in a red liquid, a black-handled kitchen knife stabbed through its middle. There's almost a hint of farce about it. The unreal fusing with the real. The young man lurches forward, looking for something to steady himself. His hand is about to grab the back of the chair when a little voice calls him to order. *No prints, man, no prints!* He steps back, turning his head to find his own face staring back at him, reflected in an oval mirror hanging on the wall to the left. It has been a long time since he's looked at himself. He is surprised by his gaunt cheeks, his complexion that looks more like soil than bronze, his six-day beard. But something else strikes him: he's handsome. Sure, the few women he had been intimate with had often said things like "You're good looking" or "Ahmed, you're a handsome guy!" Suddenly, those unimportant words from a different life take on a new meaning. His slightly frizzy hair, his full lips, his gentle eyes: they all come together harmoniously. Other features, too, that he's unwilling to detail. He is moved. He remembers Laura's gaze, and how closed his heart was to her. He turns away from his reflection and heads for the balcony.

And beholds the horror he knows he must face.

She is upright, tied fast to the other side of the railing with white electrical cable. He moves toward her big blue eyes staring into the abyss. It is as though he is seeing her for the very first time, as if death alone could show him her face in all its soft, benevolent, supreme beauty. He recalls her discreet efforts to make her feelings for him known. Pain and suffering grip him. Only when presented with her irrevocable absence does he realize his love for her, and, worse still, her affection toward him. And the closeness he felt for her, and that she understood despite his blindness. She was beautiful. They could have fallen in love. His heart is broken and enlivened at the same time. He reaches for her cheek, but stops a few fractions of an inch short. Returning to his senses, to prudence, a thought wells up inside him, a cliché, but one he claims for himself that very instant. *I will avenge you, Laura.* He moves half a step closer to the nightmare. The young woman is naked except for a crimson T-shirt.

Her mouth gagged, chest seemingly untouched. Her underbelly is nothing more than an enormous gash that has now stopped dripping onto Ahmed's balcony.

The wind blows and threatens as flashing lights fill the street. The murderers haven't hung around. Taking his leave, Ahmed is horrified to notice that the three orchids he took such meticulous care of when Laura was away have been decapitated. Only the stems remain, bunched up in their plastic pots on the kitchen counter. He looks for the heads of the flowers but doesn't find them, removes himself painstakingly from the apartment, makes his way downstairs, and shuts the door just as someone calls the elevator. He left no prints whatsoever. A rumble of thunder. The first drops fall heavily, dousing the lily. Ahmed closes the windows and shutters, removes his stained djellaba, turns it inside out and rolls it into a ball—stains on the inside—before stuffing it into a plastic bag, one from the Franprix supermarket on the corner. Tomorrow he'll get rid of it, before the police obtain their search warrant. He puts on his well-worn Brooks Brothers pajamas, the last present from his last girlfriend, the mystical Catarina, before he gets into bed, closes his eyes, and falls asleep. He needs to dream now. Laura is dead. He must live. He no longer has the choice. His dreams will mark the way. Ringing. Knocking. "Police, open up!" He doesn't hear. Pigs. Scum. Their paths have crossed for some time. Avoiding them now will be a struggle. For the first time in years, Ahmed hasn't needed a drink to get to sleep. Albeit a fitful sleep. Death, that grim tyrant, is keeping watch, looking on with glee. He resists, refusing to give himself over. Death moves aside for another: an insidious beauty, a bewitching spy, his customary nighttime visitor. There is never any penetration in his dreams. No nudity even. Just dampness. Tonight he stands firm, however, holding his seed and his nerve. And the ghosts retire in their fury, warning of worse to come. Frozen darkness, wind, rain lashing against the shutters and in his head. Lightning. Grimacing face! Iblis appears then disappears. The sleeper groans, his tongue scraping across incisors and molars. He stirs

but he doesn't wake. *Shazam.* The livid face of the killer lights up.
Ahmed opens his eyes, dazed. An unpleasant sense of déjà vu. Time
to forget. The fleeting image retires to a deep corner of his skull. He
knows it. It will guide him.

The sound of footsteps upstairs. Police officers moving around.
Detectives and forensics officers.

"What kind of crime is this? Why the pork joint? All the damn
Jews and Arabs around here, they're all as nuts as each other. As
soon as you leave the Bunker, all you hear is: '*Salaam alaikum*, officer', '*Shalom*, officer'. Fucking hell, I can't wait to get back to picture-
perfect Roscoff. I don't know about you, Rachel, but they drive me
crazy. Totally crazy. I just don't get this pork thing. It's too much. As
Goebbels said . . ."

"'The bigger the lie, the more it'll be believed'," Rachel says, cutting him short. "I love it when you quote Goebbels. It's one of the
few things that makes life bearable. Right, let's get out of here, we've
got a report to write." Ahmed hears and doesn't hear. He knows.
He sees red-headed Rachel and brown-haired Jean. They'll do what
they can, i.e., not much. Or a lot. Tomorrow at six he'll have to
dispose of his djellaba. For now, though, it's good night, Lieutenant. *Laila saida . . .*

2

3:45 a.m. If the dead of night exists, it is now. Lieutenants Hamelot
and Kupferstein are smoking light contraband cigarettes, gazing up
at the stars on the inner terrace of the Bunker, the commissariat in
the nineteenth that is their workplace.

On their return they were summoned by Mercator, who had been waiting for them in his office, a sparsely furnished room with off-white walls. He was drawing circles. His way of filling time and space. All the local officers are aware of this obsession, and they know not to interrupt it. As Hamelot has pointed out to Kupferstein, the chief always follows the same modus operandi. First the paper. He never stoops to tracing his circles on office paper. No, he goes to the stationers' at Bon Marché to buy his very own pads of Claire-fontaine "C": bright-white laid paper, three ounces. Then the pen: a Sheaffer Legacy Heritage fountain pen. As for the rest, it's just a matter of watching him in action. One circle per page, always in the center. And always the same size. The sheets piled up in a perfect stack to his right, not one out of place. Perched behind his varnished ebony desk, Mercator looked like a sort of enigmatic deity. As ever, there was that feeling with him that each gesture carried meaning. This air of mystery is precisely what makes him powerful. He's like a parchment covered in hieroglyphs—there for all to see, yet thoroughly indecipherable. This is what gets Jean going. Like any good rational communist, he cannot resign himself to not understanding. He gathers up all the clues concerning his boss, the idiosyncrasies that only deepen the mystery, much to Rachel's amusement. With an enigmatic smile, she would remind her partner that the secret is that there is no secret. She likes to think of her employer as a sort of Zen master, herself the idle observer. This is a constant source of relaxation.

Mercator has the broad chest of a tenor with the voice to match. He's no Pavarotti in either department; more like a jovial chorus member at the opera, or even a booming wine merchant on rue Daguerre. Rachel is right. The secret lies in the absence of any secret. The chief's anatomy reveals all she needs to know about him and his relationship with life and power. You can read him like a children's picture book. His eyes betray a formidable intelligence, as do his hand movements, which are precise though somewhat unrestrained. He's a *bon viveur* whose fondness for meat is apparent in his cheeks, his full lips, and his permanently flared nostrils, not to mention the folds bulging over his belt. Though he's not exactly what you might call fat. The contest between fat and muscle is more or less even-handed. A little more on the fat side to lull the opponent into a false sense of security, and just enough muscle to swoop down on any prey at the opportune moment, on the basis that this is never strictly necessary. All in all, he is handsome in a way that is very much his own. Not ugly, but rather the reflection of a handsome man trapped in the body of a police officer. A glimmer of Brando's Kurtz that has passed everyone by. Rachel spotted it immediately, and maintains it to this day. This is why Jean's obsession with the chief's M.O. makes her laugh, because for her it is merely the sum of Mercator's combination of intelligence, hidden beauty, and his policeman-like poise and sense of purpose.

That said, Hamelot's a good police officer. A very good one. And he's right on one point: the chief never does deviate from his M.O. His Sheaffer suspended weightlessly one inch above the page, he begins by scanning the surface intently. Then his eyelids close, he breathes in, and he raises his weapon so it's in line with his solar plexus. Three seconds of silence before he unleashes it, letting out a growl of sorts. In a single movement he marks out his circle, eyes still closed, breathes in again, lays down his pen, then lifts the sheet to eye level before finally opening them and surveying his work. An instant later he places it delicately on the pile to his right. It is done.

Rachel and Jean had stood rooted at the entrance to the office. Having freed his hand of his pen, Mercator motioned to them to come in and sit down. For him, reports have to describe everything, down to the most minute detail: the layout of the apartment; the precise position of the pork joint; features of the decoration (neutral and modern, no television, a bookcase where Balzac, Flaubert and Maupassant took pride of place, the Miles Davis portrait, eyes closed, lips pouting, hands framing his face, opposite a reproduction of Picasso's *Les Demoiselles d'Avignon*; and finally, the Air France stewardess uniform hanging in the wardrobe by the entrance). Rachel and Jean, struck by the horror of the scene, let him have his turn

at experiencing it. Wedged into his black leather armchair, with
its clean, sharp lines, the *commissaire* listened, distant and atten-
tive, as always. Who knows where his mind had wandered. As they
finished their report, his eyes clouded over, and he became more
serious. He seemed to be contemplating a shadow that was slowly
invading his office. A shadow he recognized, whose outline only he
could identify. When they told him about the decapitated orchids,
and how the heads had been placed in a triangle on the toilet seat,
Mercator closed up completely. He dismissed Jean and Rachel with a
few impersonal words, among them "report," "seven o'clock," "morning," "inquiry," "you two," "you two." The second time he uttered "you
two" he looked them hard in the eye, then left the office in silence.

There began the Bunker's descent into nighttime. Hamelot and
Kupferstein went for a few Kronenbourgs on the ground floor with
the officers who had finished for the evening, then back upstairs
to type up a few things. They ordered sushi and some more beers,
Asahis. Then their memory began to fade. At 3:00 a.m., Jean won a
game of solitaire. Sitting behind him, Rachel listened to "Pissing in
a River" by Patti Smith on her pink iPod nano.

LET IT ALL GO
BEGIN

In the silent night, the two detectives are sprawled out at opposite
ends of the terrace, reclining in fluorescent metal-framed deck
chairs. Green for Jean, orange for Rachel. They had encountered
overdoses, crimes of passion, ordinary baseness . . . But Laura's murder is their first experience of true horror. Right now it's a case of
confronting, of plumbing the depths of a soul. This murder must
be tamed, nourished, pondered, infiltrated. Then reassessed. They
must go beyond any ordinary fascination with evil. They are trying
now, under the delicate crescent of the moon in the starlit sky on this
night in June. Rachel is dreaming. *If we were in love, we'd be scanning the sky for shooting stars.* But that's not how it is, and she has
to make do with following the erratic path of a satellite. They think

about other things, wandering through the sky before disappearing
deep within themselves.

Jean pictures his mother in her checkered apron, sharp knife in
hand, dicing some onions. He's never had the patience to do it so
finely—he just chops them into thick slices and chucks them into
the bubbling oil, before breaking them up with a wooden spoon
and crushing the garlic straight on top. He can see her almost as if
she were standing in front of him, his nurturing mother, and the
image continues to move him, albeit less palpably than it did back
in the days when he could only just see over the edge of the kitchen
counter—did they even call them that in those days? Yes? Jean is
rambling, digressing. The word *counter* has lurched him violently
from his childhood kitchen in Brittany to a nightmarish afternoon
at Ikea. The moment in his life when he felt the most alone, lost
in the midst of families with militant wives commanding their
troops as though they were a task force on a mission in Somaliland,
mothers-in-law on lookout and fathers trying to regain the upper
hand by showering their better halves with endless technical jargon
that thwarted any sense of accomplishment. A war of movements
and positions that Jean entered, unable to dodge the stray comments loaded with pent-up resentment, more than one of which
was enough to poison his superficially tough soul. He had weaved
his crazy route through the living rooms, the baby-changing tables,
and the office furniture—carbon copy of the Bunker's—to the
kitchen department, the primary objective of the expedition that
was, as he now realizes all too well, doomed to failure. Rooted to the
spot, Jean had stared at the young, bearded, and highly competent
employee charged with designing the kitchen of his dreams. Lost
for words; voice and mind failing. He had gotten down from his
kitchen bar stool, nodding vacantly in the direction of the salesman
before going to the Swedish food shop on the ground floor to buy
himself some crackers, a tube of anchovy paste to spread on them,
and a bottle of Absolut vodka that he had begun to drink on the
RER. train and then finished at home, stretched out on the only rug

in the apartment in the twelfth arrondissement where he'd moved three months earlier. A one-bedroom so bare you'd think it uninhabited. The morning after had been as difficult as it had been emotional, but ever since, he felt calmed and contented at the sight of his kitchen's sole storage unit: a two-doored white Formica cupboard, perfectly ample for his cutlery and provisions. This thought brings him peace, helps him put some distance between himself and the murder. Soon he will be able to face it.

Rachel is following her own course. At first, the sheer monstrousness of the crime numbed her, making it possible for her to act, to do what was required of her. Cordoning off the apartment, proceeding with the first futile lines of questioning, getting curious bystanders to back off. Only when they were giving their report to Mercator did the pain creep up on her. Like after a trip to the dentist, when the effects of the anesthetic wear off. Then she and Jean had a few drinks, talked shit to each other; she'd dipped into the virtual world, listened to the music of her teenage years. Not a lack of awareness—just a distancing process. Now, at this still, latter stage of the night, she recalls in her mind's eye the events that took place before her call-out to join Jean at the crime scene. She skims over her late wake-up and midday arrival at the commissariat to dwell for a short while on what ought to have made up the main part of her day: the arrest at around 2:00 p.m. of a small gang of pot dealers on place des Fêtes. A routine operation that had been a week in the planning, and which was aimed at bolstering government statistics. The vendors—small-fry retailers—were in possession of pathetic quantities and could not have seemed more docile. Rachel stayed in the background, absentmindedly overseeing the successful completion of the operation with her *police judiciaire* hat on. And then her gaze met that of the gang leader, a handsome young man of twenty-five with kind eyes and a smooth ebony complexion. She let him check her out, just for a split second. Each looking at the other from different sides of an invisible barrier that did not block out all potential for attraction. A fleeting sensation that she had stored to one side, saved for later, and which is coming back to her now through the curling smoke of her cigarette.

A fleeting sensation that brings her back to herself, the schoolgirl at lycée Henri Bergson who would avoid the company of the overly fair-featured girls in her class, and whose best friends were Marcel and Ibrahim, the neighborhood's go-to guys for soft drugs. In July 1987, having just seen on the school bulletin board that she'd been awarded her baccalaureate with distinction, Rachel calmly announced to her parents that she would not be joining them on their vacation to Port-Bou. A memorable fight had ensued, with the result that father and daughter nearly came to blows—and it would have taken a real expert to judge who'd have come out on top in this near-miss contest, since despite all of Léon Kupferstein's 190 pounds of muscle, Rachel turned into a veritable ninja whenever she flew into one of her rages. She had managed to get her colossal father to back down, and two days later she was standing on Platform 16 at the gare d'Austerlitz, watching calmly as the 9:47 p.m. train to Cerbère carried her mortified parents off into the distance. A few minutes later, she was on Line 5 of the Métro going the opposite direction. And at 11:00 p.m. on the dot, Marcel and Ibrahim were ringing the bell of her father's workshop on rue des Carrières-d'Amérique. Rachel thinks back fondly to those hours spent slicing slabs off two pounds of Moroccan hashish and packing them into chunky one or three-ounce blocks to pass on to the petty dealers, who in turn would cut them with henna before selling them. A Butagaz camping stove was permanently lit, the huge meat cleaver passing through the flame time and again before making its clean incision through the hard, dense, beautiful dark-brown substance. Rachel loved the immense concentration that reigned in that workshop, the place she had spent so much time as a young girl watching her father ply his trade. Concentration made all the more acute by the element of danger, the feeling of doing something forbidden. The summer had gone by like that, without her even realizing. A period of pure magic. Rachel didn't smoke, she wasn't in love with either of the boys, and she had done it for free, just for the glorious sake of it. The poetry of action.

Right now, she can trace the thread between young Rachel and Lieutenant Kupferstein. The intensity of the eye contact with the main dealer earlier on is a reminder that she has not become someone else. Even if she did stray to the other side of the law, she is still playing the grand game of life. But now the rules are about to change. It's going to be like taking on death at chess.

All the while, Mercator is sleeping.

3

Ahmed wakes up at 5:25 a.m. and slips into his tracksuit and sneakers before stuffing the plastic bag containing the djellaba stained with Laura's blood into his Eastpak knapsack, along with a large box of matches, a pair of extra-thin cleaning gloves, a bottle of methylated spirits that had been sitting under the sink for years, an old cloth, a large bottle of Evian, and the bar of Ivoria chocolate. Ahmed knows the police won't carry out a search this morning. It's too early for them to have had a list of suspects approved by the *juge d'instruction*—the magistrate assigned to investigate the case. He had no interest, however, in not letting them into his apartment to interrogate him and to look at Laura's balcony from a different angle. He doesn't want to take the risk of keeping the bloodstain at his place—no doubt this would mean the start of a very long series of questions. He keeps hold of the key: the concierge knows that he goes up to water

Laura's plants when she's away. This in itself is enough to make him a witness of considerable interest, maybe even a suspect, in a crime where there is no sign of forced entry.

Ahmed gave up jogging three years ago. Running again is painful for his rusty body. But it makes him happy too. He can feel his muscles, his bones, the brisk morning air. Instinctively he heads toward canal Saint-Denis. He prefers this route—much trashier than canal de l'Ourcq with its cycle lanes, trees, and Chinese guys doing tai chi at sixteen frames per second. The embankment overlooking the quai de la Gironde is strewn with bottles of super-strength beer, torn-up Rizla packs, soiled tissues, and used condoms, all awash in the acidic stench of urine. A few yards above this wasteland, a flight of steps leads up to the *périphérique* beltway, flowing freely at this time of the morning. Not a soul in sight. He takes shelter behind some undergrowth, puts on the gloves and pulls the djellaba and methylated spirits out of the bag. He uses the cloth to wipe down the bottle meticulously before tossing it among the other detritus. He strikes a match. *Whoosh!* The rush of heat hits him square on, knocking him back. When the flame is at its highest, he scrunches the plastic bag into a ball and throws it onto the fire with the matches, chucking on the cloth and the gloves as a finishing touch. The *frrr* of the burning sulfur and the *fshhh* of the melting plastic provoke a boyish glee in him. It's pure "Comic Strip" by Gainsbourg—right down to the smell. With his right hand wrapped up in his tracksuit top he grabs a rusty piece of metal and uses it to scatter the embers around the makeshift grate, still warm with charred, melancholy remains that make his heart sink. That strange, forgotten feeling returns: he is alive; he can feel again. A heart, a soul, a body. Quick—run.

He steps out of the elevator and Jean and Rachel are there, virtually see-through after their sleepless night, taking turns ringing his doorbell. Short jabs for her; longer bursts for him. It's 6:45 a.m. Ahmed managed to buy a baguette and some croissants from a nearby *boulangerie* owned by a devout Tunisian who opens his doors after the *Fajr* prayer. The quintessential morning jogger. Ahmed is all set to play the part of the person who has seen nothing, heard nothing.

"Morning—that's me you're buzzing. What can I do for you?"

Rachel, her red hair ablaze after a night of beer, cigarettes, and memories, takes out her ID and introduces herself.

"Police. Lieutenant Kupferstein."

She points to her sidekick—tall, dark hair, haggard face.

"Lieutenant Hamelot."

Then silence. She lets the victim's neighbor register their presence. He doesn't move an inch—waiting, leaning against the wall next to the light switch. When the timer runs out he presses it again. Before, in another life, Ahmed had never been particularly chatty, but he did appreciate the company of others; he liked listening, observing. He had developed a certain talent for predicting people's characters, and sometimes their thoughts. His gaze flicks between the two police officers as he attempts to read his uncertain future in the lines of their faces. The woman is beautiful. Thirty-five at a guess. Five years older than him. Intelligent, different: her understanding of the world comes from another, more ancient time. She has sided with life, wholeheartedly. The man is the same age as her. As inward-looking as she is outward. Something is gnawing away at him, but he's refusing to find out what. Amazingly that doesn't make him bad. He is floating, remote.

Ahmed senses that they are clean and that they are not going to hurt him. He loosens up, breathes in, lowers his guard, and calmly lets himself be observed by Lieutenant Kupferstein.

Thanks to the concierge, Rachel knows that Ahmed has a copy of the keys. At this stage in the inquiry, that makes him the only potential suspect. But she is suspicious of the obvious. She takes her time to examine every detail of the face staring back at her: the sides of the nose slightly flattened; well-pronounced ears poking out from underneath an afro; an extremely prominent Adam's apple; full lips. His gaze is intense and kind, tainted by a deep-rooted sadness. An open window which she can see into immediately. It's not him.

That won't stop her from playing the game and saving face whenever necessary. But in the silence of the landing, with the light switching itself off continuously, there's no need to pretend. Just to stay quiet. For a few seconds. To let eternity play out, as forever is in front of her.

Jean is like a psychoanalyst midsession. He detects the silent link generated between Rachel and Ahmed and intuitively takes a back seat. His natural place. Hamelot likes watching, likes to take his time, to let others do the talking. "You know what you are? An observer of life!" Léna had said to him one day. He had never really understood why that was such a problem. Having given it much thought over the years, he had come to the conclusion that most women just didn't like it. Rachel didn't give a shit. Not when it came to work, at least. It made a change from the endless good cop-bad cop charade. With Kupferstein and Hamelot it was more of a present-absent thing. Rachel taking the lead; Jean detached, under cover. But right now something else is happening, prevailing.

The whole of the rest of the inquiry plays out in this instant. A minute and a half that feels like several hours for three people brought together on this nondescript landing by an unspeakable murder.

Yet the silence must stop. So Rachel speaks.

"We are investigating a murder. Your neighbor upstairs."

It's an emphatic full stop—nothing left hanging. Ahmed must react immediately. He decides to take the easy option: no playing, no pretending . . . He must genuinely realize that Laura has been murdered. That's not far from the truth anyway. He's seen the body, but has chosen to hold back the emotion that threatens to overwhelm him. He can experience the death of his neighbor in real time, in front of Kupferstein and Hamelot. A silence that at first fails to comprehend, then refuses to comprehend. Four seconds.

"What do you mean 'a murder, your neighbor upstairs'?"

"Can we talk about this inside? The corridor doesn't seem the ideal spot."

It's Ahmed's turn to fix his brown eyes on hers, which are blue-green. Without expecting it, he is thrown fifteen years into the past. The girls' toilets at the lycée. Esther's big eyes. Esther—the purest, most short-lived love of his life—on the day of the first of their seven kisses. Kupferstein holds his gaze, of course. A blue-green ocean in which he tries not to lose himself, pulling himself free as delicately as he can.

He must hold back from tasting the salt left on his skin from Rachel's eyes until later. He peels himself off the wall, takes two steps toward the door and gets his key out.

"May I?"

Jean steps aside. Ahmed opens up and goes in, followed by the others. His manner is welcoming.

"Sorry about the mess."

The two police officers are so bowled over by the strange spectacle that greets them that they don't even bother to reply. It's not so much a mess as an overbearing feeling of emptiness and fullness.

Emptiness. The bare minimum of furniture: a table consisting of a sheet of MDF held up by two white wooden trestles; a futon lying on the gray linoleum floor with a beige comforter on top (nine dollars and ninety-nine cents—Jean remembers almost buying the same cover that hellish afternoon at Ikea); a red Chinese wheeled suitcase, which Rachel can imagine containing the few essential items that make up Ahmed's wardrobe, doubling as a bedside table, with three books and a small green metal lamp on it. That's it.

Fullness. The walls of the studio apartment have completely disappeared behind hundreds and hundreds of books piled up in stacks. At a glance, they're four layers deep. Only detective novels. Pocket editions. The two officers are speechless for a moment, then Rachel gets things moving.

"Have you read them all?"

"Yes."

What more is there to say? They take a seat on some orange folding chairs, noticing a white ceramic lamp with a cream light shade, three CDs (Fela Kuti, Gainsbourg, Boris Vian), a national ID card, and a cherry Yoplait jar—empty—its teaspoon stuck to the inside. Ahmed sits next to Jean, opposite Rachel. She breaks the silence after a ten-second wait.

"Did you know Laura Vignola?"

"Did I know her?"

"Yes, perhaps I should have started with that: she's been murdered."

Ahmed repeats the word very softly, closing his eyes. Like an echo.

"Murdered . . ."

He disappears into the distance, imagining the life he might have led with Laura. Love, a child, a second child, sleepless nights, baby bottles, fading desire. Washing machine, car, vacations at a rented cottage in the countryside. After the separation, they continue to treat each other with respect. Why not, after all? A life that will not be led.

Rachel realizes that Ahmed is zoning out. She turns away and drifts off herself, allowing long-forgotten feelings to come back to her.

She is back at her father's workshop. She is nine years old, and this world apart—familiar, yet strange—has always fascinated her. Full of swirling smells, sounds, and textures that do not exist anywhere else. Freshly tanned leather. Its softness as she holds it to her cheek. Its strength. The muffled echoes of generations of ancestors from Vilnius, with her father the last one born there, the last to inherit that age-old knowledge and understanding before leaving for France. Gestures and attitudes that belonged to him alone and which she knew came from somewhere else, somewhere she would never know. She spent hours there, watching in silence, doing her homework, going over her lessons. Her father and his workshop: the only person and the only place where she could feel at peace, until she decided to cast off their protection to face the world. As she slips out of this bittersweet reverie, she glances over at Jean, who is even more absent than usual, immersed in the world of noir fiction, head tilted to one side to read the book titles. The Breton has never seen such a collection. Nights spent reading and rereading under the sheets by the light of his orange flashlight come flooding back to him, first

Chase, then Horace McCoy, Chandler and Hammett, his favorite. As could be expected for the son of a Communist from Saint-Pol-de-Léon. Whiskey and class warfare—that is his cultural stock.

The oppressive atmosphere that assailed them upon entering the studio apartment has lifted. Ahmed's apartment is like a sort of reality-free zone where Kupferstein and Hamelot are able to navigate their own inner worlds unfettered. And they reach an agreement. They tacitly communicate what they both know—this is not our guy. Strangely they feel as though they're carrying out this investigation as a threesome, rather than a twosome. An Ashkenazi Jew, a spaced-out Breton, and a loony Arab. The dream team of the nineteenth arrondissement! Now it's time to play cops and robbers.

Rachel touches down gently and Ahmed seems to come around too.

"Monsieur Taroudant, did you know Laura Vignola?"

"Yes and no. I used to go up and water her flowers when she was away."

Rachel fires a look over at Jean to make sure he doesn't say anything inappropriate. But he's still way off in Finistère. She continues.

"So you owned a set of her keys?"

Ahmed looks at her again, trying to erase the memory of Esther as he gazes at the freckles dotted across her cheekbones. She waits patiently, examining his noble face once more—very brown, almost black, more Sudanese than Moroccan—which seems stretched by life's hardships, as though he has seen too much.

"Yes, she left a spare set with me."

Jean takes over seamlessly.

"And what were you doing last night?"

"Nothing much. I read then I went to bed."

"What were you reading?"

Rachel's question takes them all by surprise, herself included.

"*My Dark Places* by James Ellroy. Know it?"

She can't help but smile slightly.

"Yes, I've read it. It's a strange book, one that conceals as much as it reveals. A book to calm the waters after the storm of *White Jazz*."

Rachel's words unsettle Ahmed. He looks at her, his head cocked to one side, and then smiles shyly.

"I've never met a woman who likes Ellroy . . ."

"Well, I am a policewoman . . ."

"Yeah, a policewoman . . . true. Almost forgot. Suppose the police are just like everyone else, aren't they? They tell each other stories. To convince themselves the world isn't as bad as all that . . . Do you know what *White Jazz* means?"

"Well, yes."

"There's the obvious translation. But according to Ellroy, the meaning is more like 'a twisted plan hatched by white guys.'"

"Monsieur Taroudant, perhaps we'll have the pleasure of continuing this literary discussion some other time. As it happens, my colleague and I are here to ask you some questions."

Rachel takes out her Oxford spiral notebook and her vintage orange pen complete with black cap. Ahmed pulls himself together and carries on the game of "what if." What if this is a real interrogation? What if it's already too late for pretending? He's talking like one of the countless characters from one of the countless novels decorating his walls.

Starting with . . . "Is there anyone who can verify your whereabouts and provide an alibi?"

Precisely.

"No, no one."

"We rang your buzzer at around 9:45 p.m. Why didn't you answer?"

Ahmed holds up the small yellow box sitting on the hessian carpet next to the tired-looking futon.

"I sleep with ear plugs in."

Jean looks at Rachel as if to say "let's leave it for now", and turns to Ahmed.

"Can we see the balcony?"

"I'll open the blinds for you."

A '70s-style metal shutter; the slats painted white. Ahmed turns the handle. Bit by bit the balcony appears before the police officers' eyes. Nothing but a flower pot with a white lily in it. Jean opens the glass door, steps outside, looks up, and turns back toward the dark-skinned Arab. His voice takes on a more insistent tone, his eyes narrowing.

"And did you go onto the balcony yesterday afternoon?"

A five-second silence in which Ahmed appears to be trying to piece together the events of the day before bit by bit.

"To be honest, I can't really remember . . . I spent the day lying on the futon, reading, drinking green tea, coffee, eating crackers; so I must have gotten up and gone to the kitchen, plus a few trips to the toilet. I usually wake up early and take the opportunity to water my lily. It's the best time for it because the soil is still cool. Yesterday morning . . . Yeah, I went out on the balcony at about 6:30. After that, I don't know. As soon as I start reading I tend to lose track of what's going on around me. Often it's not till the end of the day, when I think about making dinner, that I become aware of certain things that have happened throughout the day in my semiconscious state."

"Do you have a job, Monsieur Taroudant?"

"I'm on sick leave."

"Since when?"

"Five years. I've been on disability benefits three and a half."

"Do you mind me asking why you're on disability benefits?"

"Depression."

"Is that considered a disability?"

No response.

"Okay. . . . What was your job before?"

"Night watchman at a furniture warehouse."

The two police officers exchange a knowing look. Rachel, with her big eyes, keeps things moving.

"Great, thanks for your cooperation. I've no doubt we'll be paying you another visit. In the meantime, get in touch whenever."

Ahmed wonders if he's dreaming, but for a brief moment he detects in her eyes an invitation to call, whether he has reason to or not. She scribbles their contact details on a sheet of paper that she's ripped out of her notebook and hands it to him. He slips it into his wallet.

"By the way, you're not planning on traveling any time soon, are you?"

"I never leave the nineteenth arrondissement."

"Perfect, well until further notice, stick to that."

"Fear not."

The officers bid him farewell with a nod and leave. Ahmed closes the door behind them. It's all good—all part of the script. All he needs to do now is listen to a bit of jazz to channel the spirits of Pinkerton past. If he gets out of this he'll write a book—that's a promise. He'll call it *Arab Jazz*. Ha! Shit, what's going on—even cracking gags now?

As an air hostess, Laura often had to make stopovers in the United Arab Emirates. She hated the airport in Dubai, where she felt she became nothing more than a slab of meat on display in the eyes of the potbellied ex-Bedouins, Rolexes dripping casually from their wrists. She felt swallowed up by the shops in the tax-haven hypermarket. After her last trip there, she had brought Ahmed back a present for the first time: one of those tiny iPods, onto which she had uploaded her favorite music. Ahmed hasn't touched it for three months. He digs it out, puts in the earphones, and hits the play button. Somehow there's still a bit of battery left. The warm voice of Dinah Washington: "It's Magic." Deep down he feels a little doorway opening, one that has been hermetically sealed for so long he had forgotten it even existed. A doorway to tears. The effect of the voice, the music is magic. He weeps like a four-year-old. He thinks of his first memory—his mother taking him in her arms to console him after he'd been hit by a bigger boy. It's the only image of her he has left. The only one. Perhaps the odd bit of tenderness had managed to survive the whirlpool of her madness. Maybe, but it left without a trace. How wonderful it was to let himself go to her. How wonderful it is to let himself go now, with this soft music filling his ears. Tears stream down his cheeks. Behind the singer's voice those violins are so sweet, the backing vocals oozing . . . He is weeping freely now. He doesn't know what's come over him. Laura . . . Laura . . . What could I have done? Come now. Not the time for futile soul-searching. You will find the killer, and you will get your life back. And she will find peace. Finally. Now sleep. Dream!

With the volume turned right down, Ahmed closes his eyes and sinks into the world of Laura. Sleep. Thirty-six hours of sound left in the little gem.

4

Six floors below, Jean and Rachel come out of the elevator and find themselves face to face with the concierge. She is cleaning the windows of Building A, Laura and Ahmed's block. Fernanda Vieira is a small, thin, energetic woman with a face like a porcelain doll. Two things betray her forty-five years: the crow's feet at the corner of her jet-black eyes and the silvery strands that—either through carelessness or a remarkable display of vanity—streak through her raven-like hair. She usually wears a denim apron over the rest of her clothing. Today it's protecting a pink gingham skirt and a white blouse that are in tune with the nostalgia that has gripped her since her alarm went off. During the blessed years of her childhood, each block of apartments had its own concierge, and those that made up this exclusive club—of which her mother before her was a member—seemed to Fernanda to be the guardians of world order. Later on she rebelled, but oh how she had admired her mother! This is what she talks about with the two police officers from the moment she spots them, as though a police inquiry were some form of group therapy.

The two officers don't take offense, they just leave her to it. Things have to get going somehow.

"You know, I grew up not far from here. It's like a different planet now. My mother was concierge at a beautiful old building on avenue des Buttes-Chaumont. Just opposite the park. My father was a plasterer. It was extraordinary for them, being here. You couldn't imagine what Portugal was like back then. Ruthless nobles barely leaving a thing for the peasants to live on. My parents grew up in shacks with no running water, in complete poverty; only just had time to learn to read and write before being sent off to work in the fields at age nine. So to find themselves in a building shared by lawyers, doctors, dentists . . . getting tips at Christmas, being treated with respect . . ."

Fernanda stops short, deep in thought. Jean and Rachel, backs to the wall of the concierge's lodge, say nothing, waiting for her. She emerges from her daydream, looks at them, seemingly astonished at their presence, and continues.

"And yet they were never happy. Never. They'd suffered too much to know how to make the most of life . . . It wasn't a laugh a minute. I left home at sixteen. I dreamed of something different. I took every job going for someone without a degree: waitress, receptionist, telephone operator . . . Even worked as a dentist's secretary. And then I got married. My husband found this job, which was perfect for a young couple. So having sworn I'd never be a concierge I found myself working for the local housing association! Less than a mile from where I grew up. Two years later, my husband Laurent ran off with Samia: an unattractive, charmless girl, but she knew how to hold on to a man once she'd set her sights on one. I knew her well— we'd been at school together. And I stayed here. It was my destiny . . . That's how you've got to look at it. I don't know why I'm telling you all this . . . I'm not usually like this. Since last night . . . what with Laura . . . My mind's sort of all over the place."

Rachel looks at her kindly.

"Tell us about her. Anything, just off the top of your head . . ."

"Off the top of my head . . . She was a nice girl, Laura. I liked her
a lot. I'd have liked to get to know her better. That's what you always
say when it's too late. It gave me a real shock, her death. And murdered like that! Who'd wish such a thing on her? You know, there
are all sorts. In this job you get good at working out what people are
like. Laura . . . she was one of the good ones. Always a kind word,
a nod, a glance. I hoped she'd find a nice man. But no. I never saw
any going up to her place. Not that I was keeping tabs or anything!
I couldn't bear it when my mother did that—always nosing around
other people, making comments . . . But after someone's been here
six months or so you get a feel for who is going around to whose, and
she'd been here for three years. I could look up the exact date in my
records if you want. Speaking of men, it was obvious that she liked
Taroudant. You know, the guy below her with the keys. But I don't
think he even realized. He lives in his own world; him and his books.
He never sees anyone. I wonder how she talked him into looking
after her orchids when she was away. Maybe because he likes plants
too . . . Plus you've got to be pretty OCD to spray the right amount
of water on those delicate flowers . . ."

"And apart from Monsieur Taroudant?"

"Apart from him she had three friends, girls from around here:
Bintou, Aïcha, and Rébecca. You know, when Laura moved in here
she lived a bit like a nun . . . She never left the house unless she was
going to work, with her uniform and her wheelie suitcase. The only
place she felt okay was at Onur's, the kebab shop on the corner. She'd
stay there for hours in the afternoon just reading her books. Must
be said that it's quiet there in the afternoon. Just a few thirsty tourists leaving parc de la Villette, and a couple of worn-out regulars
watching those half-naked girls on Turkish TV channels as they sip
their tea."

Rachel takes over.

"Reading . . . Reading what?"

"What would I know? Books. Classics, I suppose. That's how
she got chatting to those girls—Rébecca was studying literature
back then."

"Would you say you knew them well, those girls?"

"They were friends of my daughter, Lourdes, at school. They lost touch after that. Lourdes trained to become a medical secretary. Rébecca, Bintou, and Aïcha went to lycée Bergson. Nowadays my daughter is married and lives down in Arpajon."

"And the three friends—are they still in the neighborhood?"

"Just two of them. Rébecca disappeared suddenly three or four months ago, not long after she started wearing an ankle-length skirt and wig. Some new trend in the neighborhood . . . Anyway, some say she's working as a waitress in New York, others that she married a rabbi from Enghien-les-Bains . . . I've got no idea. Bintou and Aïcha still live with their parents. They're at college in Paris."

"Can you give us their addresses?"

"Of course, they're just around the corner, both in the same block at 23, rue Eugène-Jumin. But your best bet is just to go around to Onur's. They go there every evening after classes to share an order of *frites-moutarde*. They've done that ever since they were small kids. Oh yes, there's something else. I don't know if it's important, but I think Laura was angry at her parents. You know, where I'm from family is sacred. Well, I've already mentioned that things weren't always rosy with my mother. After my father died she went back to Porto. She left us here—her four children—to go and live in a house that she'd built with my father. A life devoted entirely to saving money, leaving us to grow up in poverty. And all that to build a palace in Portugal that my father was never even able to enjoy. Idiotic! In spite of all that I still call my mom every Sunday evening, religiously. My siblings do too. But Laura never spoke about her family. Never. She would talk about her job, her stopovers in Los Angeles and Sydney—cities I'd always dreamed of visiting. But she never mentioned her family. Once, last May, I asked her without thinking if she'd had any ideas for a Mother's Day present. She gave me a frosty look—so different from her usual, kind self—and she went on her way without a word. That was when I realized something was up."

* * *

Fernanda falls silent. She has said her piece. The two police officers thank her for her help. As they are heading back to the Bunker, Jean notes that neither witness so far this morning had stretched to offering them a coffee. They peel off toward the edge of parc de la Villette. Once they're at Café de la Musique they can sit soft, chill out, and talk away from any wagging ears, of which there are plenty at the commissariat. Leather sofas, two Sidamo mochas—two dollars sixty cents each—on the table in front of them. Okay, who'll start? Jean steps up.

"What went on up there with Taroudant? On first impressions he's a prime suspect. In the end we barely interrogated him. I don't know . . . It was like a dream . . . I had these childhood flashbacks: Saint-Pol-de-Léon; Horace McCoy; my father. Stuff I hadn't thought about for years."

His voice is thin and reedy, his eyes glazed over. Rachel senses he is about to drift off again. She brushes his hand and tries to catch his eye.

"Grace," she says in a murmur.

"Sorry?"

"Up there in his apartment we shared a moment of grace. Something rare and fragile. A vibration. A thread so fine it's practically invisible, the smallest breath enough to disturb it. The thread that will guide our investigation."

Jean studies her with a deadpan expression, the shadow of a former smile.

"You're even more of a closed book than I thought. And the worst part is that I like it, a lot. Okay, Rachel, let's follow this thread of yours. Even so, we'll have to look into Taroudant, and then we'll go and check out the kebab shop. Oh yeah, and trace the anonymous call. We'll have to ask our friends in the eighteenth arrondissement if they can take a look at the phone booth."

"The guys in the eighteenth help us? We could always try. There's something else we need to do, a nasty thing—find Laura's parents and let them know. Heads or tails?"

"Tails says you go."

Rachel flips the quarter up in the air. She grimaces at the outcome. "Tails it is . . . You do the coffees and we'll call it quits."

Ten minutes later, they're at the Bunker. Telephone calls, gory pictures, and the pathologist's report. The works.

"Female victim, blah blah blah . . . Inner labia, outer labia, and vagina all sustained multiple stab wounds with a knife between three and six inches long. A butcher's knife. No trace of sperm. The victim died from a hemorrhage, most likely between 3:00 and 4:00 p.m. yesterday. Thighs and lower legs stained with pig's blood. Blah blah blah . . . Dr. Florence Scarpone."

On the back Rachel discovers a yellow Post-it with the words "Find this motherfucker!" written in permanent marker and signed "F." Jean arrives with two glasses of water and hands Rachel one in exchange for the report. He reads it slowly.

"Her vagina was torn to shreds with a butcher's knife," he says after a pause. "Why the theatrics? Whoever did this must feel possessed of some divine power. Untouchable. They wanted to send a message—killing to say something."

Rachel repeats those final words in a daze.

"Killing to say something . . . But to say what?"

Hamelot and Kupferstein have been working together for six months. Mercator's idea. He thought they would be well suited, what with them both being intellectual, cinephile types. Not content with just a law degree like the other police lieutenants, both of them had gone on to do a Ph.D. Jean Hamelot's was on film at Université Paris 13: "Hammett: the scriptwriter." Sociology at Paris 7 for Rachel Kupferstein: "Tony Montana, urban (anti)hero: a monograph on the *cités* of Pierre-Collinet, Meaux, 77100." Jean lasted a year while Rachel managed two before they both abandoned their theses and the unlikely prospect of a career in academia to apply for the police. Jean saw it as a way to escape being stuck in his own head, not to mention his identification with the laconic, honorable heroes of the books he had devoured since he was thirteen. For Rachel, it was a desire for action shot through with an almost erotic fixation with the pure beauty of force; she's more aligned with the samurais from a Kurosawa film than Bogart in *The Maltese Falcon*.

The chief paired them up on instinct, just to see. Naturally curious, he likes to create situations and then observe them. Nothing remarkable to their name as yet. But then the truth is that nothing remarkable has come their way yet. Basically, when he sends them on a mission, he knows the situation won't get toxic. Hamelot and Kupferstein know how to defuse situations before they get out of hand. It's a pretty good start.

They split the work up as follows: Jean will look into Ahmed while Rachel tracks down Laura's parents. She'll stay in touch with Forensics to see if any clues are revealed from the crime scene. Still working as a pair, but each with their own way of doing things. Jean's got a contact at the Maison Blanche psychiatric hospital that services the needs of the nineteenth arrondissement. Léna is an old flame from his lycée days in Brittany, who is now a social worker responsible for helping patients when they are discharged from hospital.

"Hi, Léna. How are you doing? I've got a question for you."

"How am I doing? You're really asking me that? Everyone's gone berserk since that schizo killed those two nurses. They want to turn the hospital into a prison and reduce the amount of time patients spend here. Then I've got to sort them out with benefits, accommodation, and all the rest. Try finding an apartment for a psycho on disability benefits! Meanwhile we're supplying blood samples to the INSERM research center to help them find the schizophrenia gene. I'll leave it to your imagination what'll happen when they think they've isolated it . . . As if it's not enough that they want to systematically detect deviant behavior in three-year-olds. Did you have any idea, Jean? They're going to monitor kids at day care centers and in nursery schools to see if they can pick up on any potential signs of antisocial behavior. Initially they'll offer them

American-style treatment—you know, behavioral therapy. And if that doesn't work, they'll stick them on Ritalin. I'm not making this up—it's official, approved by parliament, there in black and white in the government gazette. You remember studying *1984* back at school? Well that's what we're seeing—it's all coming true! Okay, sorry, just had to get all that off my chest. You know me . . . Your turn—what's up?"

"A murder. How shall I put it? Not your everyday one. But I'm not going to discuss it over the phone. One of the victim's neighbors has definitely been through your ward. Would you be able to look into it? And if he has, do you think you could get hold of his psychiatrist's name for me?"

"Is he a suspect? Ever heard of such a thing as patient confidentiality?"

"Let's just say he's an important witness. I know, I know. That's why I was hoping to meet his shrink . . . informally."

"Patient's name and address?"

"Ahmed Taroudant, 17, sente des Dorées, in the nineteenth."

Léna pauses for a second.

"Ahmed Taroudant. Got it. I'll call you back."

Jean hangs up.

Rachel is tidying her desk. It helps her think. The theatricality of the crime scene had to be significant. She remembers her criminology lecturers explaining that the stagecraft indulged in by serial killers is for the police; must be why it's called the "scene of the crime." Ultimately, police and murderers both have a role to play. In this case, however, it strikes her that the message left by the killer or killers is not intended for the police. Laura—pig's blood, the pork joint. Laura the impure. But why? She wasn't Jewish or Muslim, so on first impressions the notion of impurity doesn't apply. It's intended for Jews and/or Muslims. It's their imagination that'll be offended. Christians, or so-called Christians, will recognize the horror of the crime but won't be so sensitive to the defilement. Other people's taboos, even if intellectually rationalized, cannot be properly felt. Rachel is somewhere in the middle. Her parents were atheists, but that didn't stop her Aunt Ruth from lecturing her while handing her sweets. "My little china doll, you know at school you don't have to eat everything. Some food isn't good for you, okay!" Then through pursed lips she would utter the dirty words from the list she knew by heart. "Ham, roast pork, *pâté de campagne*, *rillettes*, and anything with mince in it . . . *chou farci*, stuffed tomatoes, lasagna. Be extra careful with lasagna! They'll let you think there's just beef in there— beef with plenty of blood in it, for that matter—but it's nonsense! Lasagna is full of sausage meat!" Little Rachel looked on in fascination at her encyclopedic knowledge of forbidden foods. At the cafeteria, however, she ate what her friends ate. With mixed emotions: pleasure at the transgression tinged with a slight sense of guilt. Over the years the guilt faded away. Anyhow, Aunt Ruth died, taking the old-world values of the Eastern European Jews with her. But she can empathize with those brought up as practicing Jews and Muslims—she can see where they're coming from. The visceral horror of the forbidden. She remembered seeing her Kabyle friend, Lubna, a militant Trotskyist, reprimanding her sixteen-year-old little sister, Halima. All black nails and black tights, with her lower lip pierced, she'd been eating ham in private with her Goth friends.

"At least you understand me, Rachel. I can't let her do it. It's *halouf!* Fine if she drinks a beer . . . But eating ham! We didn't fight the Algerian War so that things could come to this!"

"You were born in Colombes in 1969 . . . If you fought the Algerian War it must have been in a previous life."

Rachel chuckles to herself as she remembers the furious look in Lubna's eyes. She turns her attention again to Laura's murder. According to the concierge, the young woman had four friends: three of whom were Muslim (Ahmed, Bintou, and Aïcha), and then Rébecca, who was Jewish. Four people. Four leads. 10:15 a.m. Six hours to go until meeting Bintou and Aïcha at the kebab shop. She decides to hold off calling the pathologist and start the search for the girl's parents. After checking that Jean isn't on the telephone, she gets up and makes for his desk. A quick chat, just to make sure they're on the same page, the same wavelength. And to tell this pig from Brittany a thing or two about what impurity means to Semites. Pork, menstrual blood . . . that sort of stuff.

5

10:15 a.m. Ahmed is still asleep. Gainsbourg on the iPod.

What are his dreams made of? *Chi lo sa?* Distressed sleep. Restless. Tongue grating against teeth. Every muscle in his body tensed up. Jolts, twisted arms, eyes clenched shut. A fixed snarl. Ahmed is still fighting himself. But this morning, for the first time in five years, his confused mind can conceive of a way out. A glimmer of blinding white light in the depths of the thick darkness. As he moves toward the brightness, the battery on the iPod shuffle is starting to fade. Portishead.

The song cuts out harshly in the middle of the final riff. Ahmed opens his eyes. Beth Gibbons' lilting vocals, so untamed yet somehow controlled, are looping around his head. He'd always loved her voice. For him, "Glory Box" was the soundtrack to desire.

He's got to pull himself together before he can begin his investigation. Grubby from his morning jog, Ahmed heads for the shower. The water is almost burning, only just bearable. His senses tighten. Feelings return. Why do autistic people bite their hands? Shampoo. Shower gel. Rinse thoroughly, all parts. He hasn't spoken to anyone for years, with two exceptions. A few exchanges with Monsieur

Paul about James Hadley Chase, a writer highly skilled at describing wasters, and for whom they'd always shared a sort of guilty fascination. Last time things nearly got out of hand. The bookseller went a bit over the top and asked Ahmed to do him a favor: to go and fetch a box of books from the back that was too heavy for him to lift. While Monsieur Paul respected Ahmed for his "nonaction," the bookshop owner had in spite of everything hinted that he'd pay him if he came to help out on a regular basis. At his age he couldn't run the show all by himself, and he'd rather delegate to a proper fan of noir fiction. Then he went quiet. So did Ahmed, who didn't feel ready to take on anything resembling a job. Next time, Monsieur Paul had discreetly kept their conversation to a bit of news about Horace McCoy.

Laura was the other human being with whom he spoke from time to time. She didn't read detective novels, and their first conversation had, surprisingly enough, been about orchids. Shortly after the young woman's arrival in the building, Ahmed had bumped into her carrying an orchid. He let out an involuntary gentle sigh when he noticed the flower. In response to the mildly concerned question put to him by his new neighbor, he briefly explained that once upon a time he had looked after a South American orchid—a cattleya. Laura had assumed that there was a woman hidden among all this, but hadn't pushed him. She simply gave him updates on the plant— hers was from Madagascar—whenever she saw him. Then, one day, she plucked up the courage to ask Ahmed whether he would be willing to take care of her plant during her frequent trips abroad, since the concierge—despite her best intentions—lacked the necessary lightness of touch. After a pause, Ahmed had agreed. The orchid had settled in so well that it had been joined by a friend, and then by another. That was when he had suggested to Laura that she call it a day, since he didn't feel capable of taking responsibility for so many other living beings: a lily and three orchids . . . Enough is enough! On several occasions his neighbor had invited him up for a Lapsang souchong, or even an oolong, with a slice of blueberry, pear, or peach tart depending on the season. He had always declined on some vague pretext, promising that next time he would gladly accept. Laura would make him jam in anticipation of this hypothetical next time. Then, more recently, there had been the thing with the iPod that Ahmed had almost turned down, since music had ceased to feature in his world. But the young woman's expression, so full of hope, had persuaded him to say yes. He hadn't wanted to hurt her feelings, perhaps a sign that a chink was developing in his armor and that—who knows—with a little more patience . . . Laura was nothing if not patient. But the long game being what it is . . . Who could have predicted it? Now she's as dead as her orchids. All that Ahmed has left of her is a bit of strawberry jam, an iPod, and a burning desire for revenge.

To return to the fray he must piece together the broken fragments of his existence. He can trace the precise moment it all fell apart back to the night when, paralyzed and unable to act, he looked horror straight in the face. Two names enter his mind: Al and Dr. Germain. Let's begin by taking a walk across town. It's 11:00 a.m. Al never surfaces before midday, and there's no need for a heads-up. Ahmed no longer owns a telephone anyway. If he walks slowly along the canal he can grab some croissants and get to Al's around 1:00 p.m.

His window is open and the sun is streaming into the apartment. June 19. 71°F. Jeans, T-shirt, and into the elevator. After a few yards he runs into Sam—a sixty-year-old Jew from Tiznit—smoking a cigarillo on the step outside his barber's shop. He acknowledges his loyal customer with a slight nod—he's cut Ahmed's hair since he was four. The young man detects a glimmer of irony at the back of the barber's little light-brown eyes, and files it away in a corner of his mind for later. Three years of psychoanalysis has at least taught him to keep his paranoia in check. He heads for parc de la Villette to pick up canal de l'Ourcq, then straight down to Bastille.

Jaurès. He thinks of the red-headed policewoman as he crosses the boundary of the nineteenth. "I never leave the nineteenth

arrondissement." "Stick to that." Rachel's face comes to him with
great clarity. So many women in his life all of a sudden! Laura, who
disappears leaving behind Beth Gibbons. And Rachel Kupferstein,
who brings back the forgotten memory of Esther Miller, the first in
a short line of doomed encounters. As he makes his way he redis-
covers Paris. This city—with its canal and its stairway-bridges dotted with languishing lovers—is his.

Hôtel du Nord has reopened. Nostalgia still the order of the day.
The building, which had its glory days back at the start of the twen-
tieth century, is beyond dull. Why erect a mausoleum in the form
of a trendy café in honor of such a depressing film? Nevertheless,
Ahmed takes a seat on the terrace to soak up the vibe and orders an
espresso, the bitterness helping to revive his spirits. All these years
he has spent without thinking, book in hand more or less con-
stantly. The only time he was forced to look at himself was during
his sessions with Dr. Germain. And he didn't like what he saw. He'd
come to the conclusion that he couldn't bear himself; that he would
never bear himself. Better, then, to forget himself entirely. This is
what he had been working on. Until Laura's murder. He puts two
dollars down on the table and leaves.

At Bréguet-Sabin, Ahmed takes a left. Rue Boulle, rue Froment, rue
Sedaine. The baker's beneath Al's is open. A Chinese woman smiles
at him.
    "What would you like?"
    "Two croissants and two *pains au chocolat,* please."
    "Three dollars forty cents, monsieur."
    Five-dollar bill. Change.
    "I have a favor to ask."
    She shoots him an inquisitive glance.
    "I'm visiting a friend upstairs but I've forgotten my address book
with his door code. Would you mind giving it to me?"
    "Why don't you call him?"
    "This might seem strange, but I don't have a telephone."

The lady looks at him, sussing him out.

"What's your friend's name?"

"Al."

Her expression changes. She pauses momentarily, staring into space. Her bottom lip moistens slightly, glistening. She snaps out of it and gives him a cheery smile.

"Come this way."

She leads Ahmed behind the counter. There's a door in the back of the shop leading onto a courtyard.

"Thank you."

"Not at all."

Uneven cobblestones and oak trees with a ray of sunshine across their leaves. Fond memories. Right at the end there's a small white three-story building. Music is spilling out of an open window at the top. Guitar from the banks of the Niger River. Inspiration drawn from the Ambassadeurs Internationaux featuring Salif Keïta, to be precise. Ahmed climbs up the stairs with a new-found agility. He knocks on the door with increasing insistence until the guitar stops. A shock of red hair fills the doorway.

"*Yo, brother!*"

Palm touches palm and pulls away. Clenched fist gently knocks clenched fist. A ritual greeting from the ghetto where each man weighs up the other.

"*Yo, white boy!* What's up?"

"Hanging in there."

"You've upped your game—for a second I thought you were listening to a bit of old-school Salif!"

"Been practicing four hours a day . . . Come in!"

Ahmed steps into the den. Moth-eaten sofa covered in a tie-dye drape. Trestle table overflowing with stuff—bottles of water, rum, half-filled ashtrays, sheets of paper with words and drawings doodled all over them, books by Philip K. Dick and A. E. van Vogt, Japanese incense holders, a pack of Rizla, and more. The wall is plastered with postcards, flyers, and pictures of naked girls. An old turntable is lying on the floor in the corner. Al has never bought a CD in his life. His vinyl collection reveals the extent of his musical horizons . . . From Yes to Tchaikovsky via Hendrix and TPOK Jazz from Kinshasa. He sits down on a tired sea-green office swivel chair, a throwback to a bygone age of Bakelite telephones, imitation-leather benches, secretaries in mottled skirts, flesh-colored panty hose, and low-cut tops, tits out for the pervy boss. Ahmed takes his place on the sofa—client side—sitting a little bit lower, where he belongs. His eyes wander around the room he hasn't set foot in for three years. Nothing's changed. Al gives him a moment to come around.

"Been a while!"

"Let's just say I've had some shit to sort out in my head. It got to the stage where I could barely leave my apartment—couldn't even go beyond rue de l'Ourcq. Remember Patrick McGoohan in *The Prisoner*? Well that was me. Only difference being that no one was stopping me from leaving, and I wasn't trying to escape. I was stuck in my own head, you get me?"

"And what did you do to escape; to get out of your head?"

"I don't know. My neighbor upstairs was murdered, I went to sleep, and then I came here."

Al says nothing. He flicks some little bits of paper to one side—his latest compositions—and a small metal-inlaid wooden box from Morocco appears. Inside there's a load of baggies. He selects one that's full of handsome, dark-green grass. Ahmed can tell from the color that it's not from Holland—the weed's a lot paler. More likely from Thailand or Africa . . . Whatever, it's proper Mary Jane, none of that genetically modified shit. Al keeps that crap for clients. In complete silence, the master of ceremonies rolls a nice, smooth joint and hands it to his friend. Ahmed lights it, takes a long toke and holds the smoke in his lungs for several seconds before blowing it out in a single plume. He takes two more drags and passes the cone back to Al, who puffs away as if it were a cigarette. They sit in silence. Ahmed can see the world changing around him. Everything in its right place—the colors and smells

are the same—but all of a sudden the universe seems charged
with meaning. A glass is no longer just a glass . . . It's project-
ing its glassness onto the world, its being-in-the-world as a glass.
This new perception of things fills Ahmed with a sense that he is
magnifying, expanding, tending toward the infinite. Something
he finds intensely satisfying. For the first time in years he loosens
up and takes stock of the different pieces of his life laid out in front
of him. Give him a few more minutes or years and he'll be ready
to talk about it.

Al watches him in silence. Being a drug dealer, he smokes weed
every day, but he is careful not to give himself over entirely to
the effects of the tetrahydrocannabinol, or THC. His commercial activities serve to subsidize a personal habit of considerable
proportions. As for his other expenses, he mixes gigs on the local
Paris circuit with posting flyers. He's never gone near benefits.
Avoids all state registers like the plague. His latest song is called
"Escape from Sarkoland." He's pleased to see Ahmed again. He
sits there quietly smoking his joint, waiting for his friend to
regain the power of speech. To pass the time, Al grabs a sheet of
white paper and a pen and sets about drawing a mash-up of a Dis-
ney cartoon: Mickey is taking a hit while Scrooge McDuck, the
big daddy dealer in Duckburg, looks on disapprovingly. Ahmed
pipes up.
   "The thing is, Al, I've always killed women. You remember, the only
story I ever wrote at school was about the wanderings of a prostitute-
killer. He didn't touch them; he didn't fuck them. He got his kicks from
stabbing them. At the time it seemed perfectly innocent to me. Just a
story for the times. Then it became like an obsession. More and more
of these images of death played out in my head. I would slice women
in half as I passed them in the street; I'd gut them while in a state of
serious inner turmoil. It became almost impossible to look women in
the eye. The thought of trying it with anyone filled me with horror.
I could let things roll if a chick was really into me, but it was that or
nothing at all. How can you look at a girl, joke around with her, when

all you're doing is picturing cutting her into pieces? You read *American Psycho*, yeah? So in my head, I was Patrick Bateman."

"Listen, man, you haven't killed anyone. All this shit is just images in your mind. It's not real, okay?"

Ahmed makes as if to speak, thinks again, and swallows the words that form in his head. *The day it became real, I lost my nerve. Not here. Not with Al.* This meeting with himself is going to have happen some other time. Something has become unclogged, and that's a good thing. For the first time he lets his mind return to that warehouse. To what happened that night. The night his life ended. Al watches him calmly with an expression that seems to say *Don't worry, man. It's all chilled here. If you want to talk, talk. If you want to be quiet, be quiet. It's cool, yeah . . .*

"Deep down you're right—I haven't killed anyone. Not everyone can say that. In this world there are people who really do kill women and orchids."

Al gets to work on another cone. As he hands Ahmed the joint he explains that this weed is properly spiritual, uplifting.

"See, down here in this shithole of Paris, what are we? Twenty yards above sea level, tops. Where this *charas* is made, in Himachal Pradesh, they're five or six thousand yards up. So when you smoke this, even here in this little third-floor apartment, it sends you sky high . . . It totally cancels out the five miles between us and the roof of the world."

Two lungfuls later and Ahmed is practically teleported to that very place. He's in Tibet, Everest, the mountain plateaus of Kyrgyzstan . . . Who cares where? He's stopped knowing what it means to know anyway. If the first joint had charged him with meaning, this one was freeing him of it. Over there—far off in the distance—a shaman is reciting an age-old mantra. It's strangely reminiscent of Robert Wilson. A white Robert Wilson whose distorted chanting echoes through the smoke rings . . .

Not quite. Not quite so, oh noooo, baby, not quite so, it ain't so, no, no, no . . .

* * *

Ahmed is tripping to the rhythm of the world. The images along the way are pure. Colors, curves, light. And then letters, sometimes words, which transcend language.

He has cast off from the shore. Floating like a baby.

6

Mercator is alone in his big empty office, as is his custom. The ebony desk is clear. The Sheaffer pen is tidied away in a drawer; the sheets of paper covered in circles are nowhere to be seen. The two lieutenants—feeling somewhat uneasy—have answered the chief's summons.

"The orchids, incidentally . . . There were three?" he asks.

Silence.

"Laid out in a triangle on the toilet seat, correct?"

"Yes—we took some photos if you'd like . . ."

"No need. A triangle inside a circle—well, an oval to be precise, but a circle in the eyes of the person who took such pleasure in arranging them. The fact is you've been focused on one element of the crime scene—the most obvious one, namely the pork. But there are two. Think about it. A triangle . . . Inside a circle . . ."

"You think . . ."

"Nothing just yet. Let's each think on our own. We'll come back to it later. It's still a little early to be wondering 'aloud'. What else have we got?"

"The pathologist's report has told us a bit more about the circumstances of Laura's death. The cause of death was the hemorrhage

brought about by roughly fifteen stab wounds to the vagina. Afterward they drained her blood into a bowl, no doubt about it, though
there isn't any trace of it. I reckon it's the nastiest thing anyone's ever
seen. Rachel spoke to Scarpone, so I'll hand over to her."

"She had pig's blood smeared on her. As a matter of fact, according to the pathologist, they tipped the blood over what was left of her
vagina after killing her. To get back to the staging of it though . . . The
knife was buried in a pork joint on the table. Almost like an instal-
lation, in the artistic sense—could have been titled *The Punishment
of Impurity* or something like that. There are a lot of Jews and Muslims living in the neighborhood, a significant number of whom are
fundamentalists. For both groups, this horror has a more profound
meaning. It shows a desire to defile the dead woman—to kill her a
second time, for eternity. The murderers assumed the right to damn
her, so to speak."

"Or to make it look like that was their intention," Mercator says.

"Yes, indeed. But whether the killers were motivated by religion
or not, there's a paradox: Laura Vignola was not a member of either
community. Yet the crime scene was intended to appeal to the imaginations of Jews or Muslims."

"Or both . . ."

"That thought had occurred to me. And then there are her three
friends . . . One comes from a family of what would appear to be
Hasidic Jews, and the other two are of Muslim origin."

"And her neighbor . . ."

Jean instantly glances over at Rachel and takes over.

"Ahmed Taroudant. Manic depressive. Frankly I can't see him
doing something like this. It doesn't stick. We'll investigate him,
of course. And the three friends. The Jewish girl seems to have
disappeared, and we're going to meet up with the two Muslim ones
when they get back from college in . . ."—he checks his watch—
"half an hour."

"Perfect. You've got an 'in' with the Hasidic Jews, I believe, and
with the local mosques too. But it's too soon to go bulldozing in.
I've already ordered a complete blackout with regard to the crime

scene. As ever that won't last longer than a day or two. Someone
from Forensics or the morgue always blabs. All it takes is for a handsome young journalist to rub a receptionist up the right way . . .
Make the most of your brief head start over the media to get stuck
in. You can take some time off when this is all sorted out. I'm not
sure why, but I feel like these killers are within reach. Off you go!"

The two lieutenants are already out in the corridor when their
chief calls them back.

"Kupferstein! Hamelot! This air hostess . . . Did she have any
family?"

Rachel bites her bottom lip like a schoolgirl who has just been
busted.

"Shit! The parents—I'd completely forgotten about them. According to the concierge she had fallen out with them for some unknown
reason. I'll ask Gomes to track them down and I'll make contact with
them when we get back from the kebab shop."

Jean's head reappears in the doorway.

"Oh, boss. I asked our colleagues in the eighteenth to lead the
investigation into the phone booth in front of 37, rue Ordener,
where the call reporting the murder was made from. No response
yet. Could you keep after them? They must have groomed a few useful friends among all the dealers and junkies who hang out around
there. It would be nice if they gave us a hand on this one . . . We'll
return the favor, of course!"

A violet Post-it on Jean's red desk lamp reads: CALL LÉNA MOREL.
"Hi, Léna?"

"Ah, Jean! Listen, I get off tomorrow at 4:00 p.m. I've gotten us a
meeting in Châtelet—the Sarah Bernhardt café—at 6:30 p.m. with
Dr. Germain. He'd prefer me to be there too. If you're free why don't
we go for a Vietnamese at the New Locomotive afterward? I'll have
my car."

"Great, thanks Léna! I've got to make a move—see you tomorrow."

Rachel is briefing Gomes, a young twenty-five-year-old officer
with light brown hair held up with gel. Studious and concentrated,

he is religiously noting down every single word that passes his colleague's full lips. Find Laura Vignola's parents. Born Niort, February 25, 1978. Under no circumstances should you call them—just try to find out as much about them as possible. Apparently Laura and her parents had a frosty relationship . . . Could he make a start on working out why? She thanks him with a weary smile before turning on her heel and joining Jean in the corridor.

"Well?"

"Well the psychiatrist has agreed to see me. I would rather go alone, but he's asked for Léna to be there too . . . I'm having dinner with her afterward," he adds, a touch flustered.

"Léna! Well, if it's not broken . . ."

"You're a pain in the ass, you know! We go for dinner once a month. She's the only childhood friend I have left. You grew up in Paris. You wouldn't have a clue what it feels like, losing your roots."

Rachel smiles without saying a word. For them, seduction is a game that never plays out. One night, after a particularly tense operation in a Cameroonian squat, the two of them had gone on a bar-crawl along rue Oberkampf. They ended up in Cythéa at 3:00 a.m. After dancing for half an hour to remixed Bollywood tunes, the stress had eased completely. Slumped in front of their Abbaye beers, their conversation became flirty. Jean had looked Rachel straight in the eye, not saying a word. She turned the tables.

"What are you thinking about right now?"

"Do you really want to know?"

"Yes."

"About this . . ."

He leaned in and kissed her. Rachel responded to his lips with an energy that surprised and terrified him. A fear of not being up to it; of not wanting it enough. A familiar old defense mechanism. In general, girls didn't pick up on it. Pretended not to, anyway. Once you've kissed, you've got to push on through, right? Rachel had pulled back, puzzled.

"What exactly are you looking for?" she asked.

"If only I knew."

The spell was broken. A cloud descended over Jean. Rachel defused the situation.

"One: we work together . . . it would be a damn shambles, a complete nightmare. Two: it was worth a try, otherwise we'd always have it lurking at the back of our minds. Three: stop sulking like that or I'll leave immediately, which would be a bummer for me as my glass is empty and it's your round!"

Jean laughed. Not very heartily, but he did laugh.

"You know, it's nothing to do with you. I enjoy your company, it's fun getting smashed together. That's what life's about. But deep inside me—here in my chest—there's a burden that weighs me down and never completely goes away."

Five minutes later, they were back at the bar getting some beers. Rachel had given him a tiny peck on the cheek.

"That's why we could never be lovers. You're too gloomy for me. With all the family and ethnic baggage I have to lug around, it's a matter of surviving mentally. I will always choose life. *L'chaim!*"

She raised her glass.

"*L'chaim?*"

"It's Hebrew, it means 'to life!'"

They clinked glasses.

"*L'chaim!*"

It had come up two or three times, always on Rachel's initiative. It mattered to her that the facts were straight and that her memory of it was preserved.

Nowadays, several months later, she likes to mess around with him, tease him. She's essentially a bit jealous, in a sisterly sort of way. Neither of them has siblings and they cherish the bond that was so lacking in their younger years.

Barely a five-minute walk to Onur's restaurant, the Antalya Royal Kebab. It's the last joint on avenue Jean-Jaurès. Jean imagines a massive road sign warning drivers:

WARNING! LAST KEBAB HOUSE BEFORE
THE PÉRIPHÉRIQUE!

He loves making silly jokes, but maybe now's not the best time for this one. He decides to save it for later. They met Onur a few months back. An insignificant case involving his younger brother, Rüstem, dealing weed. They had let it slide on the understanding that Onur would handle it. Now the teenager is serving an apprenticeship as a *pâtissier* in Orléans, coming home on weekends to work at the family kebab shop. Onur—thirty years old, broad forehead, not a lot of hair left—welcomes them with a big smile.

"Salad, tomato, onions? This one's on the house!"

He chuckles to himself, as he always does. The two police officers never go for the kebabs, which are weirdly called "Greek" sandwiches. They tend to prefer his honey-heavy pastries and the kind of strong black coffee you get in Istanbul. On top of this, they always insist on paying their way, a matter of principle.

"Thanks Onur, we'll take two teas and two of your extra-sticky *gâteaux rouges.*"

Rachel lowers her voice just to be on the safe side. The only customer is a man—very pale and very thin—sitting by himself under the flat-screen, watching a Turkish music channel. A girl in a miniskirt is swaying her hips sexily on a beach. The volume is turned all the way down.

"And you're going to do us a favor, too. We need a word with two of your regulars. Bintou and Aïcha. When they get here can you tell them that we'd like to meet them somewhere a little more private. Don't worry—they haven't done anything wrong, but it's important. Reassure them and tell them to come find us at Café de la Musique. At the back on the left. Do you think they'll listen to you?"

"Yes, I'll tell them they can trust you. They're good girls, you know . . . Nothing's going to happen to them?"

"We'll make sure nothing does. As far as possible."

He looks Rachel in the eye. His voice catches slightly.

"I liked Laura very much. She was one of my customers . . ."

"Ah . . . so you've heard."

"Everyone in the neighborhood has. Go and take a seat—I'll bring your order over."

Two minutes later, Onur is back. As he serves them, he says discreetly: "There's a new drug doing the rounds. Pills similar to ecstasy, but with a different effect—stronger. They're blue I think. I overheard some customers talking about them. They'd bought them very nearby, either in parc la Villette or by rue Petit. There you go, that's it—I just wanted to warn you."

The two lieutenants sit there in thoughtful silence. Barely three minutes later, two 23-year-old girls—tall and very beautiful—enter the kebab shop. The first has dark black skin and an Angela Davis hairstyle, and is wearing a white blouse and some flared jeans. On her feet are some yellow Onitsuka Tiger Asics sneakers. The other girl has a much fairer, almost milky, complexion and curly auburn hair tied up at the back with a shiny black clip. She is sporting Indian-style clothes: a shimmering green gown over white cotton pants and a pair of leather sandals. Blown away by this double vision of beauty, Jean and Rachel watch Onur lean toward them and indicate the table where the officers are sitting with an almost invisible nod, before carrying on talking. The students don't turn around, listen to the end, and take their seats, only then stealing a glance over at Rachel. Onur tips some frozen chips into the metal basket and plunges them into the boiling oil. Jean and Rachel calmly finish their cake, get up, and pay.

"Thanks Onur, see you next time."

"See you."

Jean is so deep in thought that he doesn't notice the colossal guy hurtling past him as he steps out of the kebab shop, literally sending him back inside. Stunned, Jean's eyes stay on the man as he turns right down sente des Dorées. He instinctively makes a mental note of the man's appearance: six foot two; two hundred and forty pounds; straggly, medium-length blond hair; blue shell-suit bottoms; bright-yellow zip-up nylon tracksuit jacket. A pure '70s throwback. The image etches itself in his mind despite not catching his face. Weird. The stranger reminds him of somebody but he's struggling to figure out who. An ominous family resemblance. He sees the man pile into Sam's barber shop. Stranger by the second. He tenses up. Rachel grabs him by the elbow and drags him across the street toward parc de la Villette.

"Hey, wake up! We've got to get a move on or they'll have finished their chips. And we don't even know how we're going to handle this. I wasn't expecting them to be like that at all."

They cross the road.

"What do you mean 'like that'?"

"Serious bombshells, but not bimbos. Bright bombshells. In this neighborhood, that's hardly the norm—it kind of threw me . . ."

"You know you can be called Bintou and Aïcha, live in the nineteenth and still go to college . . . Let them do the talking first—then just follow your gut feeling. You're a girl, you grew up nearby—you can play the big sister card. In any case, they already know about Laura's death along with everyone else in the area. All we need to know for now is where they are on the fear scale."

"Wow! I'm going to write that one down. 'The fear scale' . . ."

Jean doesn't rise to the bait. They enter the café in silence.

Same table and armchairs as this morning. The two lieutenants are pushing the boundaries of presentability. They barely slept a wink last night after staying up to write their preliminary report for the chief. Today's been strange—a feeling of weightlessness as they've drifted between Ahmed, Fernanda, and a few telephone calls at the office. A day spent waiting for this meeting with Bintou and Aïcha. And now they are not even that sure what they're doing here. Perhaps that is the right approach: not knowing, knowing nothing, being sure of nothing. Being open. Silence, pause, coffees. After five minutes the two friends appear and approach them nervously. Rachel smiles and motions at them to sit down. She addresses the young black girl.

"You must be Bintou?"

"Yes."

"And you're Aïcha?"

"Yes."

The waiter arrives. Bintou orders a tomato juice and Aïcha has a cappuccino.

"Is this about Laura's death?"

"It is."

"What do you want to know?"

Rachel smiles sadly.

"Everything . . . We know virtually nothing about the late Mademoiselle Vignola apart from her job, that she was friends with you and . . ."—she pauses, hesitates, and decides not to bring up Ahmed right away—". . . and that it would appear that she'd fallen out with her parents, though we don't even know why. So you see we don't have much to go on."

Silence. The two friends look at each other. A quiet nod from Bintou. Aïcha gets things started.

"You know we heard about Laura last night around midnight. We were together at my place when Fernanda—Madame Vieira—called Bintou's cell. She asked us to come see her. She said it was urgent and very important. She seemed extremely upset and didn't want to say anything over the phone. I live around the corner—rue Eugène-Jumin. Five minutes later we were in her lodge. Fernanda looked distraught; white as a sheet. We'd never seen her like that and we've known her since we were little . . . We used to go around to her place and she'd make us bread with loads of butter and strawberry jam which we dipped in our Nesquik . . . She's Lourdes' mother—all our moms treated the other kids as if they were their own . . . She sat us down and was barely able to speak. "Laura, Laura . . ." That was all she could bring herself to say: just saying her first name over and over. We had already guessed but we didn't want to believe it. Finally she let it all out in one breath. "Dead, killed, murdered." I will never forget the way she said that, never in all my life. We wept together, all three of us, crying our eyes out. There you have it. That's it. She didn't see anything, apparently. Just heard the police talking to each other.

It sounded horrible, but she spared us the details. At 2:00 a.m. we left and went back to my place. We had to be together. We kept on crying and fell asleep in each other's arms. This morning we slept in. At 1:00 p.m. we left to go to school. We told ourselves that's what Laura would have wanted. For us not to sink into despair; for this not to stop us from doing what we needed to do. She was a strong girl, Laura. But she had no enemies. I don't get it . . . Who would do something like this? I don't get it . . ."

Aïcha shakes her head. She is desolate, she has nothing more to say.

"No enemies?" Rachel says.

Bintou and Aïcha share a rather pained look. Silence. Bintou's turn to speak.

"She had issues with her family. But I can't imagine a parent doing something like that to their daughter—this isn't Kurdistan . . ."

"What sort of issues?"

"The Vignolas are Jehovah's Witnesses. Laura was brought up as one. Completely nuts! Anyone not like them is considered a demon, the world's going to end tomorrow, no movie theater trips, no birthday celebrations . . . It's pretty straightforward—basically everything is banned. Laura left when she turned eighteen. She started planning her escape when she was thirteen. Her parents never forgave her, preferred to consider her dead. She really struggled to get them out of her head—them and the Witnesses. She was really courageous. For years she lived in a hostel for young workers. She worked as a checkout girl at Carrefour during the day and learned English in the evening. Her dream ever since she was small had been to work as an air hostess for Air France. She persisted for six years and ended up getting recruited on the day of her twenty-sixth birthday. Three weeks later she moved here. She tried to go and visit her parents at least once a year, but they chased her off as though she was the devil incarnate. Her last attempt was less than two weeks ago. Hopeless, as ever."

"Where do they live?"

"In Niort."

"Did she ever talk about her life with the Jehovah's Witnesses? Was she afraid of them?"

"Yes, she spoke about it regularly. It left its scars, for sure. But their message was mostly about fearing the world, fearing life. That's what she was so strongly against. I don't think she felt threatened by them directly. She found them poisonous, sordid, intrusive. It was as though something had stuck to her; like a sort of glue that she couldn't rub off. She never spoke about it for long; it upset her too much. And we'd never ask her questions."

"How did you meet her?"

"Rébecca met her first. One afternoon, at Onur's, she spotted a girl reading *Bel-Ami* by Maupassant. She loves that book, so she got talking to her. They became friends right away, just like that. We met her after that. She was great, Laura. Really great."

"And what did you do together?"

"Oh, not much. We drank tea, chatted about life. She was our friend, you know. Our friend . . ."

Bintou's voice catches in her throat and she starts sobbing. Aïcha grips her hand very tightly, trying her hardest to hold back her own tears. Rachel takes a pack of tissues out of her pocket and offers one to Bintou with a somber smile. Silence reigns, only broken when Aïcha, with a final squeeze of Bintou's hand, speaks up.

"Go on, ask away. It's my turn again."

Rachel leaves it a moment longer before continuing.

"And your friend Rébecca . . . Where is she now?"

"Rébecca fell out with her family. She's taken off until things calm down."

"What sort of falling-out?"

"Long story . . . Nothing to do with Laura . . ."

"Listen up, both of you. A young lady you were very close to has been murdered. She had four friends in the whole world. You two, Rébecca, and Ahmed Taroudant, her neighbor downstairs. So as far as we're concerned, anything involving any of those people has got everything to do with Laura. Rébecca has disappeared, and we need to know what's happened to her. Simple as that."

"Okay. Okay! Don't get stressed. We've got nothing to tell. But we'll do our best to put you in touch with her. Is that good enough?"

"Yes that's good enough, but I'm asking you to do it as quickly as possible. I'm sure you'll be as persuasive as you can. Anyway . . . Were there any men in her life?"

"Not really, no. You mentioned Ahmed, her neighbor. Fernanda must have told you that she was in love with him. To be fair, you could almost say that she picked a guy like him on purpose, just to be certain nothing would happen."

"Why's that?"

"Ahmed's nice, but girls . . . It's like he doesn't notice them. When we were younger we used to play this game where we'd flirt with him. Nothing. Never even realized."

"And no one in the neighborhood tried to push her buttons, as far as you're aware? She was a beautiful young woman."

Bintou looks at Aïcha, who takes over.

"No, not that I know of . . . There was just this weird thing with some of the, like . . . the over-religious guys. She had this funny effect on them . . . Was like they knew by intuition where she'd come from; what she'd escaped."

"Which 'over-religious guys'?"

Aïcha stops herself as though she's already said too much. She gives her friend a pointed look before moving on.

"Moktar and . . . Ruben. A Salafist and a Hasidic Jew. I don't know why, but they seemed uneasy every time they saw her. They looked down on her. What's even weirder is that those two hate each other as well . . ."

Rachel locks her blue eyes on Aïcha's, which are a light hazelnut. Silence. She turns toward Bintou and looks at her with the same intensity.

"What you've just said is extremely important. One of our theories is that Laura might have been killed because of her relationship with Jews or Muslims. Religious types—fundamentalists—the sort that are a bit of a specialty in this neck of the woods. Do you know them well, Moktar and Ruben?"

Bintou hesitates, beginning to answer.

"A bit . . . Through our brothers . . ."

All of a sudden, Jean sits up and looks at the girls more closely. Rachel turns toward him, holding fire. Her colleague narrows his eyes for a split second, as if to say "later." A shadow crosses Aïcha's big eyes, and she cuts her friend off.

"Listen, we've got to go now. Can we meet up again some other time? What's your number?"

Jean snaps out of his drowsiness. Rachel looks closely at the two girls, suddenly so fragile and frightened. She hesitates for a moment before tearing a page out of her notebook. She writes down her name and cell number with a black pen then hands it to Aïcha.

"An investigation is a race against the clock. We'll either catch the murderer in the next three days, or it'll take us months, years, eternity."

She turns to Jean—who hasn't said a word since the start—and continues.

"The two of us know a lot, and we're pretty patient. And you can trust us. Tonight and tomorrow, we won't be getting much sleep. Nighttime's good for talking. Think, then get in touch—even if it's 3:00 a.m., I'll be there. I know that you want Laura to be at peace now."

She holds her notebook open at a blank page.

"Can I take down your details?"

The friends take it in turns to jot down their names and numbers. Bintou Aïdarra has pretty, round handwriting, while Aïcha Bentaleb's is much more angular. A few nods goodbye and the beauties take their leave.

A pause.

"What made you react like that just now?" Rachel asks.

"Their brothers, Moktar and Ruben: 75-Zorro-19."

"Sorry?"

"A local rap group. If I remember rightly, the four members were Moktar and Ruben—the guys the girls mentioned—as well as Alpha and Mourad . . . I'd put good money on them being Bintou and Aïcha's older brothers. Nowadays they're fully paid-up regulars at the Salafist prayer room along with Moktar."

"Are you trying to tell me that Bintou and Aïcha's brothers are Salafists? Odd. Doesn't really fit. I think I've heard of Ruben. If we're talking about the same guy, he belongs to a new Hasidic circle whose name escapes me. A group set up by Jews from Tiznit in Morocco. They split from a movement that originated in Belarus and reestablished themselves with their own rebbe—in Brooklyn."

"Rebbe?"

"A messianic religious leader, if you prefer."

"How do you know all this?"

"I sometimes flick through *La Tribune Juive* at the newspaper kiosk, and every now and then I grab a coffee at the kosher *salon de thé* on rue André-Danjon, that one where all the moms meet after dropping the kids off at the Lubavitch school. I listen in on their conversations. Not long ago I heard them talking about a certain Ruben. This Moktar . . . Is he the guy that preaches at the crossroads on rue Petit?"

"The very same. An old pal of your Ruben. So, to recap: we've got three Salafists, one Hasidic Jew, and a family of Jehovah's Witnesses . . . That is one holy hornet's nest! While we're waiting, I can't even remember the last time I ate. I'd kill for a steak—how about an *onglet* at the Boeuf Couronné?"

Rachel stands up, checking her watch.

"5:30. Bit early. Let's swing by the Bunker first. Settle up and get a receipt. I can't be bothered to dither around with expenses forms again . . . Don't forget to write their names on the back."

"Yes, boss! Oh yeah . . . What are we going to do about those new pills Onur told us about?"

"Not sure yet. We haven't got time to deal with that right now. I'll ask Gomes to see if he can get anything more on it."

"Dear old Gomes . . . And to think you pick on me about me and Léna!"

"Well I've never slept with him, and there's not the slightest danger of that happening!"

"That's even worse—you're stringing him along!"

Rachel laughs.

"Touché, we're even. Can we go now?"

7

A few miles south and several orbits later, Ahmed gently touches down from his Himalayan odyssey. The walls holding up his friend's dingy pad fall back into focus: naked women; porn cartoons; Hendrix photos. The light has faded, and so too the pressure in his head. He's not far from feeling alright. Al is smoking and doodling. There are sheets of A4 paper scattered in front of him scribbled in words and drawings. He signs the bottom-right of the last one, gathers up the pages and hands them to Ahmed.

The Ballad of the Serial Killer
(an illustrated song for the times)

All the girls on the métro
All the girls in pink
Too many slappers, too many
Gotta do something
Sex makes me sick
I'm all about purity
Under their dark glare
I feel in danger.

Stronger than me
Yeah . . . it's
Stronger than me
Them with the brown hair, the big booties
I got to . . . kill them
A backyard, a box room
A blade for cuttin', shut it!
The girl lets it happen
Not so proud!
Stronger than me
Yeah . . . it's
Stronger than me
Them with the brown hair, the big booties
I got to . . . kill them
Still in ma' pocket
I got a pair of tights
Ain't nothin' better, trust
For killin' slow
In her dyin' eyes I took pleasure
In the street, I take a chance
I step lightly
Stronger than me
Yeah . . . it's
Stronger than me
Them with the brown hair, the big booties
I got to . . . kill them
A moral to the story
To kill's to live too
No philosophy simpler
For the serial killer.

The accompanying sketches are very lifelike, harking back to the golden age of the old-school *Détective* magazines. Ahmed is transfixed by the penultimate one. It features the killer seen from behind. His neck thick like a bull's. Massive shoulders. Unlike in the song, the victim is looking not at her killer but at the reader. At him, Ahmed. Exactly the same look as that night. Exactly the same shoulders, too. Ahmed looks at Al as he rolls his umpteenth joint, his eyes elsewhere. *It's cool, the dude's a shaman. Images come to him. I was totally wired when I arrived here. He got inside my head and purged me with his drawings.* He looks up from the final sheet, feeling calmer.

"Not bad, man! If only I could follow your lead and get all my obsessions down on paper, that would free up my head space for a shitload of other stuff . . . Girls, for starters . . . You know, the last five years I've completely stopped thinking about girls. Lucky enough if I even noticed they were there. Since Laura's murder it's all come flooding back. There's this policewoman . . . I don't know . . . There's something about her . . ."

"A policewoman! Yeah, boy! *Rock 'n' roll!*"

"Thanks for having me around, man. It's done a lot of good. I'll come back some time."

"In three years?"

"Maybe five . . . Or two weeks. The important thing is I'll come back."

The summer's night is falling slowly. Ahmed heads back northeast in no rush. His little stroll has allowed him to recalibrate. He thinks of Dr. Germain. It's time to get back on that couch. To talk. Talk until he can at last bring himself to discuss that night at the furniture store. And it's not like psychoanalysis was that bad. It was quite fun, thinking back, even if at the time it didn't make him laugh much. He remembers the last sentence he uttered: "The trouble with girls, doctor, is that you have to make them come!"

"You have to?"

Germain's trump card had stopped him in his tracks. Then, for a whole year, he couldn't say a single word. He replayed the film over and over in his head—a succession of different actresses but always the same scenario . . . A girl notices him and shows an interest. He won't even stop to wonder whether he likes her or not. Generally speaking she'll be fairly pretty. So he leaps on this golden opportunity, fully aware of his inability to seal the deal. He'll then set about trying to satisfy her on every level. Until it fizzles out completely and he loses any notion of who he is and what he wants in life. In the end, the girl gets fed up with spending her time with such a slippery bastard and takes off without thinking for a second why she'd set her heart on such a passive boy. But each to their own psychoanalysis . . . He knew where this imperative for making women come originated: his mother. But this, this was the abyss, the black hole. "Hole?" Germain would have said. The second he started thinking about his mother, his brain would freeze. He used to blank out, develop facial tics, and end up collapsed in a heap. This was what it was like for a whole year on the couch—nothing. Eventually he got sick and tired and stopped going. But today, something's clicked. To put it to the test, he thinks back to the shrink's "You have to?" and he starts laughing.

Wandering along the canal path he finds himself at Café Prune. Spitting distance from Dr. Germain's. Throughout his years of psychoanalysis he'd go there for a macchiato before each session, even though he never took milk in his coffee any other time. Only on Mondays and Fridays at 8:45 a.m. Today, despite the fact it's 9:00 in the evening, he enters the favorite haunt of the *bobo* hipsters in the tenth arrondissement and heads to the bar. The waiter— black hair, black T-shirt, burgundy apron—seems to recognize him vaguely. When he brings over the coffee, Ahmed, acting on a sudden impulse, asks for the telephone book. The guy gives him a funny look and fetches it. Germain Alfred, 18, rue Dieu. Tel: 01 57 91 28 73.

"Do you have a pay phone?"

The waiter looks at him in astonishment.

"A pay phone and the phone book? Not every day we get asked for that! There hasn't been a pay phone here since the '90s . . ."

"What about a landline? You must have a landline. I've got to make a call—just to another landline. It's important."

Ahmed's tone and appearance disarm the achingly trendy bar-
man, and he gestures to the telephone by the counter.

"Hello, Dr. Germain? This is Ahmed Taroudant. You remember . . . Can you fit me in? . . . In twenty minutes. Wonderful, I'll be
there."

He replaces the handset, drinks his coffee and pays before crossing the road to take a seat at the edge of the canal. Dr. Germain's
deep voice had taken him back many years to a time when, session
after session, he would relive his parents' story, which he only knew
from his mother Latifa's well-worn accounts. Until he was thirteen, Ahmed's life had been limited to one long, tragic saga. And
then—nothing.

The story begins in 1970 with Latifa Mint Ibrahim's arrival at the
Faculty of Literature at the University of Rabat. She was the daughter of a well-known Sufi religious leader. Her father was a progres-
sive. He wanted to set an example and pressed his beloved daughter
to study and be independent. In those days, the regime was harsh,
very harsh, but the people were not to be defeated. Far from it.
Young people believed in their power to change the world and their
country. Latifa felt giddy with freedom, and was naturally inclined
toward the more radical, adventurous fringes of society. She was
drawn to the Maoists of the all-new 23 Mars movement. Her heart
swelled with notions of liberty and—even more so—equality. As a
child she felt shackled by her status as daughter of the *sheik*, and
would have willingly switched places with the black-skinned young
girls who were her servants, but who were free to run wherever
they pleased. On her return from school she would eat the dates
with *smen* butter brought to her by Soueïdou, their young *hartanya*,
a freed slave girl. But she only ever dreamed of milking the goats
and churning butter in the old vessel made of animal hide. When
M'barek, Soueïdou's father, went up to gather dates from the tree
in the garden, Latifa would imagine what it was like to be up there.
As far as everyone was concerned, M'barek was a *khadim*, a slave,
barely the quarter of a man. To her he was the very embodiment of

freedom. Later, when her new Marxists friends spoke to her about Hegel and his "master-slave dialectic" she didn't need them to spell it out. But what she never understood was why they deserted her when she fell in love with Hassan. They met at a music festival. Hassan was black, like most Gnawa musicians, the Gnawa being a people descended from slaves imported—as with so many others— from the banks of the Niger River, the place the Arabs called *Bilad es-Sudan*, the Land of the Blacks. For centuries, the black slave trade had been a lucrative business, amassing great fortunes for the most distinguished families from Fez and beyond, all pious Muslims unperturbed by the fact that the origin of their wealth lay in the trafficking of human beings, most of them fellow Muslims. The Gnawa had succeeded in preserving the memory of their ancestors' music. Music that had the power to deliver the sick of the spirits that possessed them. One night—only once—Latifa had confided in Ahmed that Hassan, his father, sometimes had visions. Before he had even met her, he knew she would be coming and that their love would spell his ruin. It had been written, and it would have been unmanly of him to shy away from his destiny. This was her way of telling her son that she knew he had inherited the same gift. Then she picked up the thread of her story again . . . From the first moment Latifa laid eyes on Hassan, she had no doubt that this was the free man she had been waiting for her whole life. She lost any concept of the time and country in which she lived. Consumed by love, she never considered the risks and the price she would have to pay. As for Hassan, he loved her all the more strongly knowing that death lay in wait for him. One day, he disappeared. He never came to their tryst. This was common enough in the dark days of the Years of Lead. No one dared ask where or why he had gone. There, a Gnawa—an 'abid, a *khadr*—had loved a girl from a good family. Not often the secret police had the chance to get their hands on a case like that. Maybe it was a personal vendetta by an especially racist, jealous policeman? An intervention from Latifa's father? Right away she got the feeling that she would not see her lover alive again, and she decided to flee the country, never to return. Her comrades were so wrapped up in their revolution that they saw her plight as irrelevant. Only Ahmed Taroudant—a closeted homosexual from a middle-class Agadir family—resolved to come to her aid. He took the *sheik*'s daughter into hiding, fixed her up with a fake passport, and they left the country together across the Algerian border to the south of the country, disguised as peasants. Back in that long-distant age, Arabs and blacks could travel freely between Africa and Europe. On arriving in France, the young Moroccan girl realized she was pregnant. She decided to keep the baby. Ahmed stayed with her until the birth, met the child who was to be named after him, the only friend she had ever had. He returned to his country, and she stopped hearing from him three years later.

Ahmed therefore inherited the first name and surname of his mother's savior. As for his father, he knows only his first name, Hassan. Latifa never wanted to give him his full name. Nothing but the story. Always the same story. Two lives locked up in this one fucking story. How can you live after that without turning into some fictional character? From then on Latifa, moving from job to job, slowly began to lose her mind. First a job in a bookshop, then a florist's, then a fruit-and-vegetable stall. Doctors, psychiatrists, hospital. Ahmed had to fend for himself from the age of fourteen. Latifa was either on antipsychotics or in the hospital, first at Maison Blanche, then at Pithiviers, where the doctors abandoned any hope of releasing her. It didn't take long for him to prefer her being in the hospital. The social worker turned a blind eye: didn't put him into care, sorted out the paperwork, and made sure he got his child benefits. He started work at sixteen. At eighteen he managed to get out of military service without even having to fake it. Mentally unstable. They didn't admit him to a psychiatric ward. Just let him go like that. By the age of twenty he was a night watchman, happily removed from the world with his books and his Go board games. Human contact was limited to Al and two or three other friends. Sketchy love and sex life: every once in a while a girl would show some interest, and he would drift along with it until she got tired.

For him, love was death. Ahmed assigned words to his mother's silences: Oufkir, Tazmamart, Driss Basri. He learned about the different forms of torture. Whenever he thinks of his father, he sees a man who loved a woman and paid for it with his life, dying in agony. An endless loop runs through his head detailing every conceivable death, every conceivable torture. Water baths, parrot's perches, electrodes, red-hot pokers. Plus the ones he's read about in de Sade, and that photo of the slow-sliced man with the ecstatic expression that Georges Bataille obsessed over. This is what fills his head: the sound of screaming and ripping flesh.

Lots of images.

IMAGES

Ahmed stands up. Must be about time to head to Dr. Germain's. Time for words.

8

At the Bunker, an uneasy Gomes is updating Kupferstein on what he's found on Laura Vignola's family in Niort. Since his arrival at the commissariat last October, fresh from completing his police training, the young lieutenant has been captivated by Rachel. He would do absolutely anything to make her smile. She uses her power over him sparingly, saving it only for when she really needs a hand. She doesn't like the idea that the sorts of favors she asks of Gomes are down to the effect she has on him; they're no different from what she'd naturally expect of any colleague. What's more, she knows that the

rest of the officers at the local force—with the notable exception of
Mercator—don't like her and Hamelot. They think they're only out for
themselves—too cerebral, too unlike the others. Rachel was spoiling
for this widespread animosity, which ultimately she couldn't give a
damn about, not to taint her young admirer. But then she did like
the fact that she had this grip over Gomes, even if he wasn't her type
and his first name was Kevin; however hard she tried to put her
class prejudices to one side, that was a mega deal-breaker. Anyhow,
she's playing it very carefully so that she can keep up the beguiling
act for as long as possible. Gomes tugs nervously at his shirt collar.
Without needing to look, she can sense the reason for his growing
discomfort. She wheels her chair around regardless, if only to show
her one true enemy at the commissariat that she's not afraid of him.

At the far end of the open-plan office, old Lieutenant Meyer is swaying nonchalantly on his chair, watching them with a mocking air.
He's gnashing on some chewing gum, and pops a green bubble on
his lips at the precise moment Rachel's eyes meet his. Scum. The guy
is scum. A single look and you need a shower. This is a policeman
from the old school—fat but muscled, embittered, racist, macho,
homophobic. And all the more anti-Semitic because everyone
thinks he's Jewish because of his Alsatian surname. Just by looking
at him Rachel can feel herself turning into a guard dog, an anti-
racist angel, a militant, a *Charlie Hebdo*–reading militant. She cannot stand it. Fine if Meyer does his Meyer thing: she couldn't give a
damn. But what she can't accept is the fact that he is capable—with
that craven look of his—of touching the side of her she is least com-
fortable with. She didn't become a policewoman so she could be
confused with the teacher in that film *Entre les murs,* going all soft
on troublemakers. No—she became a policewoman to turn a vision
into a reality; to embody an inanimate ideal, namely to uphold justice through the employment of force. As far as possible, Rachel
strives to believe in that. She is lucky enough to take her orders
from Mercator, who is far from an angel, though he does retain
some notion of what it means to be a policeman—something along

the lines of "we must protect society," including against the powerful. The chief still has that bit of naïveté. If she had been stationed
at the commissariat in the eighteenth, Enkell and Benamer would
have left her with only one option: turning to the dark side.

That is what she cannot bear about Meyer—because of him, she is
forced to view her work from a more sinister angle. His presence
means she cannot forget that the police force is not just about Luke
Skywalker, but about Darth Vader too. Deep down, a part of her—
hard though it is to admit—reminds herself in a whisper that her
very being is made up of this mixture of good and evil. The incestu-
ous relationship between crime and justice is what sealed the fate of
her forebears. It's what allowed her to be born. This buried part
of her only creeps to the surface in the dead of night. It's a spirit.
One that is no stranger to the police, and which is personified by
Meyer. A demon with carpet slippers and—despite the heavy dose
of chlorophyll chewing gum—halitosis. All in all, she prefers Benamer, the torturer with the piercing eyes who taught them the most
abject of interrogation techniques, and whose advances she managed to stave off until her final month of police training. Everything
he stood for revolted her, but she was magnetically drawn to him.
She was going through a Nietzsche phase at the time, and the phi-
losopher's writings had provided her with a tailor-made means of
self-justification: "Wisdom is a woman, and loves only a warrior." It
was an encounter as brief as it was intense. Other men since have
seemed somewhat plain. She had drawn a line through Benamer.
She had not the least desire to get lost in his darkness.

Gomes is becoming increasingly unnerved by Meyer's hostile presence. Rachel looks the young officer in the eye to encourage him
to pick up from where he left off. Laura's parents, Vincenzo and
Mathilde, had been easy to locate in Niort, where they have lived in
the same house for at least twenty-seven years, since it was the same
address as the one on their only daughter's birth certificate. Just to
be on the safe side, he had also run a Google search and found an

article on the *Charente Libre* website detailing a dispute between
the taxman and the local branch of the Jehovah's Witnesses. The tax
authorities were demanding thousands of dollars that the Jehovah's
Witnesses were refusing to pay, invoking the 1905 law separating
state and religion, which affords religious organizations certain tax
breaks. Yet the Jehovah's Witnesses, who feature on a list of sects
published by the French government, are not recognized as a religious organization. Proud of having unearthed all this information,
Gomes is eager to put the icing on the cake.

"And guess who is the head of the local branch?"

"Vincenzo Vignola . . ."

The young policeman eyes her suspiciously, utterly deflated.

"You already knew?"

"To be honest, the answer to that particular conundrum was as
clear as day. And I found out less than an hour ago that Laura's
parents' religious background was the reason behind their conflict.
They've refused to see her ever since she left home. Do you mind
following up that lead, please? I'll take care of informing the parents,
or more like getting someone else to inform them. Let's hope the
police at Niort can show a bit of tact . . ."

She thanks her colleague wholeheartedly and is about to ask him
a question regarding the new drug in town when she makes eye
contact with Meyer once again. A funny feeling courses down her
spine. Is he spying on her? What for? And *who* for? Could he hear
them from over there? She saves her questions for later and heads
to her office, skirting around Jean who doesn't even seem to notice
her. Slumped in front of his screen in a daze, he looks like he's out of
service. She leaves him in his vacant state, sits down at her computer,
looks up a number and dials.

"Hello, is that the commissariat in Niort? Lieutenant Kupferstein,
Paris, nineteenth arrondissement. Please could you put me through
to the *commissaire* or the officer on duty?"

"Please hold . . ."

"Hello, Commissaire Jeanteau speaking. You caught me just as I
was leaving."

"Good evening, Commissaire, this is Lieutenant Kupferstein from the nineteenth in Paris. We have a murder on our hands. A young woman, Laura Vignola. Her parents live in your neck of the woods."

"Right. And what can we do for you?"

"Well, errr . . . We found the family's contact details on our system, and just as I was about to call them I thought to myself that I couldn't really tell them the news over the phone. I was wondering if one of your people could take care of it?"

"You know, we're short-staffed as it is, even without doing your work as well as our own."

"I understand, but imagine the responsibility—what if something were to happen? You never know how people might react. She was their only child . . . Plus we already know from the concierge in the building where Laura lived that she didn't get along at all well with her parents. The chances are—in fact it's more than likely—that this spat had nothing to do with the crime, but at this stage we have to follow up every lead. So if you or one of your more experienced officers could handle this process personally, it would be an opportunity to get the parents to talk and to shed some light on the victim's personality."

"Fine, I'll deal with it. My wife is used to me coming home late, and what's more the in-laws are around for dinner this evening . . . this gives me a decent excuse to arrive in time for pudding and the digestifs! Tell me about the murder."

Rachel briefs the *commissaire*, leaving out the most striking features of the crime scene to limit any risk of leaks. Jeanteau promises to call back as soon as he has carried out the task. She gives him her cell number before casually throwing in one last detail.

"Oh, I almost forgot, Commissaire. They're Jehovah's Witnesses."

"Jehovah's Witnesses! Serious nut-jobs, aren't they? Listen, I've investigated cases involving sects before, but this would be new for me. Maybe this'll be educational . . . I'll call you as soon I'm done there. Wish me luck!"

"Good luck, Commissaire!"

*

Exhausted, Rachel needs to get out of the Bunker as quickly as possible. She goes back over to Jean, who has risen from his torpor, and suggests they take a stroll to the Boeuf-Couronné for that much-needed *onglet*.

9

In the narrow corridor leading from the waiting area to the psychoanalyst's consulting room, Dr. Germain—around sixty, tall, slightly stooping, angular face, white hair, rounded glasses, brown corduroy pants—holds out his hand to Ahmed.

"So, you came back . . ."

Ahmed looks at the doctor, and all of a sudden he remembers what it is to go through psychoanalysis. It's not just an unburdening, an emptying; it's also a rejection of the obvious. He came back, and so right away he has to reflect on his return. He knows what he has come to say, but why does he want to say it? Ahmed remembers how once—here, in this place—he had established the parallel between psychoanalysis and confession. "Except that here there is no judgment," the doctor had stressed. Another time, when he was discussing the pangs of guilt he suffered about his mother, Dr. Germain had suggested he move toward "a mode of expression that is not that of expiation."

"Yes, I came back."

He lies down on the couch and suddenly feels good.

"It's funny, your question. 'So you came back . . .' It's not really even a question. If I had to write it down, it would be followed by a dot-dot-dot rather than a question mark. Someone needs to invent some new punctuation for psychoanalysis, in fact. Your questionless question has thrown me completely. I was going to go for a sort of confession. Tell you about the thing that took me to Maison Blanche. What I saw. The thing I've never been able to bring up. So unspeakable I ended up letting it get confused with my silence. Just three minutes ago I was still in that state of confusion."

"And now?"

"Now? I know I've got to give it a name. But I also know that deep down it's not the reason for my silence. Even if it's quite a thing to see a murder and not be able to do anything to stop it."

"A murder . . ."

"It's like there's this knot tying together my father's death, my mother's madness, and the murder of that girl at the warehouse . . . Everything's lumped together in my throat . . . It's like this thing that won't go away. Like all the images that have filled my mind for so long. It was my father who died, for fuck's sake, so why do I always picture myself killing women?"

"I see. What did they do wrong, these women?"

"Oh fucking hell!"

A heart-rending sigh. Silent tears stream down Ahmed's cheeks. He carries on, his voice strangled.

"It's the second time today. The first time was thinking about Laura."

"Laura is your neighbor, if I remember right?"

"Was."

No response.

"She was murdered. I suddenly realized that she'd been in love with me without ever saying it, and now she's dead and gone forever. And I'm sad we'll never live the life we might have had. And I decided to live. And so I came back."

Dr. Germain's voice catches slightly.

"Someone has killed Laura. Is that what you're telling me?"

"Yes, that's exactly what I'm telling you. Hey, Doctor?"

"Yes . . ."

Ahmed sits up and looks the psychoanalyst in the eye.

"How far does patient confidentiality go? Secrets from sessions like this?"

Dr. Germain looks at him squarely with his bright eyes.

"There is no limit. What's said in here stays in here. Do you want to continue?"

Ahmed lies back down.

"I was the first to see Laura's body, but I didn't say anything to the police. A former resident of Maison Blanche living on disability benefits who spends most of his time reading noir fiction about psychopathic killers . . . Not a chance! When I saw her I was overwhelmed with rage, with a desire for revenge. That's what made me snap out of it. That's what made me come here. Before doing anything I need to sort out my head. To separate the stuff with my father, my mother, my obsessions, Laura, Emma . . ."

"Emma?"

"Yeah, Emma. She's the one I've never told you about. The one I saw get murdered before my eyes at the warehouse. With Laura, that makes two."

"Did you see Laura being murdered?"

"No, I found her later. They had strapped her to the edge of her balcony. A drop of blood fell on my face. I looked up and there was her foot floating above my head. I went up to see . . . Emma—that's a whole other story."

"Maybe we'll talk about it next time?"

This is how Dr. Germain always used to wrap up his sessions, whether it was a quarter of an hour or three. Ahmed feels a bit taken aback, but he knows from the tone of the doctor's voice that these fifteen minutes carried some serious weight.

"Tomorrow I can fit you in at 7:30 a.m. Does that work for you?"

He doesn't hang about, thinks Ahmed.

"7:30, fine."

"We can also talk about payment then . . ."

"Payment, yeah, of course . . ."

"If you want to get yourself together, I don't think we can proceed as we did before. With your medical costs being covered, I mean."

"Yes, you're probably right . . . I'll think about it."

"That's right, think about it. Good night."

Dr. Germain holds out his hand to Ahmed, who shakes it.

"Good night."

The canal is strewn with young people loaded up with beers and guitars. Ahmed barely notices them. He thinks back to his mother, whom he hasn't seen for years. He remembers her slow descent into madness, and the way she took it out on him when he visited her in the hospital. Yes, he had been right to sever ties with her. A case of survival.

On avenue Jean-Jaurès, just after Ourcq Métro station, Ahmed instinctively casts an eye through the window of the Boeuf-Couronné. The sight of the two lieutenants sitting in front of their *onglets* strikes him as perfectly natural. They are meant to be in this place at this precise moment. Jean, lost in thought, brings the chunks of red meat robotically to his mouth. Rachel, however, savors each mouthful, each sip of wine. It makes him happy imagining himself with her, just like that, enjoying a meal in silence. In the meantime he thinks how great it would be to be able to call her. One last glance and he shifts off to the *tabac*. A few minutes later, France Télécom card in pocket, and just as he is stepping through the door of his block, he bumps into a tall black man wearing a prayer cap and an ankle-length *kamiss*. Moktar does not look at him. Only a murmur under his breath as he passes.

"*Halouf*-eating bastard, you'll burn in hell like a pig stuck on a spit. You stink of white man . . ."

Bewildered, Ahmed continues on his way, wondering about the reason for the insults. He stops and turns back. No sign of Moktar. Where had he gone? Which building, which shop had he entered? Strange. One more thing for him to get his head around. In his mailbox he finds an envelope with a Bordeaux postmark. News from his cousin Mohamed.

One morning, nine months earlier, a young man of around twenty-three or twenty-five had rung his doorbell and claimed to be his cousin. Mohamed Nassir was the son of Nafissa, sister of Ahmed Taroudant, the man who had saved Latifa. He'd had no difficulty finding him because Ahmed still lived in the studio apartment that Taroudant had shared with his mother at the time of his birth thirty years before. Mohamed seemed to suspect that Ahmed was secretly his uncle's son, and that he'd married, had children, and continued to keep his preference for men under wraps. The "cousin" had stayed three weeks, enough time to check out Paris while waiting for university in Bordeaux, where he was studying for a degree in physics, to restart. Ahmed hadn't thought twice about this supposed cousin he'd never heard of moving in with him just like that. Perhaps it was because Mohamed represented the only remaining link with the country of his crazy mother and his dead father. A link that he'd never delved into, but which he knew he would never let go of. He had never felt anything other than French. To him Morocco was off the radar; a forbidden, dangerous, inaccessible country. Yet he had felt singularly close to his cousin despite the fact that, on paper, they were totally different. Mohamed never missed a prayer. He tried to awaken Ahmed to the benefits of Islam, not that he ever gave him any trouble about drinking alcohol. The two of them had found a balance. Ahmed didn't want to lose this unexpected cousin by revealing to him that they weren't really related at all and that, on top of that, his uncle was homosexual.

Back in Bordeaux, Mohamed had written one or two letters to which Ahmed hadn't responded, having relapsed into his interminable reading mode. Then nothing, until today. Up in his apartment, after scaling the six flights of stairs, he places the letter on the table and his jacket on the chair, sits on the ground, and sets about thinking of nothing.

10

One hour earlier, as evening was falling, Rachel and Jean were
sauntering toward the Boeuf-Couronné. The teachers and students
were filing out of the Lubavitch school on rue Petit. White shirts,
Borsalino hats, wool tzitzit tassels trailing from black jackets. Their
eyes skimmed past Jean and Rachel. At least they did over Jean;
with Lieutenant Kupfterstein there was a moment's hesitation . . .
As if goyim didn't exist. As if the only people that were real were
Jews in general and Hasidic Jews in particular. Jean could not bear
this attitude. Rachel, for her part, was fascinated by this ability to
not see. *How do they do it?* It reminded her of her trip to India.
More than once she had felt that strange sensation of ceasing to
exist, of literally disappearing as a result of not being registered.
In order to endure it she had reasoned that the caste system
must be so entrenched that a Brahmin—when encountering an
untouchable—can alter his trajectory to keep the other at a distance and therefore avoid acknowledging him. He sees him and
doesn't see him at the same time . . . Rachel had told Jean about
this to calm him down. "Do you really think the Brahmins' craziness makes up for these Lubavitch nuts?!" came the reply. But in
fact his rage did subside.

At the next crossroads there was a change of atmosphere.
A small group of Muslims of all shapes and sizes was listening
devoutly to a tall, very thin black man. Prayer cap on his head,
white *kamiss* diligently coming down to his ankles, in imita-
tion of the dress of the holy ancestors, the Prophet Muhammad
and his companions. Rapt in a well-rehearsed trance, Moktar
spoke to them of the time when all people made up one single

community, a single body around the Prophet. "And so the Jews
and the Christians listened to the message. Their hearts were not
closed and they came to know the truth before them. Everyone
embraced the true religion." Moktar is twenty-seven years old, his
audience ranging from fifteen to eighteen. Their eyes were gleaming, lit up by the self-proclaimed preacher's spirited speech pep-
pered with Arabic words. "Following the Prophet's death—*salla
Allaahu 'alayhi wa salaam*—discord descended upon Man. *Fitna* is
the work of *Shaytan*, let it never be forgotten. And to return to the
unity of *Ummah* we must never cease to imitate the holy ancestors, the *Sahabah* . . ."

AAAAAAMIN!

With a collective sigh the assembled gave vent to the day's frustrations.

The two lieutenants had stopped and heard everything. Moktar
and the others carried on, as if not noticing them. But their pretending was even less subtle than it was back at the Lubavitch: the tension
in the bodies of the young audience; the wavering tone of the Salafist's
voice . . . Every utterance indicating that it was them, yes them, that
they were addressing—the Jews, the Christians, the atheists. Police
in the service of *Shaytan* doomed to suffer the eternal hellfire of
Gehenna. And sooner the better.

Hamelot and Kupferstein eventually continued on their way.

"Speak of the devil . . . Moktar's in fine form today," Jean said.

"Flying form! How many of them do you reckon they'll find in a
bloody mush in Baghdad three months from now?"

"So long as it's Baghdad . . ."

"It's easy to be cynical. They're local kids. It's our duty to look out
for them."

"I'm a policeman, not a nanny. And how do you propose we
protect them from themselves? Fuck, I knew Moktar . . . He was
normal. Brilliant, even. He aced his baccalaureate—got a distinction. That was before your time at the Bunker. Back then there
was some fight with a white girl he'd met at college. He was in

love with her. His family banned him from seeing her. 'You are of noble blood, a member of the Soninké people . . . You must marry a girl from the same class as you!' He flipped out—smashed up the entire house. I was on duty that day. We managed to overpower him and take him to Sainte-Anne, which was weird bearing in mind it's not the nearest psychiatric hospital. Six days later he came home. A family meeting took place which resulted in his immediate departure to their homeland, a village in the middle of nowhere on the northern bank of the Senegal River. Three months later he was back. He'd changed but he was still fairly unstable; before long it was round two in the hospital. Maison Blanche this time, for nine weeks. That stint calmed him down for good. I don't know what they did to him back in his village, but since that trip he just drifts between the prayer room and the crossroads. Preaching."

The last stop on the journey took them past the evangelical church, in front of which a small queue had formed for evening prayers and healing. Pastor from Togo; a congregation made up of Africans, West Indians, whites, and Kabyles.

"I think I've had my fill for the evening," Rachel said. "Come on, let's go. Time for this *onglet!* Afterward I've got to swing by the Bunker to touch base with Gomes one last time about the Jehovah's Witness side of things. I don't know what's behind this murder, but it certainly mirrors the neighborhood, what with these religious nut-jobs on every corner."

By chance their favorite table by the window at the Boeuf-Couronné is free. A few minutes later, they are finally tucking into their *onglet.* Jean closes his eyes for a moment. A little concerned, Rachel asks him if he is okay.

"I don't know. Feeling tired all of a sudden, thinking about the loneliness this evening when I get home . . . I'm struggling to deal with myself at the moment. Long days at work are fine by me. But when home time is approaching . . . Do you ever get the feeling you've been sentenced to life in solitary confinement?"

"No, I don't . . . This might sound silly, but if you can't stand loneliness why don't you find yourself a girlfriend?"

"Why would a girl put up with me if I can't even put up with
myself? She'd have to be a real masochist!"

"They do exist, you know . . . There are plenty of them around . . .
Come on, eat up! Cold steak's not going to help anyone."

11

Gomes is good. No doubt about it. He has managed to track down
the tax inspector who handled the Jehovah's Witness case in Niort.
He now had an almost pathological aversion to religious organizations of any kind, and didn't need to be asked twice to share
everything he could with the young policeman. Vincenzo Vignola
is the treasurer of the local branch of the Witnesses. He is also
head of the regional body of elders, a position that entitles him to
control even the most intimate aspects of his congregation's lives.
He went on to explain that the Witnesses won't talk to strangers, but
that it would be possible to find information on discussion forums
for ex-members. Which was precisely what Gomes was about to do
when Rachel arrived.

"Have you got a personal e-mail that you use at home? That way
I can send you any contacts or links I find."

"My personal e-mail? But it's personal! Oh, alright then . . .
rachelk2000@laposte.net. Hey, but aren't you going home? Haven't
you got a girlfriend, a life outside work?"

"Do you? You haven't sat down for thirty-six hours! I'm no less
of a police officer than you, Rachel! I want to catch Laura's killer

too. That's why I do this job. On top of that, you know the Jehovah's Witnesses have recruited masses of Portuguese people? They took one of the cousins I grew up with in Sartrouville. He hasn't spoken to any of us since. So all of this does concern me. Go and get some sleep. If I find anything I'll send you an e-mail."

Rachel is astonished to see Gomes getting so animated. For the first time, she looks on him as a man. Not a man she likes, for sure, but a man—no longer a boy, even if he does have a ridiculous first name she is perhaps going to have to learn to say without so much scorn.

"Okay, Kevin. I'm out of here. Oh no, hold on. I've got one more thing to ask you. Have you heard anything about a new drug in the area?"

"No. What type of drug? Have you had a reliable tip?"

"Let's just say that someone's heard about some pills . . . Like ecstasy, just a way stronger high. Reckon we should check it out."

"Okay. I think I know who to ask. I'll keep you posted."

*

Lieutenant Kupferstein's scooter is parked across the street from the Bunker. She lives in the eighteenth—hipster central—on rue d'Orsel, a stone's throw from the Théâtre de l'Atelier. In the evening, and at weekends, she has to unwind, have a change of scene and forget about the pavements she paces day in, day out. Here, at the foot of the Butte Montmartre, surrounded by tourists, Parisian night owls, artists, actors, and performers, she feels good. Her apartment—a little one-bedroom attic conversion where she rarely entertains—is her lair, her hideaway. Something nags at her on her way. Despite her tiredness, she stops on rue Ordener to check out the area around the telephone booth from which the police were called about Laura's murder. Something doesn't fit. Why would anyone go all that way? And they telephoned the commissariat in the eighteenth, rather than the emergency number where calls are logged automatically. Whoever made the call knew about police procedure. All the more reason to take a closer look. The booth is occupied by two African women, one of whom is sporting a magnificent black eye. Clearly very angry, they snatch the telephone and start yelling down the line in broken English. A few feet away, a little guy, very thin and very pale, waits his turn. In his right hand he's holding a plastic bag through which a large bottle of Heineken can be made out. He is gripping the neck very tightly through the bag. On the other side of the road, four Algerians, sitting on upturned red plastic crates, are chatting outside a grocer's, monitoring everything going on across the street out of the corner of their eye. Jean was right. Someone must have seen the anonymous caller in the booth. Tomorrow we'll see if Mercator has managed to get Enkell and his guys to chase it up.

Just as Rachel is preparing to leave, she notices that the small second-hand *brocante* shop in front of the telephone booth is still open. She has passed it many times without ever going in. The entrance is virtually barricaded by two display cases stacked with tattered copies of the worst sort of detective novels: Jean Bruce, *OSS 117, Son Altesse Sérénissime* . . . She moves closer and casts an eye over the bric-a-brac in the shop: '50s or art deco lamps, old turntables, *La Poste* calendars with gaudy '60s colors, ashtrays on stands, armchairs, wobbly seats . . . The highs and lows of a hoarding, second-hand-dealing *brocanteur*. For weeks she has been searching for a red metal lampshade. One of those ones that you can fix straight to the bulb with a metal clip. This was to be the crowning achievement of her interior decor. Maybe she would find one here? The *brocanteur* steps out from the shadows, beer bottle in hand. A truly monstrous creation. Rachel cannot help but judge him by his appearance—everything about him is grotesque. His lecherous eyes, his shuffling walk, his dubious tone.

"Are you looking for something?"

"Yes. You know one of those little lampshades that you clip . . ."

"No, I don't know anything," he says, cutting her off. "It's my one principle: to know nothing. I've got shitloads of lampshades, but I'd have to empty the entire store room to find them. And as you can see," he says, indicating his beer, "I'm relaxing. It's the end of the day."

Rachel examines the inside of the shop closely, half-listening to him. Over the man's shoulder she sees a television. On the screen she can make out a woman's buttocks, behind which a man is standing with his large, erect penis in his hand. With each thrust he takes at her from behind a tacky electronic "ping" notches up another point. Rachel's face hardens. She looks him dead in the eye.

"Yes, I can see you're relaxing. Well then, have a good evening, *monsieur le brocanteur.*"

As she turns to leave and pick up her scooter, she spots a book that seems different from the others: *Le Boucher* by Alina Reyes. Images play over in her mind for the duration of her journey home: the shop owner's repulsive face, the porn on the TV, and *Le Boucher* . . . The butcher, the butcher . . . In front of her building she locks up her scooter and decides to stop thinking about it all. Up to the sixth floor, key, lock, and *phew!* Rachel carefully hangs up her jacket on the Habitat clothes horse to the right by the entrance. She had bought it online after being won over by the description:

Valet Jeeves.
Created by Sir Terence Conran.
150 dollars.

Folding structure; black-tinted eucalyptus.
Polyurethane varnish.
Marble cufflink bowl.
Very Important Products

What really sold it for her was the marble cufflink bowl. The very definition of chic. The lieutenant scans the room: everything as it should be. She's delighted she did the housework a couple of days previously. Now she can put her mind to rest. A glass of Cutty Sark for starters. Rachel went through a brief Lagavulin phase before finally coming to the realization that top-end, peaty, sophisticated whiskey was not her cup of tea. And so she returned to the calming simplicity of the standard, everyday brands, with some dry-roasted peanuts alongside. Reclining in her sea-green, '70s-style plastic armchair, she is in seventh heaven. Empty. Half an hour and two whiskeys later, Lieutenant Kupfterstein starts nodding off.

The telephone rings—Jeanteau over in Niort.

"Lieutenant, the parents struck me as strange to say the least. As if their daughter's fate didn't have anything to do with them. It was like I was reading a newspaper announcement to them, if you know what I mean."

"I think so, yes."

"I barely got a word out of them. They listened to me very politely, totally composed, before saying that they didn't want to be rude, but that it was time for them to go to the Kingdom Hall. That's their place of worship, if I'm not mistaken. It gave me the creeps, that meeting. Only the mother spoke when I mentioned identifying the body: 'Laura chose the way of the devil—she shall remain with the devil. She only ever came here to sully us, to heap the filth of the earth on us . . .' At that point the husband gave her this look . . . That shut her up. I left it there—didn't think I'd get anything more out of her with him sitting next to her. But I got a strange feeling from that trip. I hope all this proves helpful. Don't hesitate to call me back if you need anything. This case is beginning to interest me."

"'The filth of the earth' . . . What could she have meant by that?"

"I'm not sure, Lieutenant . . . I'm not sure. But it was odd, I'm telling you!"

"Thank you very much for going, Commissaire. It may well be that I'll come pay you a little visit if we're not making any headway in Paris. Perhaps we'll need to check out the filth in Niort. Good night."

"Oh yes, one other thing before you go. The mother was nondescript and sour, but the father was extremely handsome. A bit like Robert Mitchum in *The Night of the Hunter*—know the one?"

"Yes, I see . . ."

"Well, an older version, of course. Right, that's me. Until next time, all the best!"

Into the bathroom: teeth, toilet, pee, basin, hands. Not long until bed. Pants folded, pants in the laundry basket, followed by bra and white shirt. Yves Saint Laurent—a men's shirt. Spoils from a one-night stand. Not a great night, but a lovely shirt. Crimson nightie. Bed: a futon on top of a tatami mat, thick, slightly rough sheets—the old kind—with the initials A.V. embroidered in cursive script. Still warm enough not to need a blanket. No comforter either . . . she can't stand them. Rachel's in bed. Her head is tired, yes, but it doesn't want to sleep. The ghastly face of the *brocanteur* won't go away. So she searches for a remedy. She thinks about Ahmed. Imagines him alone in his bed, in torment too. Him over there, below Laura's apartment. Her, back here in her lair. Tossing and turning in every direction. It reminds her of something. An old Wong Kar-wai film. That's the one: *Fallen Angels*. A handsome hit man working for a beautiful girl who selects targets for him and pays him. They never see each other, yet she thinks of no one but him. One scene cross-cuts between each of them alone in their beds, frantic with lust. The woman touching herself through her clothes, pleasuring herself the only way she can. Who played the man? His face is unclear, vague. So she conjures up Tony Leung from *L'Amant*. Desire starts welling up gently. The tips of the fingers of her right hand brush her left arm, up as far as the crook of her elbow. Tracing every contour, caressing its softness. It feels good. She follows it down to the palm of her hand. As if she were touching a man. As if a man were touching her. Tony Leung—elegant and dignified—swaggering through the busy streets. He arrives at the house where the lovers meet. Rachel watches as Jane March lets him in. They kiss. But they don't, because it's Rachel who has swapped places with the actress. His hands stroke her stomach lightly through the satin of her nightdress before moving down, down. Desire dictates the movements—some familiar, others new. Never before has she yielded to herself like this. Sometimes images of men come to her. Sometimes they don't. Her fingers move quickly, slowly. Playing across the surface or exploring the depths. Pleasure for her given by her. Tonight she prefers to let her touch linger through the fabric. Feeling it soak, dampen. That wetness is her—her life. Now Rachel slides up the bottom of her nightie. She needs direct contact with her flesh. Strong, fast movements. Two words return to her from some uncertain place. Two words with a rhythm all of their own. Matching her own. *In, out. In, out.* Right until the end she keeps Tony Leung in her mind, crystal clear. That powerful, slow-motion image of him in the humid street from *In the Mood for Love.* She loses herself in him. That's what real movie stars are for. After she's come, Rachel drifts, keeping sleep at bay for the moment. A thought pops up. Does Ahmed fantasize about Maggie Cheung? She laughs out loud. Then she turns on the light, rummages in her bag, and takes out her spiral notebook. She saves Bintou and Aïcha's numbers in her cell. If one of them calls at 3:00 a.m. she wants to know who they are, to gather her thoughts before picking up. Lights out. Sleep.

12

Jean is wandering, drifting, roaming. After leaving Rachel at the Boeuf-Couronné he hadn't been able to go home, despite his exhaustion. He knows he won't get to sleep before 2:00 a.m. He would love to get laid. Nothing fancy—just fuck, think about nothing and forget. Forget himself in a hole. Yeah, yeah. Guy thoughts. The words are still echoing in his mind when a vision of his mother appears. Without a word. Just that weary expression of hers which means "You men, typical . . . always about you and your needs. And we put up with it. We have to accept you just as you are—dirty." But he's aware that women need to get laid too. Shit, he knows that from experience. But they are a different category of woman. Tarts, harlots, women who like a bit of "that" . . .

THE MOTHER AND THE WHORE

The filmmaker Eustache wasn't the first to come up with that. But how do you get shot of all that? Hey? How do you love, how do you desire a woman who'll love you back? A normal woman, that's all! How? Can someone please explain that one to him? And worst of all—he can't even manage hookers. Never gone there. Conveniently enough, his meandering has taken him to les Halles and—as if by chance—rue Saint-Denis. He inspects the announcements.

THAI MASSAGE
TOTAL RELAXATION
"HAPPY ENDING GUARANTEED"
30 EUROS

Temptation itself. But no. *I'm a policeman. I'm forbidden from going into such places. Unless it's official police business. And it's bad, too. The women are exploited. It's bad.* His mother there in the background throughout. But not just her. His father was a Breton communist. Even worse than a Catholic—no confession for a commie; no means of escape. The priest is in your head; a political commissar instead of a superego. Contemplating this as he walks, he realizes he has left the high-risk neighborhood. No longer any desire to seek comfort there. He'd feel dreadful afterward. He decides to spare himself the experience.

For a long, long time, temptation has never been far from his mind, ever since those first dark nights. Before that, even. The brutal pleasure he got from toasting ants with his magnifying glass in the sun. He never felt that guilty. No, it was puberty that spoiled everything. Why? His mother's view of him must have altered, tightened ever so slightly. And it was within its limited scope that he continued to exist. Occasionally a quiet voice would whisper: "If you're going to feel so shitty, being the typical male pig that you are, you might as well go the whole way and stop feeling guilty!" But no, it was beyond him. He'd had girlfriends from time to time, until they got fed up feeling so dirty after sex. Years ago a girl once said to him: "I feel like you hate me!" He had insisted over and over that he didn't, that he'd wanted to make her come but that he couldn't—that he'd blown his load too quickly . . ."I don't give a shit about that—if I wanted a guaranteed orgasm I wouldn't ask a man! It's the way you look at me as if I'm the biggest slut of all time; as if I'd forced you to do something filthy . . . That's what I can't stand!"

He never saw her again. The conversation came flooding back to him. He was lost—totally lost. He desperately wanted to scream, to cry. Not in the street, though. And screaming, that would be fine; but crying, letting the tears flow . . . What was that like?

He stops abruptly. He feels distraught. Arts et Métiers. What am I doing here? On rue au Maire there are some old-style Chinese restaurants. Real country bumpkin clientele. Go on then, let's see if one is still open! A Tsingtao and some lychees—something to mellow him out. He passes Tango—has some memory of an Afro-Caribbean club, from when he first arrived in Paris. It was a nightmare. He hadn't been able to dance and had to watch his girlfriend grinding up against hot, gyrating West Indian guys. He looks up instinctively. A rectangular screen with flashing red lights reads: "Gay and Lesbian Club." That does it. He flops against the side of a building. He feels like his head might explode. Boom! Splinters of skull everywhere; brain smeared all over the gray wall . . . He closes his eyes and takes a deep breath. He remembers the tips on the leaflet about relaxation that Léna gave him one day when he was stressed. He holds the air in his lungs and slowly counts to five, then breathes out. Slowly, slowly. He repeats the drill three times. When he comes to, a blond uniformed policewoman with blue eyes is looking at him— strangely, with the same kind of blue eyes as the European garbage collectors employed by the city council in Paris. The police car is parked on the corner by a *tabac* where her colleagues have gone to get their provisions.

"Everything alright, monsieur?"

Jean smiles at her, employing one of his many deceptive grins, and takes out his ID.

"Yeah I'm fine, thanks. Bit of a rough day, that's all."

"Oh, Lieutenant, you're one of us! Lucky you! I'm desperate to take the exam to get to your level, but with my hours, and with work being so tiring, I've never gotten around to it. Have a good night, Lieutenant! Go and rest if it's been a tough day . . ."

"Thank you, Officer. Good night to you too."

She moves on. Jean peels himself away from the wall and takes a couple of steps before turning around and shouting out to the young uniformed policewoman.

"Hey! Mademoiselle!"

She comes back toward him, stopping half a yard away.

"Yes?"

"Don't lose hope! If you really, really want it, that is. Don't lose hope!"

There is a thinly veiled violence in his voice. It is bristling down his entire body. Without giving her any time to respond, Jean wheels around suddenly. Speechless, she watches him fade into the night, wondering whether becoming a lieutenant is in fact all it's cracked up to be. She heads back to her fellow patrol officers. At least with them she can have a bit of a laugh!

Jean really needs that beer. He falls into the first dive he comes across. No decoration whatsoever, except the obligatory shrine comprising a chubby Buddha and red lighting. Gouged wooden tables and cafeteria chairs. *No way! They must've scrounged these off the local school!* he thinks to himself. He can scarcely believe his eyes, four Chinese men are playing mah-jong. As if they'd never left Macau. The cliché strikes him with a powerful sense of unreality. It actually releases some of his tension. He's somewhere else; it's okay. Concentrating very hard, the players don't pay the white policeman the slightest attention. A young woman in a dark skirt emerges from the storeroom, her flip-flops clacking on the black-and-white concrete floor. She looks at him for a moment before speaking.

"Yes, sir, what would you like?"

To take you from behind back there in the storeroom—you pushed up against the beer crates and me fucking you up the ass. Not dry, oh no. I want to work it in with your saliva on my fingers.

"A Chinese beer, please. A large one. And some prawn crackers."

"Take a seat, sir."

The well-rehearsed smile can't conceal an old, jaded soul, one who'd seen it all before she'd even been born. Jean sits down. So many demons. He spends his life permanently ricocheting between unfulfilled impulses and pangs of guilt. Yet right now he can feel a deep-rooted violence welling up inside. He hadn't noticed it when he spoke to the policewoman minutes earlier. But that image, those words . . . They'd been so clear in his head, and they spelled something different. Something that can't just be put down to tiredness or stress. Laura's murder seems to have opened a very deep fault line, bringing him closer to the magma within, the lava of inner confusion. The elaborate crime scene, the potency of the imagery created by the killer . . . It was all speaking directly to his unconscious mind. The waitress brings over his beer and the crackers in their see-through packet. He thanks her and pours the beer himself, tipping the glass to keep the froth to a minimum. Slowly, slowly. That ritual calms him down. Should he start with the beer or the crackers? In a restaurant he'd usually have a French fry before attacking his steak. Never go straight for the main event. He forces himself to drink, leaving the packet unopened. *Vaffanculo! Go fuck yourself, you bastard! Stop giving me shit!* With a sigh Jean leans back in his chair and takes a long gulp, his eyes half-closed. Violence. His boyhood cruelty comes back to him. Toasting ants. The time he beat the hell out of a cat he had trapped in a cemetery with his friend Jérémie simply to let off steam. All reasoning had been shot to pieces. A flash. White light. Jean had never gone as far as taking heroin, but this is how he imagined the high. Kick the shit out of it. Kick it! Kick it!

SMASH IT BATTER IT
DESTROY THE FUCKING LITTLE CAT
WIPE IT OUT FUCK IT UP
KILL THE FUCKER
LET THE EARTH FINALLY BE RID OF ITS
SHITTY PRESENCE

That was the end of obedient little Jean. The kind boy who never caused a stir, who preferred to shut himself in his room, jerking off in shameful silence. He stopped there, dead. Killed in action. A deed, a movement, repeated throughout eternity, for centuries and centuries. Oh, shit!

Then, suddenly, the cat scratched. It startled Jérémie and he let go of it. He stared at Jean. The cat scurried away. "Y-y-y-y-y-you were killing it," his friend stammered, before getting up and running off. Jean sat down on the mossy gray cement tomb of Pierre Le Bouennec (1903–1971). He looked at his hands, streaked with red, and touched his neck where he could feel droplets of blood. Back to the house. The nurse, his mother, tended to him without asking any questions. She had a sense for these things. Silence was her weapon of choice, along with her all-knowing eyes. Each silence strengthening her grip on Jean. The episode with the cat marked the end of his sadistic phase. From then on he took it out on himself. In his head, for the most part. But he did hurt himself a lot of the time: scrapes, burns, bruises of various sorts. Each time his mother would soothe him without uttering a single word.

He has never told anyone about this. Maybe if he'd met Léna later on? They were only seventeen when they started going out in Saint-Pol-de-Léon. Not the age for talking. More recently he'd let slip the odd snippet in confidence. Aware of the almost palpable pain he was in, she had advised him to start seeing a therapist. She'd been in psychoanalysis herself for four years and felt better for it. They both came from Brittany and shared the same Catholic, commie heritage (they'd met at the local *Jeunesse communiste* center), and she reckoned that the treatment she had been through would not do her policeman comrade any harm.

"You know, Jean, Freud was a Jew. He lived in a Catholic country and expressed hypercritical views toward religion in general—his and ours in particular. And he never believed in communism. He knew human beings too well to subscribe to a utopian ideology. The only thing that will lighten things up is focusing on your relationship with your mother. You've only got to read Lacan and watch von Trier's *Festen* again to understand how vital it is to sort out mommy issues. In Paris, most psychiatrists are Lacanians anyway! No, I assure you, this can only do you good! Sorry, I shouldn't be talking to you like this. Psychoanalysis—just like therapy—all depends on the patient and his desire to be there. Fuck, I sound so damn serious!? Listen to me! No, forget what I said . . . We were going to have another bottle of beer, weren't we?"

Jean looks around him. He's still in the tacky Chinese restaurant. The old guys are packing up their game of mah-jong. The waitress is leaning on the bar, looking at him but not hurrying him. It's time. He's finished his Tsingtao without even realizing. He stands up, pays, and grabs his unopened crackers. He feels calmer. Crisis averted. A crack has opened inside him, and he can't let it close by itself.

13

Ahmed decided against rolling a joint. He stashed the weed that Al gave him in the breast pocket of a clean pajama top. Even if he is wary of his paranoia, he can't resist the urge to get his brain whirring and make some sense of his encounter with Moktar. He's not really one for conspiracies or for coincidences. It's been four years since Moktar last said a word to him. When they cross in the street they avoid each other: no words, but no aggression either. They had been at Maison Blanche at the same time, though not for the same reasons. They weren't friends. One of their arguments would have boiled over if a nurse hadn't interrupted. From then on they made a tacit agreement to stay out of each other's way. Ahmed had become friends with the nurse, Rita, a big red-headed lady. Another red-head! During one of their conversations she had spilled the beans about Moktar's diagnosis: degenerative paranoid psychosis. Completely incurable. Inevitably his illness had embedded itself into the spirit of the times. It was at Maison Blanche that he began to talk about God. The time spent in the *bled* had sown the seed. A vision of the crime starts to form in Ahmed's mind. Very vague; imprecise. He has to see the killer's face again. For that he must sleep. But what about that joint? It was too early. Not inside the apartment. For a second he feels tempted to call up Rachel: "Hi, it's Ahmed. I was just thinking . . . I've got some good shit from Thailand—how about we carry on that chat about Ellroy?" A short laugh. He takes in a deep breath of love and fresh air, then thinks back to Moktar. The psychotic Salafist has got to be part of the picture, but he's not the killer. He can feel it, somewhere in the corner of his mind. "*Halouf-*eating bastard." It's bonkers—why are they so hung up on all that? The pure, the impure . . . He'd never really understood it. Got to be said that Latifa was totally relaxed toward all that. She let him eat and drink anything in the house. He'd never asked his few girlfriends about when their periods were due . . . Come to think of it, he really liked the taste of blood. "The taste of blood?" He repeats the words to himself, his inner voice strangely reminiscent of Dr. Germain's. *Fuck, you've got to be kidding—now I've got a shrink in my head!* The thought irritates Ahmed a bit, before he realizes that he's a bit hungry. He decides to make a special offering to Moktar by tucking into some ham tortellini. Saucepan, water, heat. Quickly resists the sudden urge to plunge his head into the boiling water. Barilla tortellini—eleven minutes. Splash of olive oil, salt, pepper. No parmesan. As he sits down, he spots Mohamed's letter. He puts it to one side for later. For once he eats slowly, managing not to burn his tongue.

Slouched on the futon, back against an Ikea Gosa Gott pillow—twenty-five inches by twenty-five—Ahmed is straining his ears. He often does this: to forget, to escape his head. He picks up on the muffled noises from all around the poorly soundproofed building. Most of the time, like tonight, it's the television. He can't bear it when the news is on: violence piercing him through the walls, even if he can't decipher the words. The rhythm, the frequency, the tone . . . All of it is aggressive, deceitful. Ads are too shouty. No, what he likes is the anesthetizing effect of the dubbed French versions of American series. He could never bear a television in his own place, but the dull sound of the programs through the cheap concrete . . . It's like popping a Valium. Which is lucky, as he's been off that for a while now; insomnia and alcohol have to be better than an addiction to prescription drugs. He also rejoices in silence when his neighbor puts TF1 or M6 on the TV. As he listens he feels the stress easing gently. *Fffffoooooooo, vvvooooshhhh, bzzzzzzzzzissssssh, ooooohhhhh-hhhh.* Eyes shut. No need to go anywhere. Just stay put. Then he opens them and stares at the crack in the white ceiling. Opens his eyes wide. Stays still. Five more minutes.

Up he gets, slowly, slowly. He goes back to the table and drinks the untouched glass of water. Taking hold of the letter, he sits down on the orange folding chair, grabs a sharp knife, and opens the envelope. It starts with the only Arabic words he's able to read: *Bismillah ar-Rahman ar-Rahim,* "In the name of Allah, the Beneficent, the Merciful." The rest is mainly in French:

Dear cousin,

Alhamdulillah, my year at university is over and I am on vacation. So I am writing you this little note to let you know that I am coming to spend the summer with you in Paris. I hope you do not mind? Soon, then, we will have the joy of seeing each other again. I'll leave it there, dear cousin, but not before taking the opportunity to thank you as ever for welcoming me like a brother.

May God bless you. See you soon, *inshallah* . . .
Mohamed.

Deep in thought, Ahmed puts the letter down. Mohamed is coming back. Strangely he's excited about seeing him, even if sharing living space with anyone for four months fills him with dread. And even if there was a bit too much of all the *bismillah, alhamdulillah, inshallah*, and *may God bless you* nonsense in the letter. Especially after the thing with Moktar this evening. Some John Lydon lyrics pop into his head. "Religion": one of the songs he knows by heart. The first verse cuts right to the chase: *God and lies; stained-glass windows and hypocrites*. Still sitting down, Ahmed hums the bass line. *Toodoodoodoo doodoo, toodoodoodoo doodoo*, then that guitar riff that never lets up. *Tananana nananana tananana nananana, tananana nananana tananana nananana*. It's in his head now, just like it was when he was fifteen and discovered PiL through this little tune, not long after he'd first heard "Sympathy for the Devil." After that, he feels stable, immune from Moktar's bullshit. Now he's on his feet, singing at the top of his voice, body and voice disjointed.

Ahhh! Nothing like a bit of blasphemy. Blasphemy and dancing. Ahmed feels lighter immediately. Strange how Islam has been such a burden on him despite the fact his mother never taught him about it nor imposed it on him in any way. Not that she'd have been able to anyway . . .

He stretches out on his bed and calmly, unhurriedly reflects on what he's got: Moktar, his *"halouf"* insult, and the pork joint. No, no, no! Not a coincidence. He closes his eyes and lets himself drift off. The strange expression worn this morning by Sam, the Jewish barber, becomes superimposed onto the face of the black Salafist. He unpicks the scene with Moktar in slow motion. He walks past him, turns back, notices he's gone. Moktar should have gotten as far as the fruit and veg shop, just after the barber's. So he could have entered either no. 15 or Sam's. He's a local guy—nothing to say he doesn't have friends or family living at no. 15. But no. A shiver runs down his spine—the paranoiac Soninké went to Sam's. And it doesn't seem likely that it was for a haircut . . . What could this mean? Even though he can't figure out their motives, Ahmed does know what's going to happen: they'll wait for their chance to pin the blame on him by saying something to the police. Maybe not directly, but in passing—perhaps via Fernanda, or by sending an anonymous letter. He's got to find a way to get ahead of them. Anticipation and reaction. He's got to find something—a lead, anything—before he sees Rachel and Jean again. The fact he's good at playing the fool will work to his advantage. The most important thing is they don't realize he's awoken from his slumber! Ahmed the space cadet has got to stay in character: Monsieur Paul, Franprix, the baker's. And tomorrow at around 10:00 a.m., when he gets back from the shrink, he'll go for a haircut at Sam's. Been two months anyway—well overdue. Time to take off the thinking cap. Time to sleep. To sleep and dream.

11:00 p.m.

14

The man is alone in the gloomy meeting room, the weak light coming from the street lamp on the pavement opposite. He is sitting stock-still in the black office chair, leaning forward with his head in his hands. On the table in front of him, his Sagem cell starts vibrating. He looks up and stares at the telephone, his eyes wild. Unlisted number. He picks up on the eighth ring.

"Hello . . ."

"Hi, it's me, Susan."

After a short hesitation he answers in strongly accented English.

"Hi, Susan."

"I've got a surprise for you . . ."

"A surprise?"

"I'm going to be in Paris this weekend. Isn't that great?"

"But . . ."

"Don't worry! James has taken care of everything. You'll have a perfect excuse for your wife."

"I can't leave now, Susan!"

"Tomorrow you'll receive travel instructions from the Center. I'll be waiting for you at the Concorde Lafayette Hotel, room 1727. Saturday at 3:00 p.m. Ohhh, I'm so excited! Please tell me you can't wait to see me!"

He tries to steady his voice but can't stop it from cracking.

"It will be a pleasure, Susan, of course."

Susan hangs up with a kiss. He returns the telephone to its place and resumes his afflicted stance.

*

In a telephone booth, a man sparks up his lighter to make out an 800 number written on a piece of paper. He dials, listens to the recorded instructions read out by a female voice, then enters a Paris number followed by the hash key. After the fourth ring a man picks up; it's one of those old telephones with a gray receiver and '80s-style keypad. He's sitting in front of a mirror in the half-light smoking a Café Crème. He keeps on smoking and leaves it to the other guy to get the ball rolling.

"What the fuck is going on?"

"Listen . . ."

"No, you listen! You have seriously fucked up. I gave you a very simple task and look where we are now!"

"But it was that fat fuck's decision to get his brother on board. What was I meant to do?"

"Fat fuck or no fat fuck, you should have stuck to the plan. For the moment, tell your people that we're shutting everything down, then zero contact with anyone."

"Even the stuff already underway?"

"What's underway is underway. When that's done, until you hear otherwise, we lie low."

The cigarillo-smoker hangs up and then redials, this time a cell number. Two rings, then a gruff voice with an indistinguishable accent answers.

"Hello, is that you?"

"Who else would it be?"

"I'm busy, it's time for . . ."

"I only need a minute. Has my nephew left?"

"Yes."

"Good. Make sure he does what he's been told. Afterward, we're taking a vacation. We put everything on hold for a while."

"But why? We've got plans, needs . . ."

"It won't be for long . . . Anyway, that's how it has to be for now. We're following orders, *ya khouya*, we're following orders . . ."

*

The man from the telephone booth is now walking down the deserted street. A shadow appears by his side as if from nowhere.

"*Salaam.*"

"Yeah yeah, *salaam.*"

"What's up? You seem nervous."

"Someone's fucked up. You're going to have to sit tight for a bit."

"Not right now; give us a bit more time. We haven't even reached twenty percent of our target."

"Ten percent, twenty per cent . . . I couldn't give a fuck! We're stopping. We'll wait for the storm to pass and then we'll see. You've got your guys under control, right?"

"Of course I do."

"There we go. End of discussion. *I* will contact *you*."

"Peace be with you, brother."

"Yeah yeah, and with you. Right, goodbye!"

*

Rachel is sleeping like a baby—carefree, dreamless, breathing deeply—when the telephone rings. Before she even opens her eyes she knows that it's 3:00 a.m. and that it's Bintou and Aïcha. She grabs her cell, checks the time—3:06—and the name of the caller—Aïcha (VIP)—before hitting the green button.

"Hello."

"Hello . . . Lieutenant Kupferstein, it's me. Aïcha. I'm with Bintou. Sorry for calling so late."

"Don't be sorry."

"We've got a technical question for you."

"A technical question?"

"Are you on Skype?"

"Skype?"

"You know, that thing for making free calls anywhere in the world."

"No, I don't have it. Why?"

"Because Rébecca has agreed to talk to you on Skype this time tomorrow, so long as we're there too."

"I see. Well I'll get it installed for then. All you need to do is come around here at 2:30 a.m. We don't have to do this at the station . . . Tell me, did you ever hear Laura mention 'filth'? As in 'the filth of the earth'? Ring any bells?"

"Hold on, I'll ask Bintou . . . No, Lieutenant, not as far as we can remember. But it does sound like something a Jehovah's Witness might say . . . Ask Rébecca tomorrow . . . Laura confided in her the most about her past. Goodnight, Lieutenant."

"Goodnight, Aïcha . . . And since you're phoning me at three in the morning, you might as well call me Rachel."

"Okay, Lieutenant . . . Uh . . . Rachel. We'll try. Oh, er, do you know Sam, the barber?"

"As in Sam's . . . the men's barber shop. Why?"

"Well, I don't know . . . Err . . . It might be worth . . . keeping an eye open . . ."

"Is that all you're going to give me?"

"That's all for now . . . See you tomorrow, Rachel. Sorry again for waking you."

Lieutenant Kupferstein just manages to get her "See you tomorrow" in before the line goes dead.

Fully awake now, she goes online, finds the Skype website and downloads it. She hears the "ping" signaling a new message . . . Sent by Kevin Gomes half an hour ago. He's managed to have a chat with an ex-Witness from Niort who seems to have a few things to say about the Vignola family. Damn he's good! Ball's in her court . . . The guy is willing to see her, she just needs to send him a message confirming the time and place. Tomorrow, 3:00 p.m., at Le Thermomètre in République. Rachel writes an e-mail to potterlover666@free.fr before sending a quick "thank you" to Kevin. Seventeen minutes later and she's asleep again. Not so bad.

15

Watchtower Society, Brooklyn.
Twenty-one months earlier.

A file entitled "Shipments/Belarus" tucked under her arm, Susan pretends to be lost as she wanders the endless corridors that she knows like the back of her hand. Though it does take a while to familiarize herself again with the contours of this labyrinth of interlacing tunnels lit by cold, neon strips, glass-clad capillaries feeding the countless rooms and blocks that make up the complex known as the Watchtower Bible and Tract Society. Built a century ago at the foot of Brooklyn Bridge, the global headquarters of the Jehovah's Witnesses is a veritable hive, and one which the faithful never have to leave. This amniotic universe, with its central heating in the winter and air conditioning in the summer, provides them with everything they could possibly need. The Watchtower . . . Susan Barnes had lived there with her father, Abel, and her brother James since their return to New York in the month she turned four.

An expert at maneuvering the twists and turns of the building, the young lady slows her pace to give herself time to decide whether or not to go for yet another coffee in the cafeteria. She checks her watch and gauges that it's time to make a brief appearance at her work station. She forks right, nods at ten new faces and a former colleague from Office Supplies, stops and opens a door. Logistics: European Department.

Three sets of middle-aged female eyes home in on her immediately. Unflustered, the young lady—slender, beautiful, detached—heads toward her desk and sits down. Her boss whispers to her in a voice that manages to convey both venom and sweetness.

"Susan, where have you been?"

"I was fetching the Belarus file—look!"

"And that took you a whole hour . . . ?"

No answer. It's just a game. For nine minutes Susan plays the role of employee, flicks through the file, and completes seventeen lines of her Excel spreadsheet. She then excuses herself in an aloof fashion.

"Right, I've got some errands to run. I won't be joining you for lunch."

She leaves. The three frustrated women don't even look up. The boss settles for a malevolent hiss under her breath.

"That one . . . If it wasn't for her father . . ."

She walks at an assured pace, subtly taking out her cell from her black leather handbag, which is virtually identical to the ones slung over the shoulders of the mass of people packed together in the wide corridor leading to the exit. With a discreet glance right and left to make sure she's not being watched, she cups the phone in the palm of her left hand and opens the text message that James sent that morning. A smiley flashes up on the screen, causing her second giggle of the day. Susan is twenty-eight today; James is on a mission in Belize, so she's got no one else to celebrate with. No way can she confide in anyone: she mustn't let herself disobey the primary rules of the organization, no matter how senior her father is. This makes her brother's text all the more precious. It reminds her that she is not alone. Since they were nine, every September 23, she and James have found a way to do something special, something nice together. Or at least to send each other a sign or a secret message. James is away, so she'll permit herself a little solitary treat at lunchtime. A treat she prepared herself for by fussing over her choice of clothing in the morning. An unusual outfit, even if sartorial sobriety is big among the Witnesses. Full-length skirt, long-sleeved cream blouse and navy-blue anorak, and then the final touch that she pulls out of her bag once she is a safe distance from the checkpoint—a green, felt beret into which she manages to squeeze her entire head of Nordic-blond hair, a marker of her proud Estonian heritage on her mother's side.

Down in the subway, the excitement rises. She amuses herself pretending to be Agent Barnes, tasked with an undercover mission in Crown Heights. She observes the passengers: blacks, Jews, Poles, Chinese. *You don't know who I am or the dangerous life I lead. You don't have the slightest idea what's going on around you!* As she gets off at Kingston Avenue, she wonders what would happen if a riot were to break out like in 1991. She pictures herself surrounded by a group of crazed black youths mistaking her for the wife or daughter of a rabbi. The image sends a shiver down her spine. Not exactly the most pleasant of shivers, but that's what she's into—fear. That is the thing that has accompanied her and her brother through every second of their life since they were three, from the moment their father explained to them that only a few chosen ones would experience salvation and gain access to heaven, the kingdom of Jesus. The others are divided into those who will be granted permission to be reborn into God's kingdom on Earth, and those who will remain for eternity as dust, their spirits as dead as their bodies: the "left behind." For as long as she can remember, those two words have plunged her into unspeakable anxiety. She has discovered an escape route: real, physical danger, laced with the specific fear that comes with it. This is the only way that she is able to feel truly alive. In her eagerness to face concrete threats, she invents virtual ones to kill time.

A five-minute walk and she's in front of Kingston Pizza Kosher. The familiar sign details a wood fire with peculiarly blue flames. As ever, before entering, she casts an eye over the photo of Menachem Mendel Schneerson—the last rebbe, known as the Lubavitcher Rebbe—and kisses her index finger discreetly. This ritual dates back to the day of her sixteenth birthday when, lost without James who had left the day before on his first out-of-town mission, she found herself strolling aimlessly through Brooklyn. Crown Heights had had a soothing, positive effect. The men with their hats and the strictly dressed women had eased her dismay. And then she saw him, Schneerson, and he was like a revelation. He was at once the father, grandfather, and mother she had always longed for. A great ocean of kindness rippled in his eyes. All the goodness in the world. She instinctively kissed the knuckle between the first and second phalanges of her index finger, went in, ordered a pizza, and felt better than she ever had before. Today, twelve years later, this filthy pizzeria remains the one place in New York where she can find peace. Fifteen minutes on the subway and a ten-minute walk is all she needs to separate her from the isolated universe of her childhood. Twenty-five minutes to transport her to a world apart which has the extreme advantage of not being her own. Amid other people's craziness she is able to break away from her destiny. She is convinced that something major is going to happen today. Especially if the person she is looking for is there, sitting in his usual place, as she hopes he will be.

She spots him immediately thanks to his appearance, which is that of a slightly flabby quarterback. Like most of the men in the neighborhood he is wearing a black fedora, sidelocks, and tzitzits. But his hair is bizarre—more like dreadlocks than sidelocks.

Beneath his white shirt she can distinguish the outline of a T-shirt adorned with a green, yellow, and red portrait of Bob Marley. Seated at the table at the back, he pokes vacantly at his tiramisu, his eyes lost and empty, just like he was two weeks ago when she came here and saw him for the first time. That time Ariel, the pizza chef who wears a skull-cap in the colors of the Italian flag, had spoken to her about this funny Hasidic Jew who'd arrived in the area a few months before, an Ashkenazi from Kansas who was tangled up with some fairly disreputable Sephardic types, and who always wore the green, yellow, and red colors underneath his regulation white shirt. A really weird guy. She'd met Ariel, the chef, six years ago when he'd started working at Kingston Pizza. He knows she's not Jewish, but it doesn't bother him at all. Her sketchy, makeshift Hasidic costume cracks him up. He appreciates the fact she takes the time to lean on the counter and have a chat with him while he makes her pizza. Always the same: fake bacon, green peppers, tomato, and basil.

Susan subtly brings the conversation around to the Hasidic Rastafarian. Amused by the interest the pretty Jehovah's Witness is taking in this Jewish guy, who's as big as he is bizarre, the chef fills her in on what he knows about the regular at the table at the back—which is not much, truth be told. His name is Dov, he studied at Harvard, but the reasons he's turned up in Crown Heights—Hasid Central—remain unclear. The place opposite the young man frees up, and with a smile Ariel tactfully encourages her to go and sit there. He'll bring over her pizza when it's ready. She nods gratefully and crosses the room.

Dov looks up and his jaw hits the floor. When she starts coming toward him, he lowers his eyes and carries on jabbing away at his pudding. Without a moment's hesitation, the young woman sits down in the space vacated by a fifty-year-old lady who had left in a hurry—long skirt, gray sweater, auburn wig—and who patently works in the neighboring *mikvah*. Fully aware of Susan's presence, Dov continues fidgeting with his spoon without looking at her. She makes the most of the opportunity to check him out.

She is particularly gifted at initiating conversation, at coaxing people to reveal things that they would hide from everyone besides

her, and at using her newly acquired knowledge to manipu-
late their thoughts and actions. She inherited this faculty from
her father, who excels in the art of manipulative listening. She
hates her father, Abel Barnes, with all her heart and soul. She only
acknowledges this deadly genetic hand-me-down because one day
she intends to turn it against him and everything he believes in. It
was one year ago today, on September 23, that she had started plot-
ting with James; since they had realized that this man had stolen
away their very essence—their mother and their childhood. They
will only come close to being at peace when they have succeeded in
making him lose everything that is dear to him. A secret meeting
had been called at a Georgian restaurant on Brighton Beach. When
the waiters sang them "Happy Birthday"—first in their language,
then in English—Susan had been unable to hold back her tears.
James held her tight in his arms, and they had promised each other
that they would find a way to get their revenge and find happiness.

Fifteen minutes later, she has discovered the name of the man
across the table—Jakubowicz—as well as a bit about his story: brilliant child born into a secular Jewish family from Wichita, Kansas; gets into Harvard without any trouble; it's there that he carries
out his *teshuvah*—his repentance, or return to Judaism—totally
unexpectedly; before logically enough winding up here in Crown
Heights. The tale is smooth—too smooth—delivered in a tone that
is half-absent, half-amused. As if he were asking, "Do you really
want to know all this?" Sure she wants to know, but there's no hurry.
When she's done with her pizza, she proposes they make the most of
the nice weather and go for a walk—provided he has time—around
Central Park just across the river; the No. 3 line on the subway goes
direct to Columbus Circle. A proposal laden with the sort of fake
indifference that girls know how to direct at boys. She doesn't think
about what might happen next. She's not attracted to him; just eager
to figure out the secret she knows he's harboring. And for that to
happen, she's got to get him out of the Hasidic end of town. The
young man, for his part, finds this girl intriguing and amusing; this
fake Jew fallen from the heavens to deliver him from his boredom.

Today he doesn't feel like doing anything, especially not going to yeshiva. So Central Park . . . Why not?

Susan is staying true to form. Ariel hasn't taken his eyes off them since the start of their conversation. In a caring way, sure, but protective too. No way she's going to leave with Dov . . . Sliding back into Agent Barnes mode, well versed in the rules of working under cover, she instructs Dov to wait for her to leave before ordering a coffee, drinking it unhurriedly, paying, and then meeting her on the platform of the Nostrand Avenue station toward the rear of the train going via President Street. Twenty-three minutes later, they are sitting across the train car from each other. Few words are exchanged in the rough-and-tumble of the journey, which is fine. A moment; a transition. One thing's for certain: she's not going to sleep with him. She's not sure what she's going to do with this guy, but what's certain is that he is going to play a role in her life. She ditches the people she sleeps with after half a day. It's curious—at the heart of her shambolic upbringing, with all the abiding nonsense that she thought she'd managed to escape, she still can't stop herself from thinking in irrational terms, putting faith in signs and destiny. It's so deeply ingrained in her. And at this precise moment, her intuition is telling her that her life is about to change. The meeting with Dov is the moment she's been anticipating for so long. It's within reach. She just needs to play her hand right.

16

5:00 a.m. Ahmed is asleep. 6:00 a.m. Still asleep. Before he became essentially asexual, he had read the Christian mystics like Saint John of the Cross and Theresa de Ávila. A girl had put him on to them.

A sensual, spiritual girl who had liked praying, crying, and making love. Ahmed had enjoyed her company enormously. Catarina came back to him as his sleep drew to a close. He had nicknamed her "Catarina sessuale." She had taught him all about the significance of THE NIGHT in the mystic tradition, her unsettling Venetian accent thinly veiled and full of sweet promises. "THE NIGHT, it's terrible. You cannot imagine. It is to live without God. You understand, God has *turned away* from you. He is looking the other way; He gives light, love, and life to others. *La luce, l'amore solo per gli altri!* I can accept that He loves others, too. But He cannot abandon me! He cannot deprive me of His warmth! *Senza Dio non posso vivere!* But why am I telling you this? You with your chess on the computer . . . *Non capisci niente di Dio! Non capisci neanche dell'amore!* Saint John of the Cross was the greatest Catholic mystic. He was Jewish, you know, like Jesus! He endured everything, even torture. All for his God. And his greatest suffering was to endure THE NIGHT. *La notte.* Losing God. Being alone and unworthy while God's back is turned to warm other hearts!" Catarina started crying and Ahmed drank her tears, feeding on them as he consoled her. That was his mystic experience: imbibing the tears of "Catarina sessuale." As transcendental as prayers are for other people.

Tears. All of a sudden his cousin Mohamed enters the fold. "Nothing is more beautiful than the tears streaming down the cheeks of a Muslim in prayer. I pity the person who hasn't felt that blessing! But fear not—I will pray that one day you will in turn be touched." 6:01 a.m. The mood of the dream has changed. Ahmed is angry now. The Venetian lover was one thing: love always came after the tears. But that outburst from his cousin? How disillusioning! His subconscious adjusts to this imbalance, and pulls Rachel Kupferstein's face out of the bag. She leans in to him slowly, brings her lips to his, and pushes her tongue between his teeth. It sends him into a frenzy. It's been such a long time since he's made love. So long he's even stopped dreaming about it. Rachel undresses him, slowly at first, then more quickly, hastened by an overwhelming need to have him inside her. With one single movement he pulls down the zipper of his jeans and slides them off, relieved to be free of them and eager for the feeling of her wetness. Now for the best part: he is hard, she is ready—the contact. The best . . . *Fssshhh!* No more Rachel, no more dream. The young man wakes up feeling not so much frustrated as thankful he feels so alive. And overjoyed that he didn't come in his sleep. He likes the idea of saving himself for her. He savors the desire, relishing the wait. The unknown.

The digital clock reads 6:03. Saucepan, water, gas. Brown filter-holder onto Pyrex *cafetière*. Recycled filter. Three or four shakes of coffee straight from the package. Go on, let's have a fifth! Boiling water. Ahmed has a ritual to avoid getting too many coffee grounds stuck to the side when tipping the water in. It involves pouring a slow trickle of hot water before the rest of it in order to form a compact, wet lump—like at the beach to make sandcastles—at the center of the white filter. It occurs to him that this is precisely how he goes about things on the toilet. Afterward, he hoses down the inside of the toilet bowl with his urine to dislodge any skid marks. The aim is to make it tidy, but he rarely succeeds, and often has to resort to the brush to finish the job. This act of pissing on his shit to dislodge it conjures up precisely the same obsessive pleasure he gets when he splashes water on the leftover coffee clinging to the upper rim of the filter. The parallel amuses him. All about keeping things neat.

He pours himself a coffee and spreads some butter on a few crackers. By 6:30 a.m. breakfast is done, dishes washed, and shower taken. Wearing the same jeans as the day before, a white V-neck T-shirt, and blue cotton socks, he is sitting on the hessian carpet with his back to the wall. All that stuff about the coffee and the excrement has left him feeling clearer, lighter—his mind freer. Then images and faces come flooding in. Moktar, Sam. The barber's shop is at the heart of the matter. Another face is playing dead there at the very edge of his consciousness, just where it had frozen during his trance after the discovery of Laura's body. He can sense it twitching imperceptibly—slowly, like a mollusk, a crustacean, a starfish—as if it were moving toward a flicker of light between the shadows of two rocks in a stretch of calm water. He mustn't force this one. He mustn't send it scuttling away for good.

Ahmed comes back to Moktar, which in turn makes him think of that little group, 75-Zorro-19. He remembers when they started out in the neighborhood. Mourad, Alpha, Moktar and Ruben . . . Sam's nephew! That's the link between Moktar and the barber. The group has reformed and it's got something to do with Laura's death. He remembers the air hostess's idle chitchat, which he paid little attention to. Something about Ruben's little sister. She was under masses of pressure from her family. Laura was pushing her to stand up to them. Then all of a sudden she vanished and no one knew where she'd gone. But Laura, having been so concerned about Rébecca's situation, had seemed astonishingly relaxed about her disappearance, to the extent that she'd stopped talking about her. How can he find out what happened? Interrogate her girlfriends, whose names he can't even remember? He checks his watch. 7:00 a.m. He has to catch the Métro to get to Dr. Germain's on time.

Thirty-five minutes later and he's sitting in the waiting room. He had to run through the station corridors to avoid being late. Running to be on time. Feels like another life. Métro, rushing, punctuality. Now it's him waiting for Dr. Germain. Which irritates him until he realizes he is still out of breath and that he could do with the rest. The wait is part of the process, part of the well-known need to "work on oneself." Free of this little bristle of anger, Ahmed tunes in to the sounds. The pipes feeding water to the taps and then sending it back to the sewers. The purring of an extractor fan that masks both the weird noises and the delicious smells emanating from the coffee machine. Dr. Germain must have struggled to get out of bed, and considered a cup of coffee necessary prior to seeing his first patient, who happened to be closely linked to two murders. Ahmed smiles, stretches out his legs and drifts off. Thirty seconds later the door opens, he gets to his feet, shakes the outstretched hand, walks into the consulting room, and lies down. There is a eucalyptus-scented paper handkerchief on the cushion for his head. He pictures the doctor—bathing in the aura of his lofty discipline, his knowledge of the complete works of Freud and the nineteen volumes of Lacan's seminars—patting down the couch to get rid of any imprint left by the last patient before changing the paper towel. Something a bit peep-showy about the tissue—something rather intimate, rather sexual. Same with the Dalí print, the painting with Gala's naked breast that hangs above the couch.

The first time he had sat opposite Dr. Germain—it took him until the fifth session to lie down—Ahmed had been struck by the picture's energy, and had felt concern for its creator. Then he did some research and found out that the painter had been a virgin when he met Gala. He studies the picture in silence. Dr. Germain starts off.

"So, where were . . ."

"It's about omnipotence, that picture. Gala the older woman, the initiator. The one who knows."

"The powerful woman?"

"Yes, the powerful woman. What's a man meant to do when faced with her?"

"Well, let's consider him . . . What's he doing?"

"He's watching her, painting her . . . He's acting, doing something about her. And she expects that. She watches him do it. There's always something to do . . ."

Silence.

"Something to do? Yes . . ."

"Me . . . I don't paint, right. I don't do anything. Women have never hung around because I've always been too passive, too inactive. Waiting . . . Because deep down I've always been alone, caught between me and myself and my singleton ways. You know this morning I realized that I like making things tidy with my shits as well as my coffee."

Ahmed falls quiet again. The doctor draws out the pause. His breathing slows down, making his patient wonder if he's fallen asleep. So he carries on talking, saying the first thing that pops into his head, just to wake him up. Just so that he doesn't fall asleep too. Nodding out on the psychiatrist's couch!

"Apart from that, there's a killer haunting me inside my head, but I'm still too scared to look him in the eye. So I keep a distance between the dragging hours of these sessions and my overbearing need to act."

"But this need to act . . . Is it not at work on some level? It's producing something, surely? If only because it led to your return . . ."

"Yes, my return: my return here; my return to life. I've got to do something, open my eyes; not stay still. I've got to do lots of things. This murder I saw . . . I'm too scared to tell you because I'll see it all over again. As if by seeing it—even in my head—I'm starting to face up to it, making myself vulnerable, you see."

Silence.

"This is a killer we're talking about. A predator, a manhunter. Someone who enjoys killing, who enjoys making people suffer."

"Yes . . ."

"Like . . . Like the people who killed my father . . ."

"Yes . . ."

"I've got to look him straight in the eye, square on. No more of these blurred images. In the eye, I've got to look evil in the eye . . ."

"Yes . . ."

"I'm going to tell you now what I couldn't tell you before. The reason I'm here. And before that, the reason I was locked up at Maison Blanche. That murder, the one I saw, of that girl . . . Emma . . ."

"Emma. Go on . . ."

"I'll tell you like we tell anything that's happened to us. Like when you've witnessed an accident, yeah . . . Okay . . . I was at the furniture warehouse in the industrial estate in Aulnay-sous-Bois. My shift started at 8:00 p.m., when the other employees were finishing for the day. Around 9:00 p.m. I went to go and heat up a Tupperware of frozen lasagna. Half an hour later I switched on my PC to play Go against the computer. It won twice in a row. At about 11:00, as I was about to win the third game, I heard a noise at the other end of the building. That happened a lot: the odd creak, a bit of furniture falling over, a mouse nibbling a plastic cover . . . So I went to check it out to put my mind to rest, not overly worried and not thinking I needed to call it in. One thing's for sure, I didn't take my cell. I must have known what was coming instinctively, because I didn't make a sound as I tiptoed down the aisles, and my flashlight was off. I knew the warehouse like the back of my hand, don't forget. I could hear the noise more clearly, coming from an area near a side door. It definitely wasn't a mouse, no doubt about it: a rhythmic plastic rustling; panting breaths. I kept going . . . Thought I'd let them finish up, plus I wanted to get a look. There was a stool that meant I could watch without being seen. A couple were having sex on a cream display sofa that was wrapped in a stiff cover. But the woman—about thirty, chestnut-brown hair, green eyes lined with Kohl shadow—had been gagged with beige duct tape, her eyes wide open with terror. Given the position of her arms, her hands must have been tied behind her back. As for the man, I only saw the back of his head: strong shoulders like a furniture mover, long blond hair like some guitarist from a heavy metal band, and his enormous hands around her neck. All of a sudden, he grunted and he strangled her. Right then, at the exact same time, she noticed me and she died. I heard a bone break. The whole thing lasted about fifteen seconds, you know, the scene I'd had the misfortune to see. I ducked down and listened. The sounds charted the killer's movements. He straightened his pants with a 'Huh!' echoing from deep in his stomach, hoisted the girl onto his shoulder like a sack of cement, and walked out heavily. The door slammed shut and the footsteps became more distant. I stayed slumped on the stool for a good three minutes, feeling desolate. I heard the faint sound of an engine starting and a car pulling away. Diesel. Still convinced he was a taxi driver. And even though I didn't see his face, I'm sure I'd recognize him if by some cruel twist of fate, for me or for him, I came across him again. There you have it. Not the smallest trace of anything on the sofa. That plastic was solid as fuck. Like nothing had happened. 'I didn't see anything at Aulnay-sous-Bois.' So I did nothing. And I mean total 'nonaction', just not in a Zen way! That night I couldn't sleep. Same for the following nights. The girl's

expression had gotten into my head, and it's never left. I was responsible for her death. And do you know what I thought of at that exact
moment? Gainsbourg, 'Melody Nelson'. I blew it trying to lose my
virginity when 'Melody Nelson' was playing. The girl was lying there,
up for it, I was fingering her. And I didn't even take her clothes off. I
had no idea what to do. After a bit, fed up with the wait, she got up
and she was on her way. It took me another two years after that . . ."

"Melody . . ."

"Yeah, exactly. Melody . . ."

"Shall we talk about this next time?"

Ahmed sits up, stays at the edge of the couch, his mind all over
the place, like after a dream. *Next time . . . Yeah . . .*

"I've had a think . . . Since you've got nothing to your name other
than your disability benefit, what would you say to twenty dollars
per session, two sessions a week?"

"Look, I'll have to do my accounts, but I don't reckon I can manage that."

"Maybe you could find a way of managing it . . ."

Ahmed considers it, saying nothing.

"Come on Monday morning at 8:30 a.m. That'll give you some
time to think it through."

Handshake. Cut.

17

It's already 9:30 a.m. Jean arrives at the office in astonishingly good
spirits. After his Tsingtao he'd gone home. Back to one of the red-
brick social housing projects that hem in Paris. His ruinous, morbid

neighborhood with its stench of self-loathing and hatred of others had greeted him with a sense of suffocation. As he entered his one-bedroom apartment, the need to move out welled up with renewed vigor. A liberating feeling—anxiety maybe?—that transformed into affirmative action: first thing in the morning he would talk to Rachel, and she would put him in touch with an ex of hers, a formidable real estate agent. This decision had calmed him down so much that he slept like a baby under the watchful eye of happy parents. When he woke, his head clear, he remembered that he had a 75-Zorro-19 mixtape from the year 2000. On the back of the cover there was an oblique reference to Laura's girlfriends. He still had the title song on his old MP3 player.

He has a meeting with Dr. Germain at 6:30 p.m. How is he going to keep himself busy until then? Go and see Ahmed again? Had Laura's two friends—the black girl and the Arab—called Rachel back? Had they met up? No texts through this morning. Not that that means anything. Let's start with a coffee . . . Nice and simple—just need to press a button. If Rachel isn't in by 10:00 a.m. he'll call her. Mercator, back turned, is collecting the change from his espresso.

"Small with sugar, Hamelot?"

"Yes, boss, as ever."

Noise, coffee, sugar, stirrer. Mercator takes the two coffees in their plastic cups and heads down the corridor toward his office. Jean follows him. They sit down opposite each other. The desk is clean and tidy, except for a virgin pad of Clairefontaine "C."

"I know that you have dived head first into this investigation. That's what I was hoping. Full immersion in the folly of religion. In the great folly of the credulous. Or rather of those who clog up their depths, their inner space, with the concrete of certainty. Sealed up and leveled off, we can go on with life. *Tout va bien*, as Godard said. Aside from that I've got nothing to say: you and Kupferstein know what to do and how to do it. There is, however, a little something that's been bothering me all morning. A phone call from the eighteenth. My dear colleague, Commissaire Frédéric Enkell, told me that he'd had nothing back from his informants regarding the

phone booth on rue Ordener. His exact words were: 'No, no Mercator. Nobody saw a thing, I assure you.' At the time noted, nobody saw
anyone make a call from there. My question is why not? Of course
there's no reason why his rats would be on the lookout all the time,
but I still got the feeling he was lying. Amazing how easy it was to
tell he was lying! And that, Hamelot, is because he doesn't give two
shits about lying to me. I'm guessing he thinks I have to believe him
on some grounds of kinship. A caste mentality. I don't know if you've
noticed, but people beyond a certain position of power tend to lie an
awful lot. As if shameless lying is a perk of the job. It turns them on,
if you will. In our case, this lie is worth its weight in gold. It gives us
a lead. One to follow with the utmost discretion. You don't happen
to know a trustworthy officer over there?"

"No, Commissaire. Unfortunately, the commissariat in the eighteenth is murky to the core. Benamer is still Enkell's right-hand man,
is he not?"

Mercator looks up, visibly lost in his own meandering thoughts.
The lieutenant thinks his superior has started to meditate, but then
he hears his voice.

"Do you remember Van Holden?"

"Your predecessor?"

"Yes. He's heading up internal affairs at the IGPN. Been there
two years. It was him who toppled the *commissaire divisionnaire*
in Saint-Denis. You know, the guy who covered for that depraved,
cretinous gang of racketeering, prostitute-raping policemen in porte
de la Chapelle. Van Holden took his time and he nailed all of them.
Now Enkell . . . Enkell's no fool. Neither is Benamer. Evil exists,
Hamelot, and sometimes it gets itself together. You understand evil,
Hamelot?"

His words are now weaving into the fabric of his dreams.

"Enkell . . . 'Nobody saw a thing, I assure you . . .' Beneath those
words, beneath that little 'I assure you' afterthought, there lingered
a stench of death . . ."

Mercator falls silent. His eyes peel away from the wall where
moments before vivid shapes had been dancing, shapes invisible to

mere mortals. They bypass his subordinate and become engrossed in a document. At the corner of the immaculate desk the two plastic cups are still steaming.

"Don't forget your coffee," he says without looking up.

Jean heads back to his office in contemplative mood, stirring his beverage robotically. As the *commissaire*'s words etch themselves into him, he becomes aware of the inhumane nature of this work factory. Like some Ikea showroom. He remembers one of Rachel's words.

"*Ouphilanthropon*. The 'nonhuman', according to Aristotle. That which is opposed to man."

Like some mathematical concept, like zero and infinity. $1 \div \infty = 0$. And conversely. He's got to get out, quick. Got to reestablish contact with his own kind. In the toilets he ditches his untouched cup on top of the electric hand dryer, pisses, stares at the basin as though it were one of Duchamp's readymades, devoid of any function, and exits wiping his hands on the back pockets of his jeans. Telephone.

"Rachel, are you still asleep? Let's meet for a romantic breakfast at Le Gastelier . . . Up for it?"

Sleepy voice on the other end. "Give me forty-five minutes to make myself look vaguely human and I'll see you there. Read the paper while you wait and you can tell me what's going on in the world."

18

Ahmed is walking along the canal, his mind heavy with additions and multiplications. Twenty dollars per session, eight or nine sessions: it'll cost him seventy dollars a month if he decides to resume his psychoanalysis. He gets five hundred dollars in disability benefits; his rent comes out at two hundred and thirteen dollars. Food, electricity, books . . . What do we reckon? One hundred and fifty to two hundred dollars. After all the adding and subtracting, he's got somewhere between thirty-three and eighty-three dollars a month. That crook Germain has done his sums to perfection! If he wants to take up the psychoanalysis again, he'll need to earn some cash. Work . . . Work . . . But where? The question makes him uneasy, reminding him of the hardest times in the run-up to Latifa's final, definitive committal to hospital. It had become an obsession. She went around and around the apartment in circles. "Work, I must get work, all will be well if I find work." In her condition nobody was going to employ her. When she'd been a florist at marché Secrétan, she ended up deserting her stall, just like that, even though she'd been the only person there. After that she became the proper local crazy woman. *Majnouna* . . . That word brings back the nastiness of Abdelhaq Haqiqi, the most loathsome of his school "mates." The boy had begun his education in Arabic, back in Blida, and was still at primary school level when he was thirteen. He had made up for being so behind, and for his poor grasp of French, with his hulking physical superiority. From the moment the school year started in September, he made Ahmed his personal punching bag. He used to taunt him with the name *ibn majnouna*—the madwoman's son. Then he started calling him *'abid*—slave. Ahmed told Latifa, who showed up at the school gate after classes like a fury, unleashing a string of Arabic obscenities at Abdelhaq. Ahmed never found out what she'd said to him, but from that moment on, his persecutor ignored him completely, and to this day they never exchanged a word despite living in the same neighborhood. Suddenly he remembers why this story has come back to him today. Abdelhaq Haqiqi runs the prayer room frequented by Moktar. He's the imam of the small group of local Salafists. And one other thing: last week, three days before Laura's death, Abdelhaq had gone to Sam's to get his haircut. A Salafist visiting a Jewish barber . . . Definitely not unheard of, but

Abdelhaq had never been to Sam's before. Why now? What could this crossing of paths mean?

As he walks, Ahmed tries to get rid of Abdelhaq's miserable face. He finds deliverance in Monsieur Paul's features; the perfect antidote. Since Laura's death, the old Armenian is the only friendly person he has left in the world. A tenuous link, but a real one. Maybe the Armenian represents the "way of managing" mentioned by Germain? Hadn't he said something recently about helping him at the bookshop? Something about shifting boxes that he can no longer lift? Why not? In a flash, Ahmed is panicking, shaking. An irrepressible, absurd thought overwhelms him that Monsieur Paul and Dr. Germain are in cahoots and have come up with this plan to coerce him into getting back to work. He pulls himself together quickly and reflects that it really is in his best interests to resume the sessions if he is to avoid stewing in his state of semi-paranoid inertia. He'll go and see the bookseller, but first he's got to tell someone. Rachel. Without stopping to think, he dives into a telephone booth, armed with the France Télécom card he'd bought the evening before, and dials.

"Hello . . ."

"I didn't wake you?"

"No, my colleague took care of that five minutes ago . . . Ahmed . . . To what do I owe the honor of this morning call? Some news? Something come back to you?"

"No, no—it's nothing to do with the investigation. It's just . . ."

"Yes?"

"It's just I decided to go back to work. And I don't know, I just wanted to tell someone, and the only person who sprung to mind was you. In fact, I wanted to call you last night as I was passing the Boeuf-Couronné—I saw you and your colleague in there—but that wasn't really a good enough reason. So, there you go, I just wanted to hear your voice, that's all."

"So you saw me last night, and you wanted to call me; you wanted to hear the sound of my voice, is that it? Is that not some sort of declaration? I mean, I'm guessing this doesn't happen to you often, you calling up a woman to tell her this kind of thing?"

"Never. This never happens to me. I'm sorry if I bothered you, but I don't know, something came over me. I just had to call."

"Don't be sorry, Ahmed. It's always a mistake to be sorry. It doesn't bother me that you wanted to hear the sound of my voice. It doesn't bother me at all. It's just that I'm in the middle of investigating a murder, and you are—hmm—let's say . . . kind of a key witness in this investigation."

"Yes, of course. Well, there you have it—I just wanted to tell you that I'm resuming psychoanalysis and, because it's going to cost me this time around, I'm going to get back to work. At the bookshop; Monsieur Paul's. I needed to hear myself say it to someone, out loud you know, so it becomes real . . . Does that make sense?"

"Perfect sense. And I think it's really great, too. The sessions and Monsieur Paul, I mean. Listen, I have to go now, but don't hesitate to call me again, Okay? About Monsieur Paul or anything else. And don't forget . . . Laura's killer—I really do want to catch him. So if anything comes back to you that might speed up the inquiry, if you see or hear anything to do with the case, then I'm all ears. Okay?"

Ahmed is tempted—more than tempted—to mention the incident with Moktar from the night before. Just to keep her on the line for a few more minutes. Just to hear her voice, her breathing a little longer. But no. It's too dangerous. Lending too much significance to Moktar's porcine insults would risk her suspecting that he knows about the pork joint in Laura's apartment. Only the police and the killer know about that.

"Me too, I want to catch him. I'll do anything. As soon as I hear something I'll let you know—that's a promise! Have a good day, Lieutenant Kupferstein."

"And you too, Monsieur Taroudant."

On his way to the bookshop, Ahmed replays the conversation on repeat. Especially the end. "Have a good day, Lieutenant Kupferstein." "And you too, Monsieur Taroudant." He loves it. He loves it, quite literally. And he really wants to be able to say something that matters next time. Something that will help the investigation progress without putting himself in danger. Something that will lead to a meeting in person.

19

Chaim Potok High School. Fourteen months earlier.

At least once a week, Susan comes to see Dov in the exquisitely
'60s chemistry lab that he is restoring in the Jewish high school
in Queens. Rabbi Toledano found him the job as a stopgap. Over
the past six months, Susan has learned a lot about Dov, filling the
gaps in his life story with every meeting. Starting off with his stint
in prison for synthesizing MDMA in the lab at Harvard and dis-
tributing it for free to his student friends, who were all the more
indiscreet thanks to the fact that the trainee chemist's drug proved
to be ultra-powerful. Inside, Dov soon discovered that being a
geeky, rather pudgy Jewish Rastafarian was a serious handicap
with the gang leaders, especially the black or Latino ones, or those
from Italian families who were not yet totally overwhelmed by the
other ethnic groups. Scrapes, near-miss brawls, threats. The plan
was to make him suffer a long series of humiliations, more than
likely starting off with a gang rape in the showers the Thursday
after his arrival. There are no secrets in prison: Albert Bénamou, a
car thief originally from Toronto, got wind of the trouble in store
for the new detainee, a young, defenseless Jewish student. Albert
was not fainthearted and knew how to earn respect. Striking a deal
with the Dominican gang who had claimed Dov, he "bought him
back" off them. Before they met, Dov had been completely clue-
less about the Sephardim. He thought that, like his grandparents,
all Jews came from Poland, Lithuania, or Belarus at least. It had

never crossed his mind that there might be Moroccan Jews. Albert demanded nothing in exchange for his protection. Other than— and this was more a favor—going with him to the Talmud Torah classes given every other Sunday in the prison library by Rabbi Toledano. This is how he did his *teshuvah*—more out of boredom than conviction. Out of spite, too, since his family had become increasingly distant. Sure, he had let them down. Sure, Wichita was thousands of miles from his county jail in Boston. But there was a striking contrast between Rabbi Toledano's warm humanity and kindness, and the coldness of the letters that accompanied the packages from his parents. They only made a grand total of one visit in all his eighteen months inside. When he got out, Dov cut ties with his past, his family, and handed himself over entirely to the rabbi, who found him a place to live in Crown Heights, signed him up to his yeshiva, turning a blind eye to his dreads and his green, yellow-and-red T-shirts on the condition that he covered it all up with a white shirt and a black hat, and that he let his tzitzits hang loose.

In the six months she's been visiting Dov, Susan has learned how to roll joints. This is precisely what she's doing now while he's fix- ing a Bunsen burner. She admires her work with an air of satisfac- tion, lights it, takes a long toke, holds the smoke in her lungs, then breathes out. Another drag before offering the cone to Dov. Her voice changes tone slightly, her eyes shining.

"I've got a weird question for you: why have you never tried any- thing with me?"

Dov takes a toke and waits for a moment before responding.

"What about you?"

"Me? Oh, that's easy! I only sleep with men I don't like. That way I can ditch them as soon as I've had enough. Forget about them. With you, I'm not sure . . . First off I didn't find you that physically attractive, but then I think I did like you right away. I wanted you to be in my life, so that it wasn't just James . . ."

Susan feels like a little girl.

"Your turn now!" she says in a shrill voice, blushing.

"Initially I wondered why you were interested in me, and I thought that if it was something sexual, then you'd have found a way to get that across, since you were the one calling the shots. Afterward I didn't give it much more thought—the moment had gone. And then we started smoking together, and I really needed that."

"You don't have a girlfriend then? Have you ever had a girlfriend?"

"You want to know if I'm a virgin, right? Or a fag? I've never had a girlfriend, and I've never been with a guy either. It's never been a big deal to me. Not as much as dope, chemistry, and Bob Marley . . . I can't really explain it."

"I get it, I totally get it. I didn't want to . . . It's just, I'm not sure, I needed to know . . . Not even sure why . . ."

"The rabbi's finding me a wife."

"A wife?"

"Yeah, a French girl. The daughter of a follower of his cousin, who's a rabbi in Paris. A pretty girl . . . Can you imagine? Me, Dov from Wichita, Kansas, with a nice Jewish girl from Paris!"

"A Parisian—how chic! But are you going to get married without getting to know each other?"

"Yeah, that's how they do it. And I'm one of them now. You know, Rabbi Toledano . . . Uh, the rebbe, I should say. I'm still not used to it. It's only been three months since he declared himself Rebbe Toledano. So, the rebbe doesn't have a son, and all his daughters are already married, so this is his way of keeping me close to him."

"Keeping you close to him . . . He must be extremely fond of you . . ."

"He's a mystic. He believes in chance encounters and signs. From the moment he saw me, he said there was something special between us. That God was present. And then there was this dream—it's extraordinary, you know . . . It was two days before we met at the pizzeria. That's another reason I went with you to Central Park."

"A dream? You've never mentioned it before."

"No, but now is the time, because it's just come true. The first image was a girl. I didn't get a close look at her, but when you sat down in front of me two days later, I felt as though I recognized you, that you were that girl. In the dream, you were saying . . . or rather she was saying something like 'Listen', or 'Write', or 'Look' . . . Something like that. She went over to a blackboard, took a piece of chalk and drew a chemical formula, then turned back to me going 'Shhh', like this, and then left. The crazy thing is that I remembered the formula and wrote it down as soon as I woke up. Do you want me to show you?"

"Yeah, go on!"

Dov goes back to the board and draws some lines, letters and numbers. Susan, intrigued, sees something take shape in front of her. She doesn't understand it in the slightest, but she knows that it symbolizes her very future.

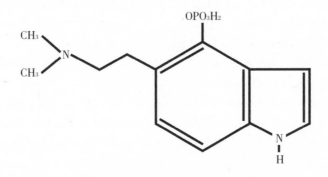

"There you go. That's what came to me in my dream. At the time, I got the impression that I knew the formula . . . A second later it came to me: it's almost identical to psilocybin, but the opposite, like a mirror image, right? Hold on, I'll draw it for you and you can see."

He scribbles another diagram super-fast, explaining as he goes to a fascinated and increasingly puzzled Susan.

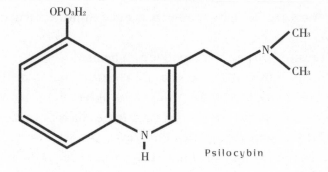

Psilocybin

That's psilocybin. Precisely the same formula, but the three bonds with the N and the two CH_3 bits on the end are stuck to the other side; on the hexagon, if you like, rather than the pentagon.

"Excuse me, Dov, this is all great—really great—but if I'm going to follow I need you to fill me in on what the hell this psilocybin is."

"It's the main active compound in 'shrooms . . . Never heard of 'shrooms? Hallucinogenic mushrooms. A wicked natural drug, a bit like peyote; you must have heard of peyote! Shamans, Castaneda?"

"Err, no, not really. Heard a bit about shamans when we were living with the Inuit . . . Pure evil in my father's eyes, something to shun and destroy at all costs."

"With the Inuit? What were you doing over there?"

"One year after my mother's death, the Jehovah's Witnesses sent my father to Greenland as a missionary. We were toddlers at that stage and we went with him. Nancy, our Inuit nanny, brought us up until the age of four. My earliest memories date back to Godthåb, the capital, where we lived. Our father was always away. Of course Nancy was a Jehovah's Witness, but Dad didn't trust her. It's weird, but the two things I remember best are her gentleness, her lullabies to help us fall asleep, and his vehemence when he spoke of the Inuit. He really hated them . . . Each time he came back, we were subjected to long, rambling discourses where he'd explain why we had to be careful around them. Above all, he spoke about his enemies, the shamans, who from his point of view were demons under the influence of drugs. At the time, we didn't understand a thing, but it left its mark on our minds. Anyway, back to you . . . Finish telling me about these 'shrooms: I prefer your story to mine. It makes me sad every time I think back to it."

"Okay, so they're less strong than the shamanic drugs, but they're still good stuff. You become bigger, you think you're . . . I don't know, somebody like Captain America or Harry Potter. So it's a drug that can be really fun, though it's important to be in a happy place when you take it.

"To cut a long story short, I went to the rebbe and I told him about my dream. He didn't say anything right away; he took the drawing and went to pray, read, do his thing. The following day, he takes me to one side at the synagogue just as I'm taking off my tefillin, tells me that he spent the night at his books, and that in the morning he'd found the sign. Imagine that! My dream had been foretold centuries ago by Isaac Luria . . . I don't know much about Kabbalah, but I do know that Luria was one of the greats. On top of this, he adds that everything that comes of this dream will be blessed as it is desired by the Most High, he who cannot be named. And then I feel this spirit come over me, and I let out a murmur, like this . . ." He bring his lips to Susan's ear, his voice little more than a caress. "'Godzwill'. The rabbi looks at me, weeping, and repeats it in his funny accent: 'Godzwill . . . Godzwill . . . It's so beautiful, my son, so beautiful. You tell me what you need. We'll take care of everything . . . Really, so beautiful.'"

Susan murmurs it too, in a daze.

"Godzwill, Godzwill . . . It is beautiful . . . But what is it?"

"Oh, a magical substance, that's all. Just something that'll give infinite joy to our fellow humans. The rebbe is remarkable—he managed to get me this job in the lab. It was in a terrible state, but it works well enough for my needs. In the afternoon, when the school is open, I do all my prep. Then in the evening, I do a few trial runs, and sleep in the morning. And here we go—three days ago I managed to stabilize the molecule and find the formula to mass-produce it."

Like an illusionist he makes two gorgeous, sky-blue pills appear in his hand. Susan looks at them in astonishment.

"Have you tried it?"

"Sure! It beats anything I've taken before. Better than MDMA, better than coke, even better than ganja! When you're on it you understand the meaning of the words 'God created man in His image'—you become like Him. You glide over the ground, creating new worlds each second. You become ultra-lucid, ultra-conscious, and ultra-wasted all at the same time. Let's try one right now, if you like?"

Susan grabs the pill out of Dov's palm, holds it between her thumb and index finger, brings it up to inspect it, closes her eyes, opens her mouth, and swallows it. He follows suit. Then the two of them sit side by side on the white, ceramic-tiled bench in the Chaim Potok High School chemistry lab. A pretend Jew and a Hasidic ex-con, with their eyes closed, waiting in the mild evening air to become gods on Earth.

20

Down at reception, Jean picks up the keys to an unmarked vehicle parked outside the Bunker. He starts it gently and follows the same route as Rachel the night before. After the bridge on rue Ordener, he slows down, closely surveying the area around the telephone booth. There's a space in a loading bay just in front. He parks, lights a cigarette, and clears his head. He lets the place wash over him. His eyes wander, stopping at a book case. There, lined up, as if on parade, are the crappy paperbacks he used to jerk off to in secret back in Saint-Pol-de-Léon. *Son Altesse Sérénissime*, his favorite, because underneath it all it was fascist, racist, misogynistic trash. Everything

that was forbidden for him. It was the really hackneyed fantasies—
like when the Air Africa stewardess sucks off Prince Malko Linge on
an airplane—that gave him the biggest boner. And they were amazing for staying hard for ages, since every two pages there was another
sex scene or, even better, some torture. Yup, the torture scenes . . .
They were the most exciting. Like with the cat.

ALMOST KILLING AN ANIMAL
A LIVING BEING
GETTING OFF ON ITS SUFFERING

The shop. Looks like a second-hand shop. Various old books and
curios in the window. Enough light from inside to see it's a real
mishmash. A huge, oddly familiar shadow comes to the entrance,
then pulls back into the cavern, followed thirty seconds later by a
second, normal-sized guy, who scrutinizes Jean for a second before
disappearing too. Bit tricky to go in asking questions like "Did you
see a murderer making a telephone call on June 18 at 9:30 p.m.?" His
watch says 10:45 a.m. Too late. If he wants to get to Rachel without
the flashing lights he needs to take off now.

At Le Gastelier, which looks out over the Montmartre funicular and
Sacré-Coeur, he orders a pain au chocolat and a double espresso. *Le
Parisien* and *Libération* are right there, but he doesn't want to get
bogged down with the din of the world. He can't wait for that wonderful first bite. The pains au chocolat here are light and flaky, not
at all stodgy. Their quality comes from their substance and texture
as much as from their taste. Every time he comes here it astonishes
him that such a place can survive, wedged between a Häagen-Dazs
ice cream parlor and a supposedly authentic old-style *bistro*. What
was it Debord said? "The true is a moment of the false . . ." Indeed.

Rachel arrives at the same time as his order. She lets the waiter
serve her colleague, asks for the same, and then sits down. Not
the customary kiss on the cheek, just a silent smile that lights
up the world.

"I saw Mercator—he managed to give me the creeps! He's got this way of speaking about evil, like something out of Dante's *Inferno* . . . No, hold on—let's begin with life, not death. Last night, I decided to move out. The twelfth is a horror show: far-right white boys and Arabs on Prozac. I want to be in a neighborhood that's alive. The eighteenth, the tenth . . . somewhere like that. Or the north of the ninth? Somewhere with some bars or clubs. People, humans, you know."

Rachel listens, still smiling.

"About time! I was really beginning to wonder why you were refusing to leave that dingy tower block on that dreadful road. As soon as this case is over I'll help you find the perfect place. The tenth would suit you, in the Tamil neighborhood, that bit between La Chapelle and Gare de l'Est. I'm sure you'd like it there. And I'll take you for a *masala dosa*—they're delicious! Before you tell me about Mercator, I've got something to tell you too. One thing in particular that troubled me this morning."

"Troubled you? You seem so happy! Like you've won the lottery, or you've met the man of your dreams. Reminds me of that Canadian song when the dude asks in his Québecois accent: 'Do you take water in your whiskey?' and she answers: 'No, I take it neeeeeeeeeeeat . . .'"

"Hey, anyone ever told you that you're a complete ass?"

"Err, yes . . . You, mainly. Okay, sorry . . . I feel like talking crap this morning, just to get it off my chest . . ."

"What makes it even trickier is that stupid remark of yours is not that wide of the mark . . . Listen, I'm going to tell you something that I shouldn't. So keep it to yourself and no lame comments. It's just I need to talk to somebody about it, and since it's linked to the inquiry, that can only be you."

"Okay Cross my heart, et cetera et cetera."

"This morning, just before leaving, I got a call from Taroudant."

"And that's what's been troubling you? If I'm seeing this right, Taroudant calls you at 10:00 a.m. and you're . . . you're overjoyed! You do realize that you're in the process of being chatted up by a half-wit Arab who's a suspect in a murder investigation that you are carrying out with yours truly?"

"Yes, I am aware of that."

"That doesn't seem to be the case. The girl, Laura, had her vagina slashed by a knife with a blade that was—what?—three, six inches long . . . He, he had keys to her place, he has no alibi . . . He is still in the picture. I'm still wondering why we haven't brought him in!"

"Because we both know that it wasn't him! Here's why: he doesn't have the build or the profile. And we're not going to waste any time going down a dead end. We don't have twenty-four hours of custody time to play with."

"I can just imagine what we're going to say to Mercator. 'It can't be him, Lieutenant Kupferstein has got a crush on him . . . Trust us, Commissaire, sir . . .'"

"Enough! You didn't let me finish. What are you, jealous? He called me to say he's going back to his psychoanalysis and that he's going to work at the bookshop with Monsieur Paul."

She stares at Jean, her eyes at once firm and imploring.

"I'm talking to you as my partner and as my friend. I'm not keeping anything from you because this is not just about my private life, it's about a criminal investigation, and I'm well aware of that. Yes, his call moved me. Especially when he admitted that the main reason for calling me was to hear the sound of my voice. It unsettled me, and that's why I need you. Ahmed . . . Ahmed has made a very profound impression on me. I could even feel myself wavering over at his place yesterday. In the evening, before going to sleep, I thought about him, I saw his face, and then this morning he calls me . . . So if we want a word for that, then maybe it's 'love', yes, I'm falling in love. Beginning to, at least. The very, very beginning . . ."

Rachel is emotional, on the verge of tears, but she pulls herself together.

"I'm asking you not to judge me, but to help me keep my judgment. Having these feelings for someone . . . It doesn't come around every day . . . But there's no question of it compromising the investigation. So if you sense I'm losing control, tell me. All I'm saying is . . . be fair!"

"Uh, okay. That's not going to be easy. For starters, I'm jealous, obviously. Even if I know things would never work between us, deep down it does hurt a little. But . . . I adore you, Rachel, I really do, and I'm telling you today that I have no doubt that I always will, so remember that . . . I adore you completely, and I'll never do anything to hurt you. But you need to know that what you're asking of me is major, really major. As far as the rest is concerned, I'm with you. Ahmed doesn't fit the murderer's profile, not for a second. But I'm still going to check . . . I've got this meeting with his doctor. Other than that, watch how you go! Keep your distance big time until the investigation's over. Imagine what'd happen if this came out . . . Just imagine . . ."

"I'll be sensible. But I did ask him to call me if he found anything out. And he told me that he'll do anything to find a good reason to call me or to see me again. I . . . I'll know how to handle it."

"Definitely let me know if that happens and we'll go and see him together."

"Alright." She stops herself, looks at Jean, smiles, mouths a "thank you," gathers her breath and continues, "Let's move on to the serious stuff. In the night I got a call from Bintou and Aïcha. They asked me if I had Skype, some application for making free calls via the Internet."

"I know the one."

"Ah, I hadn't heard of it. They're meant to be coming around tonight at about 3:00 a.m. so that we can talk to Rébecca on Skype."

"Yes! Great news. Where's Rébecca?"

"I didn't ask them for the moment. Far away, in any case . . . Straight after I switched on my computer and there was an e-mail from Gomes who's managed to organize a meeting for me this afternoon with an ex-Witness from Niort."

"Ahmed, Kevin . . . All these men at your every beck and call . . ."

"Very funny! Your turn—fill me in on Mercator."

"Hold on. Before Mercator, I've got something to show you. You remember 75-Zorro-19?"

"The rap group with Bintou and Aïcha's brothers, Moktar and Ruben?"

"Precisely. I found a mixtape of theirs from 2000. Have a look."

The photograph shows the four of them looking into the camera like gangsters in front of the Rotonde de la Villette. They're all making the same sign: little finger touching the thumb with the three middle fingers splayed apart.

"That symbolizes Allah in Arabic. They're all doing it, even Ruben. It was a pretty good way of winding people up and it worked with the white kids from the schools in the sixth. They would brave marché Malik on a Saturday to buy the latest tunes from the hot new 'ghetto' artists. The dedication is the most interesting thing: 'To our first fans, our little sisters, our homegirls Rébecca, Aïcha, and Bintou.'"

"You mean Ruben is Rébecca's big brother?"

"Yup. And you know what—I remember seeing them at a gig."

"You went to one of their concerts?"

"I went to check them out once. The girls must have been seventeen. They did a dance routine up on stage just before the first song. I didn't recognize them yesterday because I'd totally forgotten about that concert. Plus their style was completely different. They hid their curves under really baggy tracksuits. But their dancing . . . There was something wild, untamed about it . . . Everything's coming back to me now. The band started at the community school when four local kids met: two black guys, an Arab, and a Jew. They became pals, learned about life, messed around with music. They ended up at the same secondary school and decided to form a hip-hop band: 75-Zorro-19. Aside from Moktar, who you know already—he was the beatmaker—there's Mourad, Aïcha's brother, Alpha, who's Bintou's brother, and Ruben . . ."

"Rébecca's brother."

"Exactly! When I moved to the neighborhood, they'd just started college. Their tag was on every wall, their lyrics ringing in everyone's

heads. Two years later, after they'd graduated, Moktar had his breakdown and the group didn't survive after that. This morning I dug
around and I found the sleeve to their mixtape, and also one of their
rap tunes on my old MP3 player. Have a listen! Ruben is the first to
rap."

Rachel tries not to look too disgusted as she inserts the ques-
tionably clean earpuds. It starts with a stripped-down beatbox, followed by a plucked guitar riff that she could swear had been lifted
from Prince, before a Kool Shen-esque vocal kicks in.

The life of a A-rab, the life of a brother,
It's not worth nothin' round here,
Every day, wallah!
Society's vengeance on those it mistreats
Shot like rabbits, strangled between our sheets
Treated like the enemy
As if we was back in some colony
Blanking our lives from your memory
But we're in this, we're from this vicinity
We're here you hear me, fuck you to anonymity.

A break with a heavy bass line, AC/DC-style, then a new voice takes
over. It's rougher, more violent. Rachel takes out an earbud and raises
her eyebrows at Jean, who mouths "Mourad" back at her.

From the lowest of the low, I'm gonna raise my cry
We were born into a trap, suckled on fear
Nothing to lose, we can fuck it all up here
Our fathers faced the wall, waiting for the trigger
The Arab's the pariah, yeah we remember Algeria
Now the black boy's the danger, the savage they can't keep in
Way back when it was the Jew, made to purify and free the Aryan
I've not forgotten a thing, purgat'ry's my cousin
Black on Jew, Arab on brother
We eat each other, fuck each other, make each other suffer.

Another change—this time Rachel doesn't need Jean to guess that it's
Alpha, whose tone is sweeter, at times verging on a stammer.

That's enough, that's going too far, don't take me for the enemy
Unity I tell you, that's our life guarantee
The system's always lining up the next victim
Int'rested in one thing: to nail you for a crime
To shut you in a box, to put you in the dock
So eager for it they call upon their Book
What am I asking? That our lives be worth something
I'm free of hate, I'll say it again
Don't go thinking you can get us complying
With a fifty-cent coin just 'cause of the gold lining.

Rachel pulls out the earbuds.

"I don't get it . . . How did they switch from politically minded
young guys to the closed-up individuals they are now? Long story
short, Ruben joined the Moroccan Hasids, and his sister looked like
she was going the same way until her mysterious disappearance. As
for Alpha and Mourad, they're regulars at the same prayer room
as Moktar on rue Eugène-Jumin. So how come Aïcha and Bintou
never caught the fundamentalist bug?"

"Why would they? During major epidemics, some family members are affected while others aren't. One of life's great mysteries."

"A mystery, yes, perhaps. But imagine what it must be like seeing
your brother going down that path, becoming someone else? Must
be weird."

"Well you'll have all the time in the world to ask them tonight at
your little Skype-party. Tell me, do you remember who the imam at
the prayer room is? It's our friend Abdelhaq."

"Abdelhaq Haqiqi—I'd forgotten about him! His little brother
Hassan . . . He went down, didn't he?"

"No, still on remand. But I reckon it would be a plan to pay
Haqiqi a visit, just to catch up on any family news . . ."

Rachel pauses for a moment before continuing.

"Three Salafists and a fanatical Lubavitcher. One of their younger sisters is reported missing, and the other two are anything but fundamentalists. Their best friend gets murdered, the crime scene smacking of religious impurity. What does it mean? Common sense—not to mention the current climate—demands that we focus on the Salafists, but then there's Rébecca's disappearance . . . Radical Muslims and Jews involved in the same mess—doesn't it seem a bit much to you?"

"I'm not going to start quoting Goebbels again, even if you are asking for it . . ."

"On the other side there's Laura's family history. In Niort, Commissaire Jeanteau paid the parents a visit to tell them about their daughter's death, and he called me afterward. Their reaction was bizarre, as though it had absolutely nothing to do with them. The wife spoke about devils, made out that their daughter only ever visited to sully them, to cover them in 'the filth of the earth'. Something must have gone wrong when Laura last visited. Something out of the ordinary. The mother's words were too precise. We'll probably have to question her on her own because, according to Jeanteau, her husband stopped her from saying anything more."

"It's been slammed since last night! We'll have to knuckle down if we're going to follow all these leads . . . Oh yeah, about Mercator . . . He's suspicious of our dear friends in the eighteenth, Enkell and Benamer. Basically he's convinced that Enkell is lying to him, that he knows something about the call from the telephone booth, but that he's deliberately holding back some info. When I asked him if Benamer was still Frédéric Enkell's right-hand man he replied: 'Evil exists, Hamelot, and sometimes it gets itself together.' Those were his exact words. He also spoke about the stench of death. By that point I thought I was going to suffocate. I had to get out of there—meet you somewhere lively instead of at HQ."

Rachel turns pale, repeats the name, "Benamer . . ."

"What about Benamer? What is it?"

She shakes her head slowly before deciding to go on.

"Benamer . . . A brief encounter that's left me feeling grubby ever since. He ran a seminar at Cannes-Écluse when I was a trainee officer. He had this magnetism about him that attracted me right away. I wanted him—a bit like when you want to get off with the guide at ski camp. Little did I know that what I'd mistaken for magnetism was really malice. That I discovered at the end of the internship. He had no qualms in presenting the most horrific things as though they were perfectly normal, always in this insidious manner. For him, it was purely a matter of technique: how am I going to get a confession? It barely mattered whether the suspect was guilty or not. Screwing was all about technique too. He was relentless. He made me orgasm the first time. After that, I felt like if I didn't fake it, he would just keep on going, that . . . I don't know—he scared me, I think. He thought I'd faked it and he gave me this look of real scorn. He was testing me, ultimately. And I was glad I didn't pass. Deep down he reminded me of the devil . . ."

She falls quiet, closes her eyes, and then snorts.

"Alright, come on—action! How about we warm up by seeing Haqiqi? No, let me get it! My treat . . ."

21

Abdelhaq Haqiqi, self-styled imam of the semi-clandestine Srebrenica prayer room, is pissed off beyond belief. For the past two hours, since the end of Fajr prayers, he's been there, watch in hand, listening to these good-for-nothings' endless discussion of the extremist comic Dieudonné's last TV appearance. They take turns to speak, saying the same thing a hundred times over, giddy on consensus. Haqiqi's followers are developing an infuriating tendency to confuse the prayer room with the local coffee shop. And as head of this community of

true believers, he finds himself playing the part of the café owner
who's unable to chuck out the embittered soccer fan, the one who
spends the morning after a game running a postmortem on the
match, or the boozed-up, Le Pen–supporting unemployed dude who
thinks everything's gone to shit because of the Arabs and the blacks
(the Jews too, though he'd only say so in select company). No way
he can throw out this handful of unholy, hopeless down-and-outs
and losers: they're his clientele, his butts in the seats. Nothing they
like more than churning out great streams of verbal diarrhea, with
the usual suspects always bobbing on the surface like hippo crap: the
CIA and the Jews were in on 9/11; Dieudonné getting banned from
the air by Zionist media puppets; the rector of the Grande Mosquée
de Paris is in the pocket of the Freemasons; halal that's not halal . . .
Abdelhaq does his best to cling to a branch on the muddy bank. It's
strange for him, though, because not long ago he thought just like
them, bathing in the same filthy water, taking comfort from its amniotic warmth. This was before he met Aïssa. Before he developed an
interest in the material nature of the world for the first time in his
life. The fact is he does still think like them, but he no longer gives a
damn. His goals are now terrestrial rather than celestial. And that's
changed everything.

The morning regulars are there: Mahmoud, Brahim and—the
worst offender by far—Robert.

"Did you see him saying . . ."

"Yeah, but what about the Jews, the media . . ."

"Okay, obviously, man, they run it all!"

"Yeah, tell me about it, it stinks! Every time it's the same . . . He
dresses up like a Jew, so he's anti-Semitic. Just like that, yeah. Know
what I'm saying?"

Abdelhaq tries his best to leave them to it and think about his own
situation. Shit! Just when everything's starting to go like clockwork,
Aïssa wants them to hit the brakes. It's because of that girl. He's still
not sure why she was such a threat, but Aïssa seemed to know what
he was doing . . . Anyway, if everything has gone to shit then it hasn't
got much to do with him. All he did was make a small selection

error by sending his three best players to the meeting at Sam's. Only Moktar had stood firm. Time had been of the essence, Sam lost his cool and cobbled together a plan B which involved pairing up a psychotic Sahelian Salafist with a psychopathic killer from Alsace. From then on, the entire operation was a free-for-all. Right now everyone's stuck in neutral, wasting time, and it's not good. There was something divine about the way it was all panning out until this happened. But the time has come for compromise . . . Perhaps he's being tested, as they say . . . On top of this, he has to keep his people sweet, and they're not the easiest to chill out. Same for those other idiots who barely ever get off their asses. Benefit-scrounging Islamists who live with their parents and don't give a shit about anything! Fucking hell, roll on the day when someone like Sarkozy takes over . . . No jobs, no cash! These three guys wouldn't even be capable of carrying out a suicide attack—what are they good for, honestly?

"Oi, Abdelhaq! No jokes, man, the Jews, they're mocking us, aren't they?"

"You know, Robert, the Prophet, may God's peace and blessing be upon him, said that they were all liars. *Inshallah*, when the *dawla islamiya* is reestablished, they will know their rightful place as *dhimmi*. But the majority, I am sure of it, will, like you, take the right path that leads to truth."

"But I've never been a Jew!"

"No, Robert, of course not, and the Prophet himself, may God's peace and blessing be upon him, certainly preferred the Christians of all the people of the Book. What I'm saying is that you have found the way, you have opened your heart to the light, and that they will too, without a doubt . . ."

Answers like this come naturally to him. It's what he has always thought, for as long as he's been aware of his thoughts. But he can no longer bear spewing out such babble. The moment he hears himself say it he can practically feel Aïssa's look of contempt. "Don't you think that you're above all that, Abdelhaq? Why do you give a fuck about Jews,

Christians, cretins? Would you join the jihad? Would you go and blow yourself up just to kill five Iraqi soldiers and some redneck from Kansas? Do you really believe there's any sense in that? And don't tell me that everyone has a part to play in this great struggle, that everyone has the chance to attain the longed-for status of martyrdom . . . I can see in your eyes that you don't believe it anymore. The virgins, the rivers, the delicious fruit and the houses made of gold bars . . . You wanted them so much that you couldn't wait until paradise to obtain them!"

"Hey, Abdelhaq, have you seen this? Sweets with gelatin made from *halouf*. It's only come out because of that mad cow shit . . . They've been making us eat pork all along! That was their plan, yeah—to make us come here to eat pork. To turn us into pigs. Shit, man, I swear it, one day I'm getting the fuck out of here. *Inshallah*, I'll go to Mecca or Medina. I swear it, brother!"

"*Inshallah*, Brahim, *inshallah . . .*"

How much longer am I going to have to put up with this bullshit, let alone answer it? How much longer? Fucking hell, Aïssa! What the hell are you doing to me?

Sure enough the telephone decides to ring right then. It's Mohand.

"Hey, can I swing by?"

"*Salaam alaikum ya khouya*. Lucky you called—I've been so busy I nearly forgot about our meeting. I'll meet you at Onur's as planned."

"At Onur's, okay . . . I've got to go to there anyway. I'm in a rush."

"*Barak allahu fik*, my brother, see you in a bit."

A forced smile on his lips, Abdelhaq turns to the three worshippers. Sitting or half-flopped on their prayer mats, they're wearing the requisite uniform: prayer cap, white *kamiss* down to below their knee, three-quarter-length Nike or Le Coq Sportif track pants, and sneakers sporting the same logos. *How can they afford all that on jobseeker's allowance? Fair enough, they don't spend anything because they still live with their parents. Fuck, why was I born an Arab? I'd have been right at home with the* Front National!

"Brothers, I have a meeting. A young believer who is making his first steps on the path but is not yet fully ready. I've got to shut the prayer room for two hours. I'll be back in time to lead the next set of prayers . . . 1:57 p.m. today."

Ten minutes later, Haqiqi is standing outside Onur's. He smiles at the owner while he nods at a young man sitting in front of a glass of tea. Mohand—twenty-five years old, well-pressed jeans, Burlington moccasins, Lacoste polo shirt—joins him outside; they walk side by side up to parc de la Villette, the imam and the supposed brother who's seen the light. They head up the park's central walkway, dodging the crowds of people. When they reach the Grande Halle, Mohand goes on the offensive.

"Why did you change meeting places?"

"There were three idiots there I couldn't shift. The prayer room has turned into some local hangout . . . Plus there's been a change of plan. We're putting everything on hold for the moment."

"What do you mean 'putting everything on hold'? Are you taking me for a prick or what? I've got orders, clients waiting."

"There's been a supply chain issue. I've got nothing at the moment. A problem at the source, apparently."

Mohand makes to grab Abdelhaq by the throat.

"My brother, you wouldn't lay a finger on a man of God?" He looks him in the eye with a menacing smile. "You wouldn't do a thing like that now, would you?"

22

Ahmed is perched before a mug of steaming coffee. Monsieur Paul drinks his, making a racket like an old man who's beyond caring.

Ahmed ends up copying him. The bookseller finally reaches his
decision.

"How much do you need a month to resume the sessions?"

"Well . . . Between one hundred and fifty and two hundred . . ."

"Right—and since you need to pay in cash, you'll want cash from
me. No paperwork, eh?"

"No."

"Very well, very well. I don't like paperwork . . . You can come
for an hour or two a day to move books around, keep an eye on the
shop, that sort of thing?"

"Yes, okay—no problem."

"Perfect, wonderful."

Silence. He's lived with death for so long he's got all the time in
the world. Ahmed looks at him in an unhurried way. The summer
he turned thirteen, when he bought his first Horace McCoy, Monsieur Paul was already what might be described as an elderly man;
nowadays, it's a different story altogether. It's like he's from a different world, with a subtle hint of Clint Eastwood or Morgan Freeman.
The sort of person who has lived; who knows that the end is near
and that it always has been. The sort of person who loves life because
he's looking death in the face. You don't learn that when you hit
eighty. Ahmed will be like him if he reaches that age. Monsieur Paul
knows it—that's what binds them. The young man enjoys another
loud slurp of his coffee. He's like an old man. He's old. He likes it.
He keeps quiet.

"And Laura . . . Is this reawakening because of her?"

"Yes. They killed her. And I'm not sure, but it occurred to me that
I might have loved her, that I loved her in my own way. I imagined
the life we might have lived together . . . It went as far as children,
divorce . . . Most of all, I felt I had to do something. For her. For me
too, out of loyalty to what we hadn't lived. And to avoid falling into
their trap."

"How did you find out about it, this trap?"

Ahmed isn't surprised. Monsieur Paul knows everything.

"Glances, comments. Sam, Moktar, Ruben . . ."

"Good, you've learned a few things. You're ready to fight. To use your weakness as a weapon. You know they won't see you as a threat; they will be reckoning they can play around with you. That's a good start. What about the police?"

"I . . ."

Ahmed shuts his eyes and replays the police officers' visit from the day before. Everything is ingrained in his memory. The feelings come back in slow motion. Maggie Cheung's patterned dress . . . Rachel's red hair . . . Slowly, for all eternity. He opens his eyes.

"The lady's in her thirties. Ashkenazi Jew, beautiful, with the same freckles and the same eyes as Esther, the first girl I kissed at school. I'm in love with her," he adds, surprising himself. "She reads Ellroy—*White Jazz* is her favorite. Like me. You know I've always been convinced that I could only ever truly love an Ellroy fan, but believing that such a woman doesn't exist. Well, not an attractive one, at least."

Monsieur Paul says nothing, finishes off his mug, takes it all in, waiting. The beginnings of a smile form.

"The guy also likes crime novels. More into the classics. I saw his eyes stop for a long time on *No Pockets in a Shroud* by McCoy. As if it brought back memories. It's strange, I hadn't realized I'd taken all these details on board. He's the same age as her. Not Jewish, maybe a Breton, with a washed-out face . . . I can remember their names, too: Rachel Kupferstein and Jean Hamelot . . ."

"Rachel, daughter of Aaron Kupferstein, a furrier. His work-shop wasn't far from here, on rue des Carrières-d'Amérique. Originally from Vilnius, the 'Jerusalem of the North', easily the largest Jewish city in prewar Europe. Thankfully he got out of there in 1938 with his family when he was a youngster. He was hidden in Seine-et-Marne just when his parents were shipped off after the Vél d'Hiv roundup. They died, but he survived. He stayed single for a long time before marrying late, a Romanian Jew called

Alicia, whose parents had survived Buchenwald. They then fled as
quickly as they could from the anti-Semitic clampdown in Communist Bucharest. Rachel was born in '69—I watched her grow
up. Hamelot . . . he's the son of Breton Communists. Came to the
neighborhood six years ago; his first posting. He comes in from
time to time to pick up a new Hammett. He doesn't say much—
like you."

"But how . . ."

"Oh, I was there. The Nazis didn't have anything against the
Armenians, so I spent the war here, in peace. Well, more or less . . .
Aaron I knew as a youngster. Let's just say I saw certain things.
Things which have strange echoes nowadays . . . I was practically
there when Rachel was born . . . Ahmed and Rachel . . . Yes, I like
all this. I like it a lot."

The young man senses that now's not the time for asking questions. Monsieur Paul looks at him and laughs.

"You need a haircut, you do!"

It's the first time Ahmed has heard him laugh. It's a slightly hoarse
laugh that's been given a serious working over by cigarettes and coffee. This peculiar turn in their relationship knocks him off guard.
Indeed he had already decided to go to Sam's that morning; not
with any clear agenda, just to check out the lion's den, play dumb,
and test the water.

"Yes, you're going to play dumb. They take you for a harmless
imbecile, that's why they're trying to put the blame on you. Sam's
a devious idiot. He thinks mechanically, like a dominos player. I've
been watching him operate for thirty years since he arrived from
Tiznit. Always the same—one move after the other. Tack, tack, tack,
tack! And that works, of course, in this neighborhood. Everyone else
is busy surviving, trying to create some breathing space between
their money difficulties and the oppressive religious leaders. What
will be the sum of Sam's moves? The thing is, he plays alone . . . But
this is a different sort of game. This time it seems like he's out of his
depth. Quite a bit out of his depth."

"Sam—so he is involved! It's not just me going crazy in my own head? But what did he want from Laura?"

"Oh, her, nothing. He didn't want anything at all. But just as you thought, he's wrapped up in this thing you've been telling me about, this business with Moktar and Ruben . . . A few others too. The motive? The people really pulling the strings? I still can't see that clearly. But there's some weird stuff going on with the Muslims and the Jews. Stuff that's not very halal and not very kosher. You know, evil is not some single entity that can be grasped in one go. It'll all fall into place. It'll all play out in front us, you'll see. In the meantime, you shouldn't hang around here too long . . . Perfect time to go to Sam's. He'll be delighted that you're his first customer—simply delighted! What's more, it's the Sabbath this evening . . . Listen, watch, play dumb. Oh yes, and don't forget to tell him that from now on you're helping me in the shop. Then report back to Rachel. Oh, and give her my best wishes."

23

Avenue C, Alphabet City, Manhattan.
One year earlier.

The room is practically empty. Their refuge. This is the first time a stranger has stepped into James and Susan's hideout. There are three blue pills are on the table.

GODZWILL

James had been captivated by the name. He saw a gleaming future
for them bound up in it. Three magic beans; three coconspirators.
Susan introduced Dov to her brother the previous week at the Starbucks on the corner of First Avenue Loop. A chai latte with soya
milk for him (he'd eaten a pastrami pizza at Kingston Pizza Kosher
before taking the subway, and since his *teshuvah* he has scrupu-
lously obeyed the laws of *kashrut*: he must therefore abstain from
consuming any dairy products in the eight-hour period after eating
meat); mochas for them. The two guys had hit it off immediately,
which made Susan heave a huge internal sigh of relief. James knew
that there was nothing sexual going on between her and Dov; if
there had been, the meeting would never have taken place—the
idea of being around his sister's lovers repels him. This is why she
had gotten into the habit of dumping her men after half a day. No
danger of becoming attached; love falling apart. As for James, he never
mentions his sex life, leading her to believe he doesn't have one—a
bit of a loner who prefers to spend most of his time on the computer.
He needed to for work, but also to arrange the new life that tomorrow was going to bring them. Just one more throw of the dice was
needed before they could take vengeance on their father and leave
behind the fake life they had been forced to lead. It is this stroke of
genius they are about to discuss now before they drop their beautiful blue pills.

To mark the occasion, Dov has traded in his Borsalino hat for a
green, yellow, and red yarmulke. James opens a bag of Lay's Flamin'
Hot chips—guaranteed pork-free—unscrews a bottle of 7 Up, fills
the plastic cups, and takes the floor.

"Okay. To summarize: we have the product; I haven't tried it,
but Susan has explained its effect to me. The commercial potential
seems immense. All we need is a market. Preferably somewhere far
away, to ensure it doesn't get traced back to us. You have contacts
in Paris and Antwerp who could distribute it. We need to find a
way of transporting it to Europe. That's where Susan comes in. She

has many disguises—Salome, Judith, Bathsheba . . . whatever the situation calls for—all drawing from our mutual religious heritage. As we speak, a foreign elder of the Jehovah's Witnesses is making a stop-off at headquarters. Yesterday, our father, bloated with his usual self-importance, introduced us to him as a friend from France who has come on a one-week placement. 'A friend with a brilliant future,' were his exact words. Susan flashed her most charming smile, and the look he returned her proved, beyond any shadow of a doubt, and despite his devout adherence to the strict precepts of the organization, that he is ripe for the picking. Now it's just a matter of logistics—I'll take care of all that."

James finishes as abruptly as he started. Over to Dov.

"The rebbe has confirmed that plans are gradually falling into place in Paris. Seven or eight months from now the dealing network will be operational across France, Belgium, and Holland. Aside from that, at a wholesale price of twenty-five dollars per pill, we should easily reach our targets in the first six months." Then he turns to Susan and says, "Um, listen—I really like you. I don't know how to put it, but . . . Are you sure you want to go ahead with this? Maybe there's some other way . . ."

Susan smiles cheerfully, like a little girl.

"It's fun, you know. You're sweet to worry about me, but I've never done anything I didn't want to do. Sure, he's a bit old, but that doesn't bother me. The truth is, I love leading these old guys astray, the ones who think they're above everyone and everything, as though they've already got one foot in heaven! And there am I, waiting to trip them up, to deny them peace. Forever. Mmm, can't wait! Nothing better . . . Right, we've covered everything, I think. Shall we go and get him?"

A moment's contemplation. The three partners in crime swallow their pills with a 7 Up chaser. A ritual made all the more magical by its profound ordinariness. Each of them gets ready, waiting for ascension to commence. Dov sits on the floor, his back against a slightly grubby white wall. The Barnes twins slide onto a pair of canary-yellow plastic chairs. They exchange the odd sentence, more

or less devoid of meaning, just to maintain contact. The strangeness
sets in. It's a new sensation for James; Dov and Susan are rediscover-
ing the joy of that omnipotent state. Two dimensions, one superimposed on the other. That's the incredible thing: being the Barnes
twins in this world and in another at the very same time. Nothing
like acid, where the high is so intense it makes you lose the power of
speech. Not like coke, either, which makes you think you're cleverer
than everyone else. No. They are completely and utterly present in
the shitty apartment where they are, 7 Up bottle and ridged white
plastic cups in hand. And they are gods. No, they are *God*. This is a
monotheistic drug: Christian, to be exact, with its Trinity of Gods,
or early Jewish, with its YHWH, Adonai and Elohim. They divide
the roles between them: Susan plays Elohim and the Holy Spirit—a
woman, plural and playful . . . yes, that works. Like a good Hasid,
Dov is YHWH, G-D—he who cannot be named—the tetragram-
maton, the spirit of Kabbalah made flesh . . . and Jesus, because,
regardless of any misgivings, he's not letting some goy take that
role. Then James is Adonai and God the Father, suiting his loner
profile nicely.

Seeing double. Feeling double. Above, below, everywhere. Perfect
harmony. Thoughts, words become one—they finish each other's
sentences without opening their mouths. Beauty, plenty, fullness. An
alternate creation: Eden basking in the innocent glow of its garden-
ers; heavenly boredom.

TO BECOME GOD
WE MUST FIRST ACCEPT
THE NEED FOR EVIL

No free will; a monotone eternity. No evil, no action, no story. God
created Man in His image. Murder, envy, adultery, theft. God created
Man to stave off boredom. All three of them, all six of them understand that. They are God! They know! They have eaten of the tree of
knowledge. They are God, they know. They are Man and Woman,
they know.

TO DO EVIL IS TO DO GOOD

It is to ensure that God be kept from boredom. To ensure that everything keeps moving for the sake of eternity. An infinity of years
where nothing happens. Absoluteness. Their plan is on high. They
know that Dov-YHWH-Jesus was divinely inspired to dream up
this drug. *The tree of fucking knowledge.* And their eyes are opened.
Human. So human. With their fizzy drinks—seventy-five cents for a
half-gallon—their French fries and their love of trivial worldly plea-
sures. Swimming pools, weed, flat-screen televisions, skateboards,
forbidden DVDs . . . *Whatever.* And they laugh.
 They laugh.

24

Since first thing in the morning, Mathilde Vignola has been repeating herself. One single line, over and over, in a sinister nursery-
rhyme hum. "The little whore, dead and buried . . . The little whore,
dead and buried . . . The little whore, dead and buried . . . The little
whore, dead and buried . . ." Tall and willowy, all skin and bones,
she might have been beautiful, but her features hardened with her
ineffable hatred of the world. Horrified as much as intrigued by his
wife's patent lunacy, Vincenzo wanders from one room to the next in
the stone house. As soon as he catches sight of Mathilde he shudders,
unable to conceal his panic despite knowing its cause. It is his mortal
fear. This gnawing sense of fear is threatening to take hold of him
completely, just as madness has gripped his wife. At 7:30 a.m., when
he woke up, she was sitting on the right-hand side of the bed in her

synthetic burgundy nightdress. When he foolishly tried to explain to her that Laura was dead, yes, but not yet buried, Mathilde's hawk-like eyes bored into his own, so much so that he felt as though they were burning the inside of his skull. Then she slowly lowered her face toward him until it was one inch away, and said:

THE—LITTLE—WHORE—
DEAD—AND—BURIED

A ghastly mixture of hatred, garlic, and bile. At that precise moment he realized his whole life had been determined by his fear of this woman. If it wasn't for her he'd have taken his business studies degree from La Rochelle and would now be a big mover and shaker in the insurance world, maybe chief accountant at MAIF, or even administrative director at Matmut. Instead of that nicely mapped-out career, he has become, without ever really leaving France (not counting his regular stints in Brooklyn), locked in a parallel universe governed by its own laws. It has been a good life in many ways, above all by letting him wield a disproportionate amount of power over the other prisoners of this strange world that Mathilde plunged him into on their second meeting. Contrary to his naive expectations, they had not ended up back at his place (Italian tunes, glass of Asti Spumante, violet satin bedcovers), but in a Kingdom Hall. Since that evening he had risen to the highest echelons, eventually becoming the organization's number one in the Poitou-Charentes region. Members' lives were entirely under his control: camping trips, pets, lovemaking . . . No aspect of their existence escaped him. Despite his power, he always succumbed to his wife's will. The same wife who is now spitting her vile breath and insanity in his face.

It's 11:30 a.m. Vincenzo Vignola, head of the council of elders, is pacing around in circles, not daring to leave the house, despite knowing that Mathilde, even in her delirium, is monitoring his every move. She's lying in wait like an animal, ready to pounce at his throat the second he attempts to call an ambulance. Vincenzo knows she's capable of anything to avoid going back to the hospital. The more he tries to act naturally, the clumsier his gestures become, and the closer his wife gets to incandescence. Yet even the psychotic have their needs. Mathilde stands up, her litany unbroken, heads to the toilet and locks the door behind her. Vincenzo immediately grabs his car keys and cell and leaves without a sound. As soon as he's on the move in his car he dials the emergency services: a vehicle will be there in ten to twelve minutes. Avenue de La Rochelle, rue du 24 Février, rue de la Gare, avenue Charles de Gaulle, avenue Louis Pasteur, avenue de La Rochelle. Eighteen minutes later, he parks three houses down from his own. The ambulance is there, flashing lights on. Two nurses stand either side of the stretcher onto which Mathilde is strapped. One of them has a scarlet wound streaked across his right cheek. When she sees Vincenzo get out of his car, she erupts in a wild frenzy.

"Devil, the sign of the beast . . . Filth, muck . . . Laura . . . Same blood . . . Damnation . . ."

She's slobbering, momentarily silent. A cloud slides across the sky and the sun is freed, lighting up her miraculous smile, so pure and loving. That same smile he remembers from the first time he saw her. Soft, mellifluous words follow.

"You are going to die, Vincenzo. You do realize that, don't you— that you're going to die? It's your turn . . . That is how it is to be."

Another cloud passes overhead, black, eclipsing the brightness and obscuring her face.

"The little whore, dead and buried . . . The little whore, dead and buried . . . The little whore, dead and buried . . . The little whore, dead and buried . . ."

With the paperwork over and done with, Vincenzo is back in the sitting room staring eternity in the face. Mathilde's words are dancing a saraband around his head. "You are going to die . . . Die . . . You do realize that, don't you? Do you realize that? Do you?" He'd like to think that her intention had been to embitter his life, to avenge the madness the world had dealt her, to deny him enjoyment of his newly won freedom. He'd like to think that. But a little voice whispers in his ear. *She's right, Vincenzo, she's right. She knows . . . Do you see? She knows . . .* Tears start to flow and he sobs, his body shaking. For thirty years he has earned his living skillfully instilling the fear of the end of the world—Armageddon, Apocalypse—into the credulous hearts of his flock. And that dreaded abyss is now swallowing him whole. He's been hurled into empty, infinite space. Alone and naked amid the nothingness.

A primal, primitive sense of foreboding hooks itself on to the very immediate concerns he already has about the unfolding operation. No word from the people who should have been and gone an hour ago to pick up the consignment. Every thirty seconds Vincenzo checks his watch. Outside the sun is shining with a mocking brightness. His black Sagem vibrates on the table. Private number.

"Yes."

"Are you in place?"

Vincenzo recognizes the voice as belonging to the man he's only met once. Bad sign.

"What's happening? I'm waiting here like a fool."

"Calm down. Stay put . . . Two hours from now all will be well."

"Two hours! But I've got stuff to do. I can't sit around waiting! This is not how it was meant to go!"

"But this *is* how it is going. Is that clear? You have no control over any of this. So be good and wait patiently—it's not hard. Got it?"

"I'll be here on Saturday. We'll talk on Saturday."

"Saturday, eh? Okay, on Saturday we'll talk."

The line goes dead. Vincenzo bends backward with a sigh. Now he realizes. His destiny is right here, and he has no other option than to submit to it. That's all he's ever been: an instrument, a cog. He knows that he should have followed Mathilde's crazy but somehow reasonable ambitions. But he chose to bow to another mistress who was even more demanding, even more dangerous. Mathilde can see clearly in her dark state. Of course she knows what'll happen. As for him, how can he change that which has been written?

* * *

He picks up the T.G.V. ticket lying on the table next to the telephone.

Departure: Niort, 11:37
Arrival: Paris-Montparnasse, 14:00

How can he change what has already been written?

25

Ahmed has been waiting his turn at Sam's for twenty minutes. Flicking through a copy of *Auto hebdo*, he strives to follow the conversation between the barber and Albert, an old Egyptian Jew swamped by an enormous yet immaculate cream suit, who has spent the last thirty years trotting out the same story. As a tailor in Zamalek—a Cairo neighborhood favored by expats and the old post-Ottoman bourgeoisie, who longed for a return to the days of King Farouk—he had succeeded, by adapting his style, in establishing a clientele made up predominantly of officials from Nasser's government, making elegant clothing to measure that at the same time strictly adhered to the revolutionary code. He turned a blind eye to late payments from his frequently cash-strapped customers, relying instead on Western diplomats to keep the shop afloat. In return for his unreserved discretion—letting anything slip would have constituted a major faux pas in the tailor's eyes—Albert had hoped he would be rewarded with some kind of immunity should the going get tough. Alas! This was 1967, and the going was not so much tough as non-negotiable. The only special treatment he received at the outbreak of the Six Day War was a warning that came through a few hours before the imminent expulsion of all "Jewish foreigners." Now that second word was superfluous, since virtually every Jew in Egypt had European nationality, many of them British or French, dating back to the period of Ottoman rule where non-Muslim minorities were "protected" by Christian powers—France, England, or Russia (fortunately for Albert, the Russians only protected members of the Orthodox faith). So the Jewish tailor had half a day to put his affairs in order before leaving the only country he had ever lived in, never to return. He wasn't rich—he had served the rich. The meager savings he had scraped together was just enough to allow him to open a small workshop on rue Riquet. He'd barely opened his doors when the prêt-à-porter boom hit him like a truck.

"You know, Sam, the Six Day War . . . I survived it, at the end of the day, and I had no hand in it. I was neither Egyptian nor Israeli. I was French. Never before had I considered myself French, but . . . ah, *maalesh*, when I look at what happened later, I tell myself that I did well to leave that region of madmen. No, my real Six Day War, the one that really laid me out, was against that prêt-à-porter muck. That, old friend, was worse than any tank, any bombardment . . . The worst of all! An unstoppable machine. Imagine a machine taking over your job! Imagine, Sam, *ya sahabi!* Some laser-beam contraption to cut your customers' hair. Same style for men and women. What would you do if those started springing up all over the place? A kiosk down at the supermarket, between the photo booth and the photocopier, with a range of styles to suit any hairdo: you just choose which one, then scissors, clippers . . . everything done automatically! You just plunk yourself down, even choose what music to listen to: a bit of Dalida, some Maurice El Medioni, Enrico Macias, Lili Boniche, the works . . . What would you do if things came to that?"

"I couldn't give a damn anymore, Albert, *ya khouya!* I'll be retiring in a year's time . . . And Sholem, my son, has been in Brooklyn for a good while now, at Toledano's yeshiva, you know, our rabbi's cousin, the one who's just been declared rebbe by his followers. My Sholem is going to be a rabbi, not a barber. And quite frankly, what more can I ask of God, eh?"

"My goodness, yes . . . Well, as for me, my Six Day War, my anti-prêt-à-porter campaign, brought me to my knees, and I've finally decided to call it a day. *La belle France* is generous, you know . . ."

"And so is the Unified Jewish Social Fund. Us hard-working folk picking up the tab for your indolence. But that's okay, because you come here and repay my donations in part. That'll be seven fifty."

Sam whips off all the paraphernalia with a sharp movement and Albert gets to his feet. They settle up and the barber stands on the doorstep to shake the hand of his elegant client.

"*Shabbat shalom!*"

"Ah yes, that's right, it is the sabbath today, I almost forgot. Good job you reminded me."

"Don't pretend that's not why you came here. As if I'm not going to find you down at the synagogue later, sucking up to the rabbi and the faithful Jews who are bailing you out, you unbelieving rogue. Typical Egyptian Jews! Us Moroccan Jews are savages in your eyes, but you all, you're just a bunch of sly old dogs! Go on, off you go, my brother. See you tonight. Enough harping on—now it's my boy Ahmed's turn; come on and get your haircut by your old papa Sam."

The tone is ever-so-slightly false. When the old barber closes the door behind Albert, Ahmed gets up in meditative mode. The name of a book he's seen kicking about Dr. Germain's comes back to him suddenly: *L'Imposture perverse*. The perverse deception. The perverse Sam. Sam laying into Laura, or rather watching while some other sick bastard does. The scene comes to Ahmed easily. An empty space—a warehouse, perhaps—the knifeman at work with his back turned, and Laura gagged. Her legs apart but bound together. Eyes wide open. Horror. Not the sort of lightweight nastiness you get in Japanese bondage mangas. No—we're talking the depths of human depravity. Dante, Pasolini. Sam standing to one side. His face contorted in a state of arousal that is at once extreme and contained. And then the knifeman starts to turn around. Ahmed blinks rapidly to shake off the vision. Not the time or place to come face-to-face with the murderer. He's seen him from behind, knows that he recognizes him, but he can't put a name to those broad, sloping shoulders.

Will he have the courage to confront him when the moment comes? So close. He's brought around by a short burst of unidentifiable rap pouring out of a Mercedes coupe with Hauts-de-Seine plates and tinted windows, something about speaking with a Glock in your mouth.

A Glock, a shooter. That's what he needs. How can he get his hands on one? He can deal with that later. For now, let's look happy! Play the idiot, the same old oddball. Ahmed has known Sam since he was a child. His mother used to bring him here to get his haircut every other month because it was just next door and because Sam was Moroccan. She'd speak to him in Arabic, which calmed her down. The youngster didn't understand a word. Ahmed realizes that this was the only place where his mother spoke her native language. With him it was French from day one. What could they have talked about, the Jewish barber and the young, estranged, ex-Maoist daughter of a religious leader? Not the faintest idea . . . He also remembers Sholem, Sam's son. They'd barely ever spoken despite being in the same class at primary school. Bizarrely enough Sholem was really tight with Haqiqi at the time. Funny to think now that one of them was a Salafist and the other had left for Brooklyn, the mecca for ultra-Orthodox Jews. Despite being removed from the world for so long, it was impossible for anyone who grew up in this neighborhood not to have heard of Schneerson, the Lubavitcher Rebbe, who preached the coming of the Messiah over there on the other side of the Atlantic. Sholem got set up there through the local Hasidic rabbi's cousin. Ahmed can't think why, but the Brooklyn connection is arousing his curiosity. A lot. But how can he mention it to Rachel without letting on that he knows about the pork joint? How? He's going to have to find something on Sam that brings everything together. He's not normally very talkative, but he decides to make an effort to keep the conversation going in the hope of gleaning some information, a clue, a confirmation. Not so much he blows his cover. Just enough to keep it flowing if necessary.

Which it is not. Sam is on the attack immediately.

"So, my boy, it's been a long time. How is everything? Still not back at work?"

"All good, same old. The doc said it wouldn't do any harm to start working a bit again. So I'm probably going to help out Monsieur Paul in the shop."

"Is that right, you're going to help Paul. Dear old Paul . . . Well, that's great, my boy. *Mabrouk!*"

Sam falls silent. He sprays Ahmed's hair. Snip, snip, snip with his long, sharp scissors. The young man tries to imagine the crime being done with scissors, but they wouldn't have worked—too fine. They'd be perfect for gouging out eyes, for a different type of murder. Sam catches a vague glimmer in Ahmed's eyes. He tenses up a little. *Careful! Don't give yourself away!* Ahmed switches to standby mode.

"And your *ma*?"

"My mother? Still in the hospital. They've said it's not going to get any better."

"Ever see her?"

"Err, not for a while . . ."

Ahmed's turn to pause. His Go-playing instincts come to the fore, alerting him to the danger of a Meursault-style attack. Camus's outsider was sentenced to death for not crying at his mother's burial. Sam doesn't know it, but Latifa's son is covered on that front. The last time he saw her, four years ago, she tried to strangle him. It took two nurses to pull her off him. Dr. Germain advised him to stop going after that. "It's too damaging for you, and there's nothing you can do for her. Latifa is out of reach at the moment. In her eyes, you are nothing but an afterglow, a reminder of her misfortune. It's no great surprise she wants to obliterate you." The incident was recorded in a hospital report, but it's better to let Sam think what he wants. The young man says nothing, lets the old barber fill the silence.

"You know, Ahmed, I can talk to you like a father; I've known you since you were a kid. Nothing can replace a mother. Even if it's hard sometimes, you've still got to keep in touch. God orders us to obey our mother above all else. Okay, fine if you can't for the moment . . . But one day you will go back, won't you?"

No response.

"And that girl, the one who got killed, she was your neighbor, wasn't she?"

Now we're talking.

"Yes. She lived in the apartment upstairs."

"Didn't you tell me about her once?"

"Me?"

Ahmed doesn't remember. He'd never spoken to Sam about anything other than the length of his hair and, every now and then, his mother. He's beginning to figure out the barber's tactics.

"Yes, you. Oh, with that medication of yours, perhaps you struggle to remember everything, but me, I don't forget a thing . . . Just upstairs, eh? Horrible business. Who could have wanted to kill her? It's unbelievable, no?"

"Err . . ."

Ahmed can feel the barber's interrogating eyes on the back of his head. He's beginning to find the situation singularly unpleasant. But his unease is working in his favor—it'll make Sam think he has him at his mercy.

"Did you see the police? Did they talk to you?"

"Yeah, they asked me some questions."

Sam's laugh is like a creaking door.

"And you're not a suspect?"

"No! Why? You think that . . ."

Ahmed is feeling increasingly uncomfortable. He can feel beads of sweat forming at his armpits and on the nape of his neck. The old man tightens his grip, ruthless, lowering his voice.

"You didn't screw up, did you? You're still taking your medication? No confusion, no memory blanks?"

The attack is full-frontal. Ahmed is sweating freely now.

"Yes, I'm taking my pills. And . . . I think I remember everything. The thing is I'm always reading. When I'm not, I'm drinking tea, coffee, maybe eating something, or going for a jog along the canal."

Sam nonchalantly mops the perspiration from his customer's neck before reaching for the clippers.

"A bit of booze every now and then—I see you coming back with your shopping from the Franprix. Got to be careful mixing things, you know . . . Anyway, this girl, I don't know if there was something going on beneath the surface. Maybe she got caught up in some weird business. She was an air hostess, wasn't she? Did she use that to get involved in a bit of trafficking? You never know . . . You don't get yourself killed for nothing, do you? Or maybe she led some guy on who ended up flipping out? You quite fancied her, didn't you?"

Ahmed gulps. He's never felt so bad in all his life. This twisted old barber turning him over, razor in hand, coolly pushing him to take responsibility for an abominable murder.

"Oh, me, women . . ."

Sam sharpens the razor and goes for his sideburns.

"Yeah, women. Everyone likes women, my boy! Me, I obey the commandments, but all the same, I can't keep myself from looking. God gives me the strength to resist them. And then as you get older, you settle down. But that one, she was beautiful . . . Did she like men? You see all sorts nowadays . . ."

"Laura liked orchids. That's all I really know about her. She loved orchids. I think I liked her a lot because of that. Because women, to be honest, with my meds . . . I haven't really been able to think about any of that."

Ahmed's voice catches. He decides to leave. He's got what he needs, and he wants Sam to read his panic as a confession of sorts. He looks at himself in the mirror. Pulls himself together a bit.

"Great, that's fine, I reckon. Good job, thank you."

"But wait, I haven't done the back of your neck with the razor!"

Ahmed's voice is still faltering, just the right amount to let the barber think he's snared his prey. He gets up without giving him time to react.

"No, honestly, it's fine as it is . . . Great, bye—I'll swing by when it's grown back . . ."

"Farewell, my boy. And don't forget, if anything's wrong you come see me. If you get the feeling you've screwed up . . . Your old papa

Sam is here for you. I know a lot of people. People who might be able to help you. Even police officers . . . Go on, *salaama ya walid . . . Barak allahu fik.*"

Flustered and soaked in sweat, Ahmed pays, leaving Sam to wonder if he might just have said three words too many, and takes off without waiting for his change. He needs movement to get back to normal. He makes for parc de la Villette with its Rastas, its joggers, and its public pay phones.

26

Avenue C, Alphabet City, Manhattan.
Three months earlier.

Gasping for breath, Vincenzo Vignola opens his mouth and closes it again, unable to take in the air. His pelvis seems possessed by a frenzied life of its own as he finally releases himself inside his partner. His skin is wrinkly and rough. Susan studies his face until he flops back onto the mattress with his eyes shut, tugging a green and white striped sheet on top of him as he struggles to regain his breath. Always the same with the handsome older ones, she thinks to herself: fully clothed they're passable, but the moment they're naked . . . But actually, she hasn't minded sleeping with this one. It's been an exciting, emotional journey. There's the desire to bring him down, sure, but not just that. There is also the human weakness he betrays at the point of orgasm, the ultimate abandon that always seems to take him to the furthest reaches of his being. He doesn't think of her for a second during the act. She finds this fascinating, and it means she is at complete liberty to spot some new detail of him every time he thrusts into her in the missionary position: the folds of his neck; the drop of sweat that forms on his top lip before crashing onto her chin; the gray hair protruding from his right ear; the small, discolored mark just below his left nipple. And many other images which—thanks to the Jamaican weed Dov brought around earlier in the morning—appear to her disconnected, pure, rich with meaning.

They had shared a joint, leaning shoulder to shoulder against the window, looking out on the city and the world. Dov had done most of the talking: he was agitated, worried. The rebbe had informed him that his engagement celebration had been postponed just three days before he was due to take his flight to Paris for the ceremony. Toledano's explanations were sketchy, but after some eavesdropping and a session grilling Sholem Aboulafia, the young new arrival from Paris, he eventually found out that his fiancée had disappeared and that they were doing everything in their power to find her. He was beginning to smell a rat: if the girl was happy to marry him, why would she have taken off? The wedding no longer meant anything to him. He loved the rebbe, who was the most profound, most spiritual being he had ever met. But Dov was troubled by the idea that the rebbe had arranged a marriage with a woman who didn't want to be with him. He took a photo out of his wallet, muttering his betrothed's name softly. "Rébecca." Susan looked at the young woman in silence: she was beautiful, serious in her Hasidic clothing. Almost too serious.

"I don't know, something's not quite right about this photo. She doesn't look like the girls you see around Crown Heights. It's like she's in character, but what's going on in her head is something else entirely. Speak to Toledano—tell him you don't want to get married now. Say it's nothing serious, that what matters to you is him, the rebbe, and what he has done for you, and what you have done for him and the group. If she doesn't want you then fine, you don't want her—that's that. What's the big deal? They should forget about it. Most of all, they shouldn't go hunting her down. We absolutely cannot draw attention to ourselves right now!"

Susan looked at him. He was on the verge of tears, distraught.

"You're sad? You're sad, hey?"

Slowly, almost clumsily, her hand rose to stroke his cheek. She'd only ever reserved such gestures of tenderness for her brother.

"He's let you down . . . Listen, Dov, when our plan has worked out, you won't have to stay with your rebbe. Come with us! James, you and me, on the island—we'll be fine, you'll see . . . We'll have more money than we could possibly need. Tell me one thing: can you make sure he realizes that we have to stay calm and discreet to avoid jeopardizing the operation."

"Yeah, he realizes, no worries."

He looked at her with a sad smile, planted a kiss on the top of her head, and stepped outside her plane of consciousness. Susan had already reverted to her role of Jehovah's Witness gone bad. She took a final toke on her joint before flicking the roach down onto the taxis, buses, and passersby of Avenue C.

Susan watches Vincenzo getting dressed. White Y-fronts, blue nylon socks, nondescript suit, and black leather briefcase. On a sudden impulse she chucks on her undercover outfit: Levi's, Pumas, LAPD hoodie.

"I'm coming with you to Grand Central."

Vignola's flight takes off from Newark at 5:30 p.m. He's just got enough time to take the shuttle and be at the airport on time.

"No, no, it's not worth it, honestly."

"Yeah, I want to. I'm going to miss you so much. When are you coming back?"

"I don't know. Nothing's been scheduled yet."

"Okay. I'll see to it. And in the meantime, I'm coming with you. Half an hour more with you . . . that's better than nothing."

On the way, she makes sure that Vincenzo has fully understood the plan ahead. The first shipment is already en route to Europe. It'll arrive in Niort in a fortnight. When it gets to Charles de Gaulle, Vignola has to meet the two French handlers and see to the final details. In the cab he is nervous, on edge. He smiles nervously throughout. How could he ever have guessed that the daughter of Abel Barnes—one of the Jehovah's Witnesses' most respected leaders—would be such a perfect demon? A devil in a thong that he can no longer resist. He knows he's cursed and that she has him entirely at her mercy. However much he tries to understand how events have unfolded, he keeps drawing a blank about what happened between the innocent smile from the reserved young girl sitting opposite him in the cafeteria ten days earlier, and the moment barely forty-eight hours later that he was screwing her to death like the damned soul he had become. The following day he was her accomplice in an international drug trafficking operation whose cover was being provided by the very organization he had devoted his entire life to serving. And when Susan had whispered the word "Godzwill," the name of the substance he was to help her peddle, as he was desperately trying to recover his breath, a shiver had rushed through him. His body, in the clutches of orgasm just seconds before, had been reduced to sheer terror.

Overcome by an ominous feeling, he tries to make his mistress stay in the cab, but she insists on accompanying him to the shuttle. One final kiss and the door closes. A final kiss watched by two young women buying a bottle of water and a newspaper. One, dressed in an air hostess uniform, stands there speechless.

27

The prayer room is closed. No sign of Haqiqi. They have reached that point in the investigation where everything is scattered and reassembled in one and the same moment. Dispersed rays of clues, names, faces. Many bad vibrations that certainly need to be factored in. Jean shuffles this pack of imaginary cards over and over in his head. He splits the pack and deals them out. Haqiqi, Mourad, Moktar, Alpha, Ruben. He doesn't realize that he has uttered the names aloud. Rachel is listening in silence, then hears herself add Sam.

"Sam, for goodness' sake!" she says. "I nearly forgot the most important part of the conversation with the girls! As we were wrapping things up, Aïcha threw Sam's name out there, just like that, as if it were nothing, and advised us to keep an eye on him. I asked her if she meant Sam the barber, she said she did, but that was it. In any case, it clearly wasn't some casual slip. Let's go!"

A few minutes later, Jean and Rachel are stepping into the barber's shop. Sam is smoking one of his Café Crème cigarillos. He watches the two police officers come in. He knows them from a couple of conversations back when they were investigating a theft on a neighboring street. Barbers are a bit like concierges: they hear things. Jean and Rachel must be tactful. They mustn't let Sam think he's on their list of suspects—suspects of what, they're still not even sure themselves . . . Another simple, routine visit. Jean is about to get things off to a gentle start, but Sam beats him to it.

"Good morning, Lieutenant. Let me guess . . . You're here about the murder of that girl—Laura—aren't you? You said to yourselves, 'Let's go and pay the barber a visit, because barbers always know what's going on.' Am I wrong?"

"No, that's spot-on, absolutely spot-on."

Rachel keeps her distance. Textbook stuff: let the Breton question the Jew. Log every detail, every reaction. Sam plays his role as the obliging, slightly bragging Sephardi down to a T, like a well-oiled machine. But all it takes is the blink of an eye, a tic—the shrug of a shoulder, the index finger scratching the temple, the thumb coming down to wrap itself around the belt—to alert the police officer. Then it's her turn to pretend she hasn't seen anything . . . As she flicks between observing and thinking, her colleague fills the silence.

"So, what can you tell us about Laura Vignola?"

"A beautiful young lady, Lieutenant, in all honesty. I used to see her walking past the shop with her pristine uniform and her little wheelie suitcase. A straightforward girl, who used to take the RER to get to work. Except that her nine-to-five went on up in the sky. I couldn't tell you anything else about her life. I cut men's hair, let's not forget. Old Jewish men, mostly. So a young goy woman . . . not really my department."

Sam puts a bit too much into his pause. A real pause, like a concierge from a Simenon novel. Jean has no choice but to pretend to play along—one of the rules of the game.

"Anything at all, Sam? Even something seemingly insignificant: a throwaway comment from a customer, for example . . . At this stage, anything could be of help. And you do know everyone around here . . ."

Rachel watches him swell with pride. It always amazes her how far flattery can get you. Especially with really shady characters.

"Well, Lieutenant, I'm not one to sneak. But this . . . this involves someone close, someone who's like a son to me. On top of that I know he'd never harm anyone. You'll have met him already, I'm sure, Ahmed, and made up your own mind? A nice, gentle boy, but not always easy. His mother was a close friend of mine, you know. Poor lady . . . Her life hasn't been a walk in the park. Right now she's in the psychiatric hospital, all on her own . . . Very much on her own."

Jean ups the ante.

"So, about Ahmed . . ."

"Ahmed also had a stint there. But that's not what this is about. Listen, can I say something that stays between us; off the record?"

"Why off the record? If you have information about a murder, Sam, then you have an obligation to tell us."

"It's no big deal, just a story. Not proper information, as you say. It's not an official testimony on Ahmed . . . No, I could never bring myself to do it. He's like family, you understand?"

Jean glances at Rachel. She closes her eyes in agreement.

"Fine, go ahead."

Sam smiles at Rachel.

"Once, a few months, ago, when he was in for his last haircut, Ahmed was sitting in this chair. Laura went past, air hostess outfit and all. He saw her in the mirror and his face went bizarre, as though he was in some sort of pain. I think he even said her name quietly under his breath—'Laura, Laura'—but I might be wrong. You see . . . Nothing major, but I wanted to tell you, just in case. It's funny—he was here just this morning. You must have bumped into him; he'd only been gone three minutes when you arrived."

"Did he talk to you about Laura?"

"It was me who asked him how he was doing, what with the murder in the apartment upstairs. He didn't say anything, but I got the feeling he was distressed, out of sorts. Quite right, I say . . . A crime like that, what a shock!"

"Yes, a shock indeed. Sam, you've known Ahmed for a long time . . . Do you think he's capable of . . ."

"No, no, that's not what I meant. He wouldn't hurt a fly . . . Not in his normal state. But why did they bang him up, eh? I never got to the bottom of that. His mother, and then him . . . Something about that family . . ."

All the while Rachel has been examining the room. An object attracts her attention, a wrought-iron, art deco lamp topped with a turquoise bulb. She interrupts Sam's rambling.

"Hey, that's weird—I've been looking for a lamp just like that. May I ask where you found it?"

Having kept his cool until then, the barber can't stop himself from pulling at the frayed collar of his lumberjack shirt with his index finger and thumb, lifting it up and letting it fall back down.

"Oh, er . . . I can't really remember, I've had that for a while . . . Maybe . . . At marché aux Puces, must have been the flea market . . ." he says, pulling himself together. "Sorry, but I gave up bargain-hunting long ago, so I couldn't tell you how to find another one like it . . . Forget what I told you," he says, turning back to Jean. "It was just a random memory. Poor Ahmed would never be capable of committing such a crime. I hope you find the killer, truly. A thing like that in the neighborhood—it's horrible."

"Horrible, indeed. Have a good day, Sam. We may call again. And if by chance you remember anything else . . ."

"Have a good day yourselves. *Shabbat shalom*, Inspecteur."

The barber's ritual farewell really grates on Rachel's nerves. With one foot still in the shop, she changes her mind and pokes her head back in through the half-open door.

"By the way, Sam, we've been 'lieutenants' since 1995. Columbo's the only person who still gets called 'inspecteur'. *Shabbat shalom!*"

As soon as they've rounded the corner of the street, Jean turns to his colleague.

"That two-faced bastard! What was all that crap about Ahmed? What's he trying to make us think?"

"He's simply trying to serve us up a suspect on a plate. The question is why. What's he covering up? What's he hiding from us? And what did the girls not tell me? We can't wait till tonight to find out. It's quarter to twelve—I'm meeting the ex–Jehovah's Witness at three. I'll call them and try to see them as soon as possible. I'll go alone: better that way, I think."

"No problem. As for Ahmed, can we ignore Sam's accusation, even if it is hazy?"

"You're seeing his psychoanalyst this evening, aren't you? We'll work out what to do depending on what he says. For the moment, let's not tire ourselves out with a sketchy lead. The further we get, the more I'm thinking this is a race against the clock."

Rachel is about to fish out her cell when Jean interrupts her.

"Hold on, I almost forgot: can you explain why you asked him about his lamp? It really threw him, but I didn't have a clue what you were going on about . . ."

"I saw the same one last night on my way home. At that weirdo's second-hand shop."

Jean looks confused.

"Sorry, let me explain. By the telephone booth where the crime was reported from, there's a second-hand shop owned by some pervert . . ."

Rachel tells him about her visit to the *brocanteur*. "The more I think about it," she finishes, "the more he reminds me of this serial molester I came across toward the end of my training. His way of speaking, his walk, his eyes. Everything about him screams pervert. He and Sam have the same art deco lamp. Not so much a freak coincidence as just plain freaky . . ."

"Definitely. That's weird, I almost went in to take a look around the same shop this morning." He stops, a darkness crossing his face. "Not too bright of me, to be honest. I parked right in front of the telephone, just long enough to smoke a cigarette and get a feel for the area, the atmosphere. I got the impression that there were two guys inside the shop. The first one was massive and cagey, and disappeared as soon as he saw me. The other must have been your *brocanteur*. He took his time getting a good look at me. He'll be on the alert now after our two visits. Léna, who comes across her fair share of perverts, has told me a few times that they're like schizophrenics: they can sense everything."

"Well, if Léna says so!"

"Yeah, yeah, okay! Whatever, at this stage we haven't gotten any evidence to charge either him or Sam. Just a tip-off that may not hold water. Let's touch base after you've seen your Jehovah's Witness."

"Ex-Jehovah's Witness!"

"Of course, ex– . . ."

28

Aïssa Benamer is alone. Crew cut, green eyes, broad wrestler's shoulders, off-white Lacoste polo shirt, impeccably pressed, pleated beige pants from the Gap. He's sitting with his legs outstretched, his sky-blue Timberland boat shoes crossed on his empty desk. By all appearances, an ex-Phalangist militiaman from Lebanon turned sailing club manager in the Vendée, or a former Israeli army officer who has reinvented himself as the head of security at a provincial shopping center. But no. Benamer was born to peaceable Kabyle hoteliers from Saint-Chamond. He joined the police in 1983 (the year of the pro-equality, anti-racism march that he followed on the television absentmindedly and without the least interest despite his brother, Lounès, being one of the spokesmen) after securing his law degree from Université Lyon 3 and completing his course at police training college. Nowadays, as *commissaire central adjoint* for the eighteenth arrondissement, he's not far from the top.

But he is aiming for something more than that. Benamer is too scornful of other people to take any interest in honors. Or in order, or goodness. Or even in money. No, his reason for being is power. To hold it and wield it in all its forms. As chance would have it, his first posting meant serving under Frédéric Enkell, who immediately recognized in him the disciple he had always hoped for. Despite being a devout atheist, Enkell was, in his own way, a mystic. For him nothingness was evil. After observing him for three months, the Alsatian arranged for the young Kabyle to commit a fatal blunder, just so he could cover it up. This murderous initiation was the perfect rite of passage: it gave the promising pupil a taste for blood and, more importantly, for the unpunished crime, a field in which Enkell had been quite outstanding for the past twenty-five years (twenty of which with Benamer by his side), trafficking and murdering away without even the stirrings of an internal inquiry. All the while Enkell never stopped climbing the ranks with every new posting, each one in a challenging neighborhood. From Aulnay-sous-Bois to the fifteenth arrondissement in Marseilles, from Vénissieux in Lyon to the eighteenth in Paris. Benamer had followed him everywhere, his apprentice in every department of the criminal world: procuring; dealing stolen goods; trading sketchy favors; trafficking arms; drugs; blackmail . . . No gaps in their repertoire. Their strength? Always knowing when to pull the plug and take out the two or three civilians (never more) who had acted as their middlemen. And, every time trouble really started brewing, Enkell always managed to nip any investigations in the bud. Benamer didn't know who was protecting him or why. His guess was that it had something to do with his role in liquidating certain people on request during the rather turbulent period straddling the Giscard and Mitterrand presidencies, just before he met Enkell. It didn't really matter: sometimes it was no bad thing to be in the dark about the odd detail.

Currently, and for the first time, a sort of evil eye is on them. It started with the Vignola girl seeing something she ought not to have seen, which forced them to silence her for good. Not really the evil eye as it all comes down to the fact that they strayed from their usual prudence by agreeing to let a colleague in on their enterprise. Agreeing is not the right word. Francis Meyer, known as "Le Gros" on account of his great fatness, twisted their arm. He had some very precise information relating to a big part of the duo's activities over the past fifteen years or so. Information that he can't have gleaned by himself. Enkell knew Meyer's father by reputation. "Handsome Roger" had been mixed up in every murky affair in the Parisian police from 1942 to 1973 and, in spite of his ninety years of age, he continued to ensure his son enjoyed considerable degrees of protection. So there was no chance of getting rid of the killjoy. And, in fairness, the business venture Le Gros brought them via Sam Aboulafia, a Jewish barber in the nineteenth, was gold dust. From the start, Enkell had been clear about the rules of the game: eliminating any nonpolice accomplices who could link it back to them, starting with Sam. Le Gros loved the idea. With the exception of the deviant Jehovah's Witness, this deal involved a bunch of Arabs and Jews who he'd be delighted to take out—or at least have someone else take out. Because Francis Meyer had "forgotten" to warn Enkell and Benamer about one detail: he was in the habit of entrusting such matters to his younger brother, Raymond, who had unjustly failed his police entrance examination despite his evident skills in handling bladed weapons. The problem was that Raymond was extremely partial to every type of drug. And his big brother, who never refused him anything, had provided him with a few of the pretty blue pills that were to make them their fortune. The result? While the plan had been to make Laura disappear without a trace, Raymond—under the influence of Godzwill—had turned the young woman's murder into a veritable work of conceptual art. And this made it impossible to hush up.

The previous day, standing among the crowds of tourists at Sacré-Coeur, confronting a livid Enkell, who had summoned him after the discovery of the grotesque theatrics surrounding the air hostess's corpse, Le Gros seemed totally unfazed: "It gives him such pleasure, and anyway, it's up to him to take care of it . . . He's a guy that likes to make himself useful." The *commissaire central* had thought it wise not to respond, and instead swore to himself that, however well-protected they might be, he would skin the two brothers alive when the time was right. He then charged his right-hand man with the task of "sorting out this fucking mess."

Sorting out this fucking mess. Benamer takes a deep breath and recaps. The delivery to Holland had been successfully completed by Ruben, who had then gone to collect the latest batch from Vignola's house in Niort before stashing it at the kosher products warehouse on boulevard MacDonald. A warehouse which connects to another—much more secret—via a door which only he and Enkell know exists, and to which only they have the key. If need be, they will be able to dissolve the pills in a few minutes and with the utmost

discretion. As things stand, Ruben and his Hasidic pals are operational. Blissfully ignorant, not least because they're convinced that the
boxes contain tefillin, mezuzoth, and Torah scrolls. They could
transport anything, with their beards, sidelocks, and hats placing
them beyond all suspicion. Who would suspect a bumbling old
rabbi? Anyway, the American woman has opened a new distribution
network in Antwerp. Until things calm down, retail will have to be
limited to Belgium and Holland. As for Paris, they'll have to wait and
see. Benamer's plan had been to take out Vignola, Sam, and Haqiqi
in one. Not such a sensible idea now thanks to the delirious antics
of Meyer's brother, which have served to put both Jews and Muslims
in the spotlight, not to mention the Jehovah's Witnesses, given the
victim's identity. Sam and Haqiqi can wait—nothing substantial
links them to Laura. Plus, without them there's no way of getting
business back on track after this upset: the Jewish barber controls
Ruben and the Hasidic mules; the Salafist preacher manages the network of dealers. Not so for Vignola, who's pretty much no use to anyone anymore, and he wouldn't last an hour and a half across the table
from Rachel in the interrogation room. So he'll need to be quietly
taken out of the equation as soon as he arrived in Paris the next day.

The telephone rings. It's Sam. Still living, albeit on borrowed time,
Benamer thinks to himself, the morning's first hint of a smile playing
across his lips.

"Yes."

"Can we meet?"

"Thirty minutes."

"Okay."

Half an hour later, in the back room of a couscous restaurant on
rue de l'Aqueduc, Sam is playing the smartass.

"Had the full lineup this morning! First there was Ahmed
the dreamer, then your friends from the nineteenth, the Jew and the
Breton. Ahmed bolted before his haircut was done. He was sweating.
I made him think he was the ideal suspect. I can't see him holding
out in front of the police, especially if he hasn't taken his meds: they
could made him confess to anything."

Benamer has never liked Sam, the idiot who reckons he's cleverer than everyone else. He has to try hard not to betray his scorn at the man's lack of judgment in thinking he's capable of flogging an ideal suspect to Kupferstein and Hamelot, let alone in imagining that Benamer would be able to convince his colleagues that Ahmed is indeed guilty: that it's an open-and-shut case . . . Thank you and good night! Maintaining an expression of intense, almost reverent concentration throughout, Benamer reflects upon how he's going to kill Sam. Something simple, like a bullet in the back of the neck, but not without a little speech, some words to avenge all those long minutes spent entertaining his delusions of intelligence. Completely oblivious of what is going through Benamer's mind, the barber brings his self-satisfied monologue to a close.

"In the end, I told Hamelot and Kupferstein that there was something suspicious about the way Ahmed had spoken about Laura the last time he was in for a haircut. The rest you know already. What do we do now?"

Benamer lets out a flicker of a smile.

"For the moment, you can just sit tight and do nothing—that would be an excellent start."

29

Stretched out on the grass, Ahmed drifts off to the sound of the *djembe* drum being played by a white Rasta sitting behind the embankment. After Sam's, shaken up by the barber's aggression, he had wandered around parc de la Villette before deciding to spark up a joint beneath the belly of a giant dragon slide which was out of service until further notice due to vandalism. He needed to zone out, free up his thoughts. He was cruising at ten thousand feet, flying Thai Airways, enthralled by the TV programs in which he was the sole, omnipresent character. Channel 1—rom-com. He and Rachel move toward each other in slow motion. He offers her a bouquet of purple roses, and she offers him her lips. Channel 2—film noir. Dressed in a trench coat in the cold winter rain, finger on the trigger of his Glock, Ahmed steps into the tunnel at porte des Lilas. A Porsche is waiting for him, hazard lights on, parked in the right-hand lane. He gets a bad feeling, so he ducks into a gap in the wall. A bullet whistles past his ear. He lifts his weapon and fires blindly. Channel 3—snuff movie. Sam is tied to a chair in his barber shop. Ahmed approaches him, a sadistic smile on his lips. His gagged victim looks at him pleadingly. With a false air of remorse, Ahmed shakes his head slowly and starts stabbing him calmly with the scissors—*snip, snip, snip*. Blood starts pouring down his face. Channel 3—second film. Laura's balcony. She's already dead. The killer, seen from behind, is almost done trussing her up like a joint of meat. His muscles bulge through his olive-green T-shirt. That neck. That back. Since it first flashed up in his dream thirty-six hours ago, Ahmed has dreaded seeing the killer's face again; now it's that back, full screen, that is making him tremble. He already knows what the next shot confirms. The warehouse at Aulnay-sous-Bois, the scene he has played back in his mind so many times. The killer's back. The same back. The same killer. Since the day before yesterday he has refused to let in the truth that has been knocking at the door of his consciousness: Emma and Laura were the victims of the same man. That man is now turning toward him, looking at him from his drug-skewed screen, fresh from strangling his young victim of five years ago all over again.

FACING THE KILLER

An unfinished face, an absurd blond brute, whose expression lurches between madness and idiocy. The spirit of a naughty twelve-year-old child locked in the body of a solidly built forty-five-year-old man.

Monstrous. Ahmed shudders. Something drains from within him. For five years he has been possessed by this faceless killer whose back came to embody his perpetual fear. A concentrate of his father's suffering and his mother's torment. Evil in all its ordinariness: the back of a bulky porter from Les Halles market wrapped in a stripy polo shirt. It was this image that had driven him into exile and made a ghost of him for five years. Finally, he is liberated as he sees the face he has feared above all else. Finally, he knows who and what he is fighting.

FEAR—HATE—WILLPOWER

Escape, breathe. Leave behind the vision of the killer in order to dominate it. His spirit soars, not knowing which direction to take now that he has been banished from the desert, the place of his roots. So he takes a different approach, going down the route of his past. The rare, precious moments in his early childhood when Latifa would reel off the chain of his forebears as far back as the thirteenth generation. Although Ahmed hasn't thought about it for years, the names of his ancestors come back to him effortlessly. "You are the son of Latifa, daughter of Ibrahim, son of Mohamed-Ansar, son of Ethman, son of Mansour, son of Abdallah, son of Omar, son of Suleiman, son of Anwar, son of Ethman, son of Ibrahim, son of Saif al-Islam, son of Nur al-Dîn, founder of the Ahel-Dîn dynasty, who came from the Kinawaïn Mountains on the other side of the desert." He couldn't say where they were located, these mountains. In Mali, or Mauritania perhaps? Not at all far from the land of his father's fathers, somewhere between Mopti and Gao. This long line of unknown ancestors whose name was lost centuries ago during the crossing of the desert. The name, maybe, but not the gift—or is it a curse?—that he inherited: the ability to see things better left unseen. The story of his parents anchors him in a far-off, unfathomable world. It is no doubt why he has never told anyone about it, except Dr. Germain. For the first time he realizes the weight of this silence, which brings him back to Laura.

He imagines her listening, captivated. He pictures her lying on the grass, floating in the clouds, her big eyes staring at him, drinking up the words that send her to a more distant place than any long-haul Air France flight. Light years from the suffocating world of her childhood that she struggled so hard to escape from. On the landing of their apartment block, Laura had recounted her early years to her neighbor on more than one occasion. The horror of growing up with Jehovah's Witness parents. He had listened to her patiently, not saying a word. That had been enough for her. A recent memory comes to the surface, almost a revelation. It happened in the stairwell barely ten days earlier. Laura had just gotten back from Niort. For a full fifteen minutes she told him how she had called her father a liar, an impostor. He had poisoned her childhood with every sort of absurd prohibition; had made it his business to control the sex lives of others. And now he, who was beyond reproach, had a mistress in New York, and she had seen her with her own eyes. She was the same age as Laura, his daughter! She had told her mother everything on the front steps of the family home she was no longer allowed to visit. Mathilde Vignola had called her a lying whore. She had yelled and tried to claw at her. In the end her father had stood between them, pronouncing the irreversible verdict. "Vile, dirty girl! You will regret this insolence! Bitterly. In this world, not in the next!" At the time Ahmed hadn't paid it any attention. Just like the other times, he was content with listening politely, not reacting, half absent, half present. It was only today, freed from his prison, his mind enlivened by the smoke in his lungs, that he understood the true meaning of the phrase. Laura's father had explicitly threatened his daughter. This made him a prime suspect. But what's the link with him and Sam? No matter. Time to call Rachel.

Once, he can't remember where, he read that in Yiddish the suffix "lé" is added to form a sort of affectionate diminutive. Rachel, Ra-che-lé.

RA-CHE-LÉ

30

Lincoln Center, Manhattan. Thirteen days earlier.

Ten minutes he's been following her without her noticing, so absorbed is she in her search for the books listed on a printed sheet. Frantz Fanon, Malcolm X, W.E.B. Du Bois, Toni Morrison, V. Y. Mudimbe. Dov observes every minute gesture, records the title of each of the books she places in her basket. Looks at the photo, then looks at her. And again.

In the photo: light brown hair, long skirt, wool coat. A look of contrived humility.

In the flesh: darker brown, curly hair loose on her shoulders, jeans, camisole top. The picture of calm assurance.

And yet the same full, slightly pouting lips, the same beauty spot between her cheekbone and her right eye, the same piercing, electric-gray eyes. No doubt whatsoever.

Black Skin, White Masks joins *Beloved* in the basket. When Rébecca settles into the queue, Dov stations himself in the court-yard outside, three yards from the entrance. What's he waiting for? For her to explain to him why she didn't want him, the tubby American Hasidic Jew? Hopeless! He's understood perfectly from watching her move, breathe, just be for the last ten minutes. There's nothing—absolutely nothing!—ultra-Orthodox about her. Susan was right. Rébecca was in character. Why? Who cares why? He could just forget it and disappear from her life forever, a life in which he will represent nothing more than a fleeting image, and a future in which he will not play the slightest role. But Dov stays.

Just so he can say to her *I'm here, I exist, I'm not like the person in the photo either*. A sense of boyish indignation. This whole thing has left him hurt.

She emerges, her plastic bag full of course books for the Center for Black Studies at Northern Illinois University. He goes up to her.

"Rébecca!"

Taken aback, she looks up at the stranger who's addressing her by name in this vast city where she doesn't know a soul. He is wearing jeans flapping over green Converse sneakers, a Marcus Garvey T-shirt so baggy his tzitzits are barely visible, a green, yellow, and red skullcap. Never in her life has she been confronted by such a phenomenon: an ultra-Orthodox Jewish Rasta built like a chubby rugby player. And he is smiling at her. Somewhere in her head—right at the back—a little light comes on that she'd like to switch off.

"Yes?"

He hands her the photo without saying a word. Rébecca turns deathly pale, like she's seen a ghost. Making no attempt to deny the evidence, Rébecca grabs hold of the image and studies it carefully before turning back to the funny-looking man. The outline of a soundless question on her lips. "Dov?" He too answers in silence.

Had he looked awkward and surly in his Hasidic garb like in the photo Ruben had given her, she'd have known how to react. She'd have mocked him and then left him standing there. All over and done with in a couple of minutes. But now she's stumped. Sure, he's got the skullcap and the tzitzits, but she can tell immediately that something's up. He's about as hard-line as she is. What does that mean? What's this all about? How have two Jews clearly more attracted to hip-hop culture than to the Torah ended up on the verge of an arranged marriage that harks back to the shtetl or the *mellah*? "What the fuck?" She's uttered these last words aloud. Dov, deep in thought, echoes her.

"Yeah—what the fuck! Come on, let's grab a table in Starbucks and talk. We owe each other that at least."

Half an hour later, Dov has detailed his journey from Wichita to Brooklyn via Harvard and prison, omitting only the part about how his chemistry skills have enabled him to manufacture a new drug that is starting to flood the French market thanks to a distribution network in which Ruben, her own brother, is unwittingly playing a vital role. The union that Rebbe Toledano was hankering after was a business contract of sorts. It sealed the transatlantic links between the two branches of the Sephardic Hasidic movement which was without a doubt about to experience a new and dazzling prosperity with the money brought in from the sales of Godzwill. Dov keeps quiet about all this. For the first time he feels a bit ashamed about it. The girl's sincerity touches him in a new, unfamiliar way. It almost irritates him to realize how affected she is by his story. Because his tale of family breakdown and the abandonment he felt in prison moved Rébecca profoundly. Trying to curtail this unfamiliar outpouring of emotion, he asks her how she came to have her photo taken in full Hasidic getup and how she nearly went ahead with an arranged marriage.

So she sets about explaining how her mother had found comfort in religion after her husband had left her, as had Ruben, who had reacted very badly to the breakup of his hip-hop group. An ultra-Orthodox synagogue had opened down the road from where they lived, run by Rabbi Haïm Seror, a Moroccan like them. Within a few months the whole family was under his influence, including Rébecca, who was worried about losing the two people, besides her girlfriends, she loved most in the world. She changed the way she dressed, observed the Sabbath as much as possible, but still went to school and on to college. For almost four years they left her alone, though one by one all the girls her age in the community started getting hitched. Then they began talking marriage. She played for time, maintained that she wanted to finish her studies, that she wasn't ready. Her mother insisted, Ruben too, and her resistance was worn down. She gave in because of her love for them. Their sadness made her feel desolate, that the world was tumbling down. Her marriage had become like an obsession, the focus of their lives, as if it would turn back the clock, erasing all memory of her father's flight. The rabbi's wife joined forces with them, talking about a young Jew from Brooklyn—Ashkenazi, of course, but educated at Harvard—who was Rebbe Toledano's protégé. That really did get them going, those Moroccan and Tunisian Jews living in the nineteenth in Paris, all this talk of the rebbe and Brooklyn! To them it was the Messiah and New Jerusalem! So in the end she agreed, anything to see her mother smile at last. The photo was taken that same day.

After that she quite literally blanked it from her mind. She didn't even tell her girlfriends, with whom she shared everything, and who were so worried about her since she started following—or at least pretending to follow—her mother and brother on the family *teshuvah*, the return to the "true" Jewish faith. The subject wasn't broached again for another three weeks until, a few days after her midterm exams, her beaming mother announced that Dov was coming to Paris in six days' time to mark their engagement. This was her wake-up call. The Rébecca of old came back with a jolt, and she called her friends.

An emergency meeting was held at Laura's with Aïcha and Bintou. The immediate, unanimous decision was to get Rébecca onto the next flight Laura was working on. By an ironic twist of fate, its destination was New York. As chance would have it, her passport had been renewed for a trip to Israel four years earlier. On the Thursday morning, after scribbling a note for her mother and brother, and without looking back, she left the apartment, the building, the street where she had grown up. At Laura's she got changed, became herself again. Sixteen hours later the two friends were getting off the Newark–Grand Central shuttle.

"I was so happy! The skyscrapers all around me! I felt more free than ever. And—if you'll excuse me—all the more free because this had meant to be a place of confinement . . ." She stares at him in amazement before continuing. "And here we are today sitting and chatting in Starbucks . . . It's so weird . . . I should have run a mile when I saw you. But I came in here with you instead. It's nuts! Like some kind of dybbuk story. Spooky! But it's been like that from the word 'go'. When we got off the bus at Grand Central, we hung around five minutes to buy some water and a paper from a Pakistani guy's stall. And all of a sudden Laura went white as a sheet, staring straight ahead. I saw her mouth the word 'Daddy'. I followed her gaze: a beautiful young blonde was passionately kissing an old, awkward, graying man of about fifty. He didn't spot us. He got onto the bus to the airport and disappeared. My friend was petrified. Arriving in New York only to find her father—a super-strict Jehovah's Witness—in the arms of a girl the same age as her. It was all too much!"

"Your friend's a Jehovah's Witness?"

"No, she got out of there. Her childhood and teenage years were a living hell . . . Her father is head of a local branch of the organization somewhere in France."

Rébecca loses herself in thought for a moment. When she tunes back in she sees that Dov is in a state of shock.

"What's up? Something upset you about my story? You look like you've seen a ghost!"

Dov pulls himself together, manages the hint of a smile, and checks his watch.

"No, no, I . . . I just realized I'm running late for an important meeting. I'm sorry, Rébecca, but I've got to bust now. Can we do this again?"

"I'm leaving town tomorrow. Listen, Dov, I'm not sure I want to see you again. This chapter of my life is over. Give me your number . . . If I feel up to it, I'll call you. But you . . . I'm asking you not to look me up. Can I trust you?"

"Yeah, of course, don't mention it. I'll leave you in peace."

Five minutes later and three streets away, standing stock-still before a pedestrian crossing, Dov stares at his telephone. Contacts: the name "Susan" on the screen. His hesitant thumb hovers over the green button, an unsure look in his eyes. He blinks and presses the button. Perfectly aware of the consequences.

31

The girls are standing in front of Le Point Éphémère club. Its name a metaphor for the temporality of existence in general, and for theirs at this particular moment. They are tense and fidgety as they wait for Rachel. All their hopes, all their trust strangely resting on this one policewoman. They want to see Laura's killers punished, of course. They also want to lift the shadow that has overwhelmed their beloved brothers. It's still a mystery to them. Why the boys and not us? At what point did they start crossing over to the dark side? As kids and teenagers they admired their big brothers more than anything. The 75-Zorro-19 days were like one long trance. Bintou, Aïcha, and Rébecca didn't miss a single show, tagging the group's name on every wall in the neighborhood. Until that unforgettable, exceptional evening when they got on stage in front of all the local kids and did the dance routine they'd rehearsed for months, inspired by the start of that Spike Lee film *Do the Right Thing*. Five minutes of pure energy and fun. It felt like right then, at that precise moment, their lives had officially begun. After that they got their heads down to review for their baccalaureate. They forgot about hip hop and their brothers for several months. Then there was that strange period when Moktar started going crazy. Hawa, Bintou's mother, said that it all stemmed from there. Fair enough, she couldn't stand Codou, the beatmaker's mother. The mere mention of her name would make her face shut down and her mouth harden, little lines appearing at the corners of her lips. "It's her, it's Codou. I knew her from back home. She's always been jealous, envious. She didn't even want her son to succeed. So she cast a spell on the whole group. That's why you've got Moktar hanging around the crossroads dressed in that stupid long *kamiss* of his, and Ruben with his bizarre gangster hat. As for Alpha and Mourad, they spend half their time in that tiny prayer room with their phony imam. I tell you, every day I pray they'll snap out of it. And they will, you'll see. They're my children, all of them. I nursed them, I watched them grow up. As for that Codou, let me tell you! She'll get her comeuppance in Paradise!" Aïcha and Bintou only half believe in charms, prayers, and protection spells, in all that stuff from the *bled*. Their brothers' gradual decline remains a mystery to them. *Why them and not us?* The truth is they do know why, even if they've never said so out loud. It comes from their parents, their way of being, moving, speaking. Words, gestures, and ways of seeing that the girls wanted to adopt, while their brothers only sought to adopt them in part, mostly craving the validation of others. They were more prone to focusing their energies on countering a section of society's scorn toward "Muslim youths," that danger-ous new class of the postcolonial Republic. They were frequently tempted to reverse the feeling of stigma, to brand themselves proudly with the very religion that brought them such relentless contempt.

Bintou and Aïcha never felt the so-called war against Islam had anything to do with them. They quite simply couldn't have cared less. It had no bearing on the way they defined themselves in the universe. Aïcha's worldview was largely influenced by her father. Arzeki had spent his entire career as a pâtissier at Dalloyau, just opposite the jar-din du Luxembourg. A decent man, she had never known him to harm or speak ill of anyone. A calm man too, never one to pray, fast, or say anything about God. Of course she loved her mother Khadidja, a reasonably pious lady, but she felt much closer to her father. It was his example she followed. Instinctively and without question. Bintou's role model was her mother, Hawa. A spirited woman who had her own reasons, deep inside her, for railing against a world order that she felt was grossly outdated, though she seldom spoke of it. Except once, to her daughter. A conversation that left an indelible mark on Bintou's memory.

* * *

Lieutenant Kupferstein approaches the two girls with long strides. Rachel is the precise representation of what they want to be "when they grow up." Not a police officer, no; just an upstanding woman. She pauses when she reaches them, looks both of them in the eye, then nods to the towpath. No time to sit down before the next meeting, so a little walk together down the canal will have to suffice. It should be enough to talk everything through. Almost, at least.

Bintou takes a deep breath before starting, like she used to back at primary school before diving into the blue water of the swimming pool with its trembling lines.

"We were there, on the corner of the street, and they filed past us without noticing us, one after the other. What time was it? One in the morning. It was hot. We hadn't gone our separate ways yet. We needed to talk some more. To be together, the two of us, a bit longer. We'd just been on Skype with Rébecca for an hour. Laura wasn't there. She was meant to be coming back from Los Angeles the following morning, after we left for college. We never thought we wouldn't get to see her again. Why would we have? How were we to know that her fate was playing out right there under our noses?"

Bintou stops, lowers her head. When she looks up her eyes are filled with tears. Rachel takes it on board, but subtly keeps things moving.

"Did you try to see her after she got back?"

"We called her but her cell was off. We didn't insist too much because she worked on long flights and got jet lag really badly. She needed to recover. Anyway, we weren't worried about anything."

Rachel urges the girls on again.

"So who appeared that night on the street corner?"

"75-Zorro-19: the whole gang. It was surreal. Moktar, wearing a three-quarter length Adidas tracksuit that was a bit too long, his *kamiss* and his prayer cap, followed thirty seconds later by our brothers, Alpha and Mourad, looking like your average computer geeks.

Then, after five minutes, there was Ruben, with his skullcap and tzitzits. All heading into Sam's. We had to pinch ourselves. But we were both there, and we both saw the same thing. Our instinct was to hide as soon as we saw our brothers. Over the four years they've been going to Haqiqi's prayer room with Moktar they've belonged to another world, and we've lost touch. They tried loads to convert us, but it didn't work, so they dropped it. Since then, we've barely had anything to say to each other, and we've kept out of one another's way. When Ruben went into the barber shop he sat down next to Sam and just nodded to the others. There was no warmth in it, but it'd been ages since they'd spoken a word to each other . . . We left them there, went home feeling pretty confused. It was all so weird that at the time we didn't talk about it. But since Laura was found dead we haven't been able to stop thinking about it . . . We can't let it go: it doesn't add up. Why are these former friends who had a bad falling-out all meeting up like that? And why at Sam's?"

"Have you asked them?"

"We haven't dared. We wanted to get your thoughts on it. We need to know who killed her. We don't want to get our brothers in any trouble, but we need to know."

Bintou stares at Rachel, tears streaming down her cheeks. The policewoman takes her hand in her own and grips it hard.

"You don't want them to get in any trouble, but you want the truth. Unfortunately I think you're going to have to choose between the two. I have to go now. I'll think about what I can do. Thank you for talking to me. Not just for Laura, but for you too."

She touches Aïcha's back softly and moves away before turning around again.

"See you at two in the morning. I'll stock up on coffee."

What now? Bringing in the brothers would risk alerting Sam. For the moment, neither she nor Jean is in possession of anything tangible. Rachel decides to leave it to bubble away, gathers her thoughts, breathes, and prepares to take on the Jehovah's Witness defector, who'd requested they meet at a brasserie in République. Her telephone rings. It's Ahmed: she can tell from the number. No one else calls her from a landline.

"Ahmed, I'm a bit tied up. Is this just to hear the sound of my voice, or was there something else?"

"Well, there's nothing wrong with the sound of your voice, but it's not that. Something came back to me. I was lying on the grass in parc de la Villette, and there was this djemba drummer and, err . . . basically . . . I've got a lead on Laura. The motive, I mean. The motive for the crime."

Ahmed sums up in a few sentences the threats her father made when she told him she'd seen him with his mistress in New York. Rachel goes quiet and feels the blood drain from her.

"Ahmed?"

"Yes."

"Thank you so much for calling me. I need to contact Niort right away. Can we meet up at the police station at four o'clock?"

"Err . . ."

"Okay, not at the police station, but Jean will have to be there . . . How about the café at the MK2 cinema in quai de Seine?"

"I'll be there."

Rachel dials another number without breaking her stride.

"Commissaire Jeanteau."

"Lieutenant Kupferstein, I was about to call you."

"Has something happened?"

"Your victim's mother is in the psychiatric hospital. It was Vincenzo Vignola who signed the request to have her admitted."

"Commissaire, it's emerged that when Laura last came to Niort, ten days ago, her father made an explicit threat against her. I'll have confirmation in less than two hours, but in the meantime, it's absolutely essential that we find Vincenzo Vignola and that he doesn't disappear into thin air."

"I'll call you back."

A man is waiting for Lieutenant Kupferstein on the terrace of Le Thermomètre. Around thirty-three years old, wearing an impeccably ironed white shirt, a black jacket, and a well-groomed beard, he looks at her without smiling. In front of him there's a half-finished bottle of Perrier and a copy of *Le Monde* carefully folded in half. She shakes his hand, sits down, calls the waiter over and orders a macchiato before wading straight in.

"Any other time I would have wanted to hear all about the Jehovah's Witness organization, but this is something of an emergency: what can you tell me about Vincenzo Vignola?"

As potterlover666 starts telling her about how this man took control of his whole life, destroying him painfully and slowly, Rachel writes a text to Jean:

MK2, quai de Seine, 4:00 p.m. News on L's father, Sam and 75zorro19.

"It all started back in the summer of 1999, just before I took some leave. I was working at the post office in Niort at the time. I'd saved up five thousand dollars to pay for a dream vacation in Andalusia. At the end of a meeting in the Kingdom Hall, in front of all the others, Vincenzo Vignola asked me how I could spend all that money on myself when I hadn't put any aside for Jehovah. He called me selfish, asked me if I wanted to be one of the 'left behind'. He always said that in English, with this strange accent. 'Do you want to enter the Kingdom of Jehovah, or return to dust like the other 'left behind?' I cracked: I gave all five thousand dollars to Jehovah, or should I say Vignola."

He pauses, spent. Seven summers later and still the same bitterness. Everything ruined. Not yet thirty-five and already completely at sea, lost, his lifeblood drained. But Rachel doesn't have time for sympathy.

"So he's like a professional manipulator?"

"Yes, you could say that. In fact all he was doing was applying the rules. Jehovah must come before everything. He was sort of like the head of a team in a vast company. And we were the sheep, getting fleeced but ultimately not minding. We were content with that. Like, for seventy hours each month we had to go around handing out copies of *Watchtower*. And we did it, we went along with it. Three times a week I hung around the train station in Niort to recruit new unfortunate members . . ."

"Did you know Laura?"

"I came across her early on. She left home on her eighteenth birthday, so only about six months after I joined. From then on we were forbidden from mentioning her name. As if she'd never existed. We talked about her a bit behind closed doors, but after a while that was it. She was pretty, as I remember, and kept very much to herself. I don't think I ever said a word to her."

"Her father didn't say anything? Didn't ever bring her up again?"

"No."

"Do you remember seeing Vincenzo Vignola behave violently?"

"No. His tongue was his weapon. He killed you with words, that's all."

"I'll rephrase my question. Can you imagine him killing someone?"

"No. Can you tell me what's going on? Your colleague mentioned a crime when we were messaging, but didn't go into any detail. Is it Laura? Has something happened to her?"

"Yes. Do you think her father would be capable of that?"

"Vincenzo Vignola killing his daughter . . . No, I can't see it . . . No . . . But . . . I don't know why I'm telling you this . . . I'm not sure he'd particularly mind if somebody else did . . . The man is . . . what's the word . . . cold. Just thinking about him makes me shudder. Right, that's enough—anything else you want from me?"

"No, thank you . . . Actually, wait! A purely personal question, if you don't mind?"

"Fire away."

"What's the significance of your username: potterlover666?"

The ex-Witness smiles.

"Potter is because of Harry Potter. We weren't allowed to go to the movies. But the most forbidden films of all were the Harry Potter ones. All that irrational, magical Hollywood stuff caused too much friction with the fantastical world that we had to inhabit, with its own cast of demons. So: potterlover. And then 666—the number of the beast—for good measure. To remind myself that I've picked my side: the demons. You know, when I left the Witnesses I was overcome by a powerful need to transgress, to prove to myself that I'd really escaped. The first meal I had was blood sausage, some good old *boudin noir*."

"*Boudin?*"

"Yes, I had to eat some blood, another thing that was strictly forbidden."

"Blood? You mean like for transfusions?"

"Yes. It's illegal to let any foreign blood enter your body. In any way whatsoever . . . It's strange, you know, all this talk of forbidden things. I can picture him now, Vignola. And five years on, hard as it is to admit, I'm still scared of him."

32

Vincenzo Vignola has stopped in his tracks. A police car is parked outside his house and the *commissaire* who questioned him the day before is repeatedly ringing the bell. He had just stepped out for a walk to get his thoughts straight after sending Ruben off with the consignment of Godzwill. And now the police are badgering him again. Luckily he has his wallet, credit card, and cell on him. Maybe not that luckily as all he has to do is withdraw some money or make a call and they'll locate him right away.

Jeanteau gives up ringing the doorbell, returns to the police car, says something to the officer at the steering wheel, and sets off on foot. Vignola waits for a bit, then heads down a perpendicular street on the double. Five minutes later, he's at a Crédit Agricole cash machine. He takes out two thousand dollars—the maximum amount—before crossing the road to a *tabac* where he buys a telephone card. On his way out he switches off his cell phone, takes out the SIM card and deposits them in two separate bins.

He has to get to Paris via the back roads. The police will definitely be monitoring the station in Niort and arrivals into Montparnasse, but not much else. He'll take a bus to Poitiers, the train to Orléans, then another to Étampes, and eventually the RER C into Paris. To Susan. He's fully aware that she'll ditch him. He knows it with every inch of his being, but he does want to be with her one last time. And perhaps his innermost dream? To die by her hand. On his way to the bus station he finds a public pay phone and dials the number he knows by heart. Susan answers on the second ring, listens to his account of the latest developments, then suggests a new rendezvous point now that the Concorde Lafayette is no longer a safe option. He recalls a café in porte de Clignancourt near a Kingdom Hall where he did a temporary placement the year before. A heavy weight is crushing his chest. Vincenzo lets out a sentence that he never thought he'd hear himself say.

"Susan, do you still love me?"

"Of course, Vincenzo! Would I be flying across the ocean tonight if I didn't?"

"You'll never leave me, will you?"

"Never. I'll be with you till the end, my love. See you tomorrow. I've got to run to the airport now . . ."

"Alright, Susan . . . See you tomorrow."

A quarter of an hour later, the fugitive arrives within sight of the bus station. Two policemen are patrolling it. They are visible from a mile away. Vignola manages to get on the bus for La Crêche, the next station to the northeast. From there he'll take a TER train to Poitiers. The last thing he sees in Niort is the MAIF head office, the place where he'd be working today if once upon a time he had not met Mathilde and careened into this parallel world in which he has built his life and his

modest empire. Yet he has no regrets. He feels that he's done everything required of him in the service and defense of Jehovah.

Auchan shopping center, Courtepaille bar and grill, Castorama
DIY shop, Monsieur Meuble furniture store, Total service station.
Corn fields. Cows. He thinks about Susan. He can't bring himself to
resent her. She has destroyed him, and she ordered his daughter's
murder. But somehow he wants nothing other than to see her and
rest his head on her shoulder, to breathe in her scent. As if that
would fix everything, erase it all. As if it were possible to return from
beyond, to the time he abandoned his status as an elder and became
one of the "left behind," a member of that multitude who will remain
dust for eternity, never to see the kingdom of Jehovah.

33

Meyer, Le Gros, is slumped in his chair, black boots on his black
desk, champing down furiously on some green chewing gum. Three-
day beard. A telephone is ringing but no one is picking it up. It's
Rachel's. After fifteen seconds, and since neither of the other two
officers present seem in a hurry to answer it, Meyer gets up, walks
across the open-plan office, and picks it up.

"Lieutenant Meyer."

"Good morning, Lieutenant. Does anyone ever pick up at your
station? I was about to give up! This is Commissaire Jeanteau from
Niort—is Lieutenant Kupferstein not around? I tried her cell phone
but it went straight through to her voicemail."

"She's gone out. Leave a message with me and I'll pass it on."

"Tell her to call me back urgently. Her suspect has done a runner."

Meyer can't keep himself from blurting out.

"Vignola!"

"Yes, Vignola. Did she mention him to you?"

"Yes, of course . . . Obviously. Don't worry, I'll pass on the message. Goodbye, Commissaire."

Meyer is sweating. He's not so thick that he doesn't realize he's just made a mistake that Enkell will not forgive him for. He knows what he and Benamer will do to him. He has to play for time. Distract them. Lie, but without burning his fingers this time.

One text and forty-five minutes later, and Le Gros is sitting with the *commissaire adjoint* of the eighteenth arrondissement on the Montmartre funicular. He tells him about Jeanteau's telephone call, omitting the part about how it was him who mentioned Vignola's name. Benamer senses the error, says nothing, and divvies up the tasks.

"We're entering the cleanup phase. You take care of Haqiqi; I'll deal with Sam and Vignola."

"But he's disappeared."

Aïssa Benamer closes his eyes for a second, lets out a gentle sigh, continues.

"Right, let's start with the easiest part: your brother does the *brocanteur*. He's got him under his thumb—it'll be easy. Just stay with him from start to finish. Make sure he does the job properly. It's got to look like a junkie did it, alright, not some clown tripping his balls off on acid."

A steely look from the green-eyed Kabyle.

You and your brother are going to be payback for me and Enkell. A little treat at the end of this fuck up. Whoever's covering your back, they won't be able to do a thing for you . . .

When they get to the foot of that overblown wedding cake of a church that takes pride of place at the top of Montmartre, they go their separate ways.

Meyer heads for the alleyway that crosses the garden downhill from the Butte before joining up with rue Muller. Instead of going back to the police station he decides to blow off some steam on the *brocanteur*. That fuckwit who thinks he's in the clear because he's been putting up his idiot brother for months. That meddling bastard who gets off on the secrets of the killer under his roof and who thinks he can get away with it. He'll get his dose of pain. Even though Benamer's instructions mean he's getting off lightly. Junkies don't torture people to death. They kill with knives, sure, but they do it quickly. After turning the shop upside down for a couple of hundred dollars, if they're lucky. On rue de Clignancourt, Meyer smiles. By the time he has reached rue Labat he is laughing to himself. It's been a while.

In the area at the back of the second-hand shop, Raymond—wearing a vest of dubious cleanliness and tracksuit bottoms of indeterminable color—is sitting on the foam mattress that has served as his bed since his return to Paris from Alsace three months earlier. The *brocanteur*, sitting opposite him, slams down a nine of spades and declares in bellicose fashion: "War!" Someone knocks on the window pane. Tock, tock . . . tock. The code. Georges gets up, crosses the main room, opens the glass door and finally the padlock on the metal gate.

"Hey Le Gros, how are you doing? What's new? We were playing cards while we were waiting."

"Waiting for what?"

"You know, just waiting."

They cross the dimly lit room jam-packed with shelves and tables loaded with all manner of objects from the '50s and '60s. There are several lamps and fans which take on a sinister personality in the half-light. Francis Meyer knocks into a safe lying on the yellowed linoleum floor.

"Fucking piece-of-shit junk shop!"

"Piece-of-shit junk shop? Oh, that's nice! How long have I been putting up your little bro in my piece-of-shit junk shop?"

His voice is frosty.

"Shut it, you!"

The two men reach the room at the back. Raymond is about to reel off the standard formalities, but sees his brother's face and keeps quiet. One of those decisive moments in a murder when a dramatic change occurs. A glimpse of eternity. Killing as a metaphysical act.

TIME

IS

SUSPENDED

Francis—arms crossed, motionless—positions himself between the door and Georges. On the other side, Raymond's right hand is gripping a Laguiole knife that's appeared as if from nowhere, all his senses on alert.

"But why? Why? I'm your friend. I've always helped you. I've always been on your side, both of you. Why? Why?"

Georges desperately attempts to catch the eye of either one of the brothers. No point. He's moved over to the other side now. Beef, mutton, chicken, something like that. He's left the human race, and his incessant pleading doesn't affect the brothers any more than the cries of a piglet would upset a butcher in an abattoir.

"A junkie murder. No screwing around this time," Francis tells his brother.

"Okay, no problem. Random knife wounds. Stomach, neck, chest, and an accidental one to the heart to finish?"

"There you go—perfect."

Georges used to love listening to Raymond talk about his murders. He always wanted to know more, reveling in the detail. How did you tie up his wrists? And the duct tape over the mouth—does it have to go right around? How many knife wounds? And where? That one in the warehouse, did you strangle her when you were coming, was that it? Now it's his turn. He knows it. He knows it just like he knows that all his feeble strength has left him. Georges has never been much of a fighter. Just good at taking pleasure in the suffering of others, by others. He's not capable of saving his own skin. He slowly slides to the floor, curls up in the fetal position, and lets out a long, unintelligible groan, the timeless lament of the condemned man facing death. Raymond delivers a kick to the small of his back. Not too hard; just enough to make him unfold himself. Quick as a flash he spins him around and stabs him in the stomach first. A scream. The second blow of the knife goes to the neck, then the chest and heart. It takes all of nine seconds, by which time Francis—having slipped on his leather gloves—has started trashing the place, tipping out jars of Nescafé and powdered milk, packets of biscuits, emptying everything. The fury of a drug addict looking for anything to pay for his next hit . . . Really got to be a stupid junkie to burgle Georges the *brocanteur*. Job done.

All over within five minutes, and the crime scene is perfect. Raymond looks up at his brother, his eyes gleaming.

"See, I did just as you said. One, two, three, four. Stomach, neck, chest, heart. Are you happy with me? Are you?"

"Yes, Raymond, you did well."

"How about another of those Godzwills?"

"Not just yet, Raymond. Not just yet."

34

Avenue C, Alphabet City, Manhattan.
Thirteen days earlier.

Susan is alone, smoking a joint by the window. She's thinking about the girl she doesn't know, but over whom she has the power of life and death. She doesn't feel anything. Something needs to be done, and she's going to do it. That's what it boils down to. But this is no trivial thing.

DEATH

She's been expecting this first murder, not that she'd ever thought about it. The act itself does not interest her. Apart from anything else, it's going to happen thousands of miles away. But the sense of power it gives her . . . It's particular, new, reminds her of the Godzwill experience. Brings her to the level of the wicked God under whose glaring eyes she grew up. She comes to the sudden realization that her mother died when she was roughly the same age as this Laura. There's a link. The girl's blood for the blood her mother was denied when her father said no to the transfusion. She remembers the day when she discovered the medical file with James. They were nine and a half. And she thinks back to what they promised one another after all those tears: no more believing in Jehovah; celebrating their birthdays in secret; never being apart; taking revenge on their father and on the organization.

A tear runs down her cheek. Whether she's sad or happy she's not sure, but she does feel alive. More alive than ever. Nancy, in her strange Inuit accent, often used to talk of soul eaters with a mixture of fear and respect.

POWER

Throughout those years she hated her father for killing her mother out of obedience to Jehovah. Now, as she is about to push the green button that will seal Laura's fate, she finally understands. It was from this first murder that he drew all his strength. The man who had devoted his life to hunting down "demons" had become one himself at the precise moment he told the doctor that his faith prohibited him from introducing the blood of another human into his wife's body. Eternal salvation up there instead of life down here. It was that gesture that transformed him and made him into a missionary in a league of his own, bringing him to the attention of the Governing Body. It was thanks to this inaugural murder that he became the strange being who was able to present his best side to the Inuits, managing to touch them and convert them at the same time as hating them as much as he did. This was how he had worked his way to the very top of the organization.

She still hates him so much. And yet she feels close to him, very close. On her telephone screen there's a number starting 01133, the dialing code for international calls to France. She takes one last toke, stubs out the joint, checks her watch, works out that it's 2:00 a.m. over there, and presses the green button. After the fourth ring someone picks up.

"Hi, Aïssa, it's Susan. I'm afraid we've got a serious problem and I need your help to fix it—how should I say?—terminally . . ."

"Hi, Susan. Sure. Tell me what's going on."

Five minutes later, she pours herself a glass of 7 Up and breathes in slowly. She's been waiting for this moment her whole life. She's going to call James and Dov and tell them to meet her at the Starbucks on the First Avenue Loop. She's really craving a brownie and a frappuccino. In their company. She's happier than she's ever been.

35

Ahmed has dropped in at home to take a shower and change before meeting up with Rachel. Oh, and Jean too. Fernanda is sunbathing in front of her lodge. She waves him over.

"Monsieur Taroudant, there's a young man here to see you. He's waiting for you up on the landing."

"I'm not expecting anyone . . ."

"I've seen him before; he came last autumn. Your cousin if I remember rightly."

"Mohamed . . . Ah, okay . . . Thank you."

He'd totally forgotten about the letter where his cousin had told him he'd be back in Paris for the summer. When was it again? Yesterday—it only got here yesterday . . . He didn't hang around! What am I going to do with him? As he comes out of the elevator he sees Mohamed wandering down the corridor wearing jeans and a flower-print T-shirt, and greets him with a smile and a hug.

Ten minutes later, with a coffee in front of them, Mohamed fills him in on the past eight months. He settled in well to life in Bordeaux, and the year went by without any trouble. He likes France a lot, he feels calm, far away from family stuff. He breathes in.

Only one thing is eating away at him: his mother, Ourida, cannot understand why he doesn't want to return home. However much he tells her he wants to get to know Paris she doesn't buy it, and she's decided to find him a wife—letting him live his life across the sea without a ball and chain is out of the question. Everyone knows what happens in the land of the *nasara*, the "Nazarenes." You get a degree, a Master's, and then, once you're settled, you marry a nice French girl and you're never seen again. Another one lost . . . Ahmed listens but keeps one eye on the time. Something doesn't stack up in his cousin's tale. Not that it matters much for the moment. But he's got to leave in fifteen minutes and he needs to explain to Mohamed how his life of introspection has been suddenly and radically shaken up.

"Listen, something major has happened: my neighbor upstairs was murdered. Laura. Remember I used to look after her orchids?"

"The air hostess who was in love with you?"

Ahmed's face hardens.

"In love with me? Well . . . Maybe, yeah. How did you know that, anyway?"

"It was obvious to everyone except you . . . Even the concierge knew—we spoke about it once. Laura . . . That's sad. She was a nice girl, no doubt about it. Why did they kill her? Have they found the murderer?"

"They don't know why and they haven't found who did it. You know, I should have been the prime suspect—I had keys to her place—but the two officers on the case seemed to realize that it couldn't have been me. I don't know, something strange happened when we met. Then there's Rachel . . . Basically I've got to go and see them now. I remembered something that Laura said to me. I've got to tell them. I've decided to get involved in the whole thing. To help them find the killer. I can't go back to how I was before. If I hadn't been sleepwalking through life, Laura would still be alive, you see what I'm saying? Now listen, right—being with me now is dangerous. All the more so because I've got this bad feeling that some people in the neighborhood want to do me harm. They're mixed up in this murder in one way or another and they want it to look like I'm the main culprit. Dead or alive. It's properly dangerous, Mohamed—do you understand? I'm really happy to see you, but it's not wise for you to stay here . . ."

Clearly very moved, Mohamed grabs Ahmed by the arm.

"I'm here for you, cousin. When the going's good I'm with you— same when it gets bad. Your enemies will find me at your side if they come for you."

He breaks into a smile.

"So Rachel, hey?"

The terrace at MK2 is jam-packed so Jean and Rachel have settled inside at the back. Ahmed sits down without a word. Rachel looks up. She seems somber, very somber, distressed. Then his presence fully dawns on her and she breaks into a big smile which dispels all his anguish, all that's bad. Ahmed's heart is flooded by her. New, fresh blood courses through his veins. One word is imprinted on his soul and it contains all the love in the world.

RA-CHE-LÉ.

Jean eventually pipes up. His expression bittersweet. He can't help but feel jealous, resentful of at least part of their happiness. And then he thinks of Léna who he'll be seeing in two hours, smiles, pulls himself together, and gets on with his job.

"Ahmed . . . so, Ahmed. We don't have much time. Everything's gathering speed, taking shape, and backing away all at the same time. You had something important to tell us?"

Ahmed's smile loses some of its intensity but doesn't disappear altogether.

"Yeah, I'll be quick . . ."

In as few words as possible he recounts the conversation he had with Laura ten days before. Jean takes notes.

"Why didn't you tell us yesterday?"

"I didn't think of it yesterday. My head was still all over the place. It came back to me this morning and I called Rachel—sorry, Lieutenant Kupferstein—immediately to tell her."

"It's okay, you can call me Rachel, it's no problem."

That smile again. Jean leaves it at that and is getting ready to ask his next question when his colleague's telephone rings.

"Hello . . . Who have you spoken to? . . . No, he didn't pass on the message. What exactly did he say? . . . Okay, thank you, *commissaire*."

She turns to Hamelot.

"That was Jeanteau, the *commissaire* in Niort. Laura's father has disappeared. And something else weird has happened: my cell phone was going straight to voicemail, apparently, so Jeanteau called the Bunker and Meyer picked up. As soon as he said that the suspect had gotten away, Le Gros blurted out 'Vignola!'"

Rachel pauses and Jean looks stunned.

"What the fuck? How could Meyer have known about that? We're the only people who know, and we only found out two hours ago!"

He turns to Ahmed and, for the very first time, talks to him like a police officer interrogating a suspect.

"Did you tell anyone else? Who are you talking to apart from us? Do you know anyone else from the police?"

Jean's tone is threatening. Ahmed's face closes right up—Rachel can sense him disappearing far away, quickly. She tries to calms things down with a voice that's at once gentle and firm.

"Jean, if Ahmed hadn't called me, we wouldn't have had any reason to suspect Vignola. Ahmed, there's just one thing I need to be sure about: no one else besides us knows about the conversation between Laura and you, right?"

Ahmed swallows hard, takes a deep breath. He looks at Jean.

"It's fine, I get it; it's normal for you to ask me this. No, I didn't tell anyone else. I didn't say anything to Monsieur Paul when I saw him this morning, nor to Sam, not even to my cousin Mohamed who rolled in from Bordeaux this morning for the summer. As for Laura, apart from me there's a chance she might have told Bintou and Aïcha, but I don't know, I don't think so. She was more the sort of person who'd want to protect them rather than seek protection from them."

Rachel cuts in.

"Sam? Hey, that reminds me—Sam told us about your visit this morning . . ."

"Of course . . . I bet he tried to make you think that I'm crazy enough to kill Laura . . . That was the worst haircut of my life. He stalked around me, clippers in hand, and tried to convince me that I could be the killer. He really reckons he's a big shot. And he really takes me for an idiot."

Jean again.

"So Sam wants to pin you as the killer. Why?"

"I don't know. Weird stuff's being going on in the neighborhood the last few days. I could feel it even before Laura's death. I think there's a link between Sam and Moktar. Might seem really strange to you, you might think I'm a bit nuts, and you wouldn't be wrong. But nutcases can sense this sort of stuff . . . Nothing more to it than that: just sensing stuff."

"Moktar. 75-Zorro-19 . . ."

"Moktar became a Salafist after they sent him to the *bled*. After he was forced to give up on his love . . . I bumped into him in the street yesterday. He insulted me, said I stank of white man. But it has been years since we've said a word to each other. Not since Maison Blanche, to be exact."

"Maison Blanche?"

"Yeah, we were admitted there at the same time, but not for the same reasons. I can't work out why he started on me for no reason five years later, even though we see each other once or twice a month, around and about, without saying a word. After a few yards, I turned around and he was gone. I'm pretty sure he went into Sam's . . . There you have it, for what it's worth . . . A lunatic's intuition."

Rachel looks at Jean.

"That squares up with the girls' story about how the former members of 75-Zorro-19 met up at Sam's in the middle of the night three days before the murder . . ."

She turns to Ahmed, any trace of a smile vanished.

"You didn't hear anything—is that right?"

Without waiting for a response, Jean gets up to go and pay. Rachel stands up, sliding away from the bench, but a lot more slowly.

"Can I call you again tonight, from a pay phone? That wouldn't bug you?"

Rachel blushes, feels like she's seventeen all over again.

"No, Ahmed, that wouldn't bug me . . . Not at all. Call me at . . . eleven. Hopefully I'll be finished by then. Hopefully. By the way, it's not really any of my business, but . . ."

"Yeah?"

"Ever thought about getting yourself a cell phone?"

36

Raymond, still stuffed into his vest, is buzzing like he does after every murder. The *brocanteur*'s body lies slumped in the faintly ridiculous position common to most murder victims. The blade is wrapped up in a plastic bag—prints wiped down—ready to be tossed into the Seine, the last thing he needs to do before leaving Paris for Guebwiller in Alsace. They'll be safe over there in the family stronghold while things calm down. They'll stay there long enough for the old man to placate the furious Enkell. Raymond is particularly excited to get going: his brother promised him a Godzwill upon arrival, and not a moment before.

They slip through the half-open gate. Once they're out in the street, Francis straightens up and takes a large gulp of air. And nearly chokes as he feels the steel of a gun barrel against the back of his neck. He can make out the languid smile in Aïssa Benamer's voice.

"Off we go. The car's just over there."

It's always difficult to accept when your number's up. People try to grab on to anything they can . . .

"But Haqiqi . . . I was meant to deal with Haqiqi . . ."

"Ah, of course! Well, in the end I decided to take care of him myself. Seemed the logical thing to do. Right, are you coming? Or shall we do this here?"

Less resigned to his fate than his brother, Raymond attempts to escape. He's barely started to run when a shadow emerges from the darkness, the barrel of a Glock shoving into his side. He turns to find himself face-to-face with Enkell's icy glare. But he doesn't want to die—no . . . He tries to barge into him and wrestle the gun off him. Before he knows it, barely two seconds later his arm is locked behind his back and his face is being scraped against the wall of the shop. For several days now Enkell has been waiting to take revenge on the person responsible for the grotesque theatrics of Laura's murder. As he marches Raymond toward the mouse-gray Scenic, whose four doors are all open, he whispers into his ear.

"So, Meyer the Younger . . . You like a bit of a performance, do you? Choose the wrong career, did we? Our real calling was to be an artist but we ended up as a murderer? Because when it comes to murdering, you see, it's best to keep it discreet. I mean, if you want to stay employed . . ."

The *commissaire* is reveling in the moment. He twists Raymond's forearm up, slowly at first, taking pleasure from the thought of the pain rushing through the body of the younger Meyer brother, the man's face reddening, sweat streaming down his neck in filthy rivulets. Then Enkell yanks the arm up with an abrupt movement that is followed by a crack and a muffled cry. Dislocated shoulder. All he needs to do now is fling Raymond into the back seat of the car like a rag.

Francis couldn't care less about his brother. From the moment he stepped out of the shadow, Enkell had—rather surprisingly—reminded him of his grandfather Meyer. An old *vigneron* from Alsace who didn't like it when his son, Handsome Roger, became a policeman and a pimp in the capital. Every summer, he and Raymond would spend two months there, terrified of this man who'd never say more than twenty-five words a day in French. And fifty in Alsatian, which the young boys flatly refused to speak. That would have meant forfeiting, renouncing the dubious glamour of their status as little Parisians. This is what is running through Francis's mind when he lets them cuff his hands behind his back and place him gently next to his brother who is crushed with pain and despair on the rear seat of the car about to take them on their final journey. If he'd been able to understand what old Meyer had been saying, maybe he wouldn't be here today.

Enkell starts up the car. Benamer, sitting in the front passenger seat, keeps both brothers in view. The car drives alongside the murals that run the length of rue Ordener. Two graffiti artists, armed with gas lamps and cans of spray paint, are drawing an American cop—his cap and gun totally out of proportion—pursuing one of the Beagle Boys as he hightails it out of Scrooge McDuck's vault-swimming pool with a sack bursting with gold coins. Francis Meyer has always felt an indifference laced with a degree of scorn toward those the *bobos* refer to as "street artists." He watches as the last human scene he'll ever behold plays out in front of him: two kids—one black, one white—wearing tracksuits, sneakers and bandanas, digging up one of his fondest childhood memories from those summers in Alsace, awaiting the arrival of the *Mickey Mouse Weekly* each Thursday at the village shop. He would impatiently comb through the magazine to make sure that the Beagle Boys were in it. By far his favorite characters, even if Chief O'Hara did always catch them.

Enkell takes a left down rue de la Chapelle, heading north. Raymond opens an eye and looks around him; lets out a yelp at the faintest of movements as he tries to sit up straight. He collapses in a heap. Benamer smiles at him.

"With that dislocated shoulder of yours, I wouldn't move too much if I were you. Tell me, just between the two of us, and since we've got some time on our hands, I wanted to ask you to clear something up for me: the three orchids laid out on the toilet seat . . . What was that about? I get the pork joint, but the orchids . . . I can't figure them out . . ."

Raymond gives him a look of pure hatred. Shuts his eyes. Silence.

Francis can't stop himself from laughing.

"Something funny?"

"Do you really want to know?"

"Yes."

"Okay, I'll tell you, on one condition."

"Go on then . . ."

"There's a Godzwill in the breast pocket of my coat—let me pop it? May as well, right . . ."

Raymond opens his eyes and hisses, "Francis, no!" He lurches toward his brother but falls back heavily into the seat with a terrible groan. Benamer ignores him, reaches for the pill and places it on his colleague's tongue as if he were performing the Eucharist. Francis swallows the Godzwill dry, inhales deeply, and pauses. Enkell turns right at porte de la Chapelle. On boulevard Ney, Benamer asks his question again.

"So, the orchids?"

Francis smiles, as if there's some in-joke only he gets.

"You didn't notice the little tattoo on the inside of his wrist?"

"No."

"Three dots. That mean anything to you?"

"'Death to the pigs!' His father and brother are in the force, and the police cover him for all his crimes."

"Jealous. He's always been jealous. He couldn't handle it when he flunked the entrance exam. Too thick to even direct traffic. So one day he got himself that tattoo. My father unleashed one of his major beatings. It was his last, but it was one hell of a walloping! And then most recently, with that drug . . . I don't know, he was inspired.

There was something beautiful about it, wasn't there? Something poetic."

Francis Meyer falls silent, the pill starting to take effect. He feels good. Happy that he is able to reflect upon his end. The corrupt, criminal officer resigned to his fate. He understands. His consciousness is reaching the cosmos. His role on Earth has been and will be to inflict harm, which is no small matter. He'll have his place in the Great Scheme, the infinite Oneness. Enkell and Benamer are at a higher level. It is their lot to continue. To do evil for evil's sake; to fulfill their destiny as they halt his. He realizes—albeit a little late— that crime is a serious business. It's not a vacation. They're professional evildoers, while he was just an amateur. Step aside. Give way. Case closed.

FINAL JOURNEY

Too thick to even direct traffic! Francis's words are spinning around his younger brother's head. On boulevard MacDonald he sits up gently, trying suppress the pain. The car slows down, turns left, and heads down an alleyway. Raymond is pure, cold fury. He doesn't want to die. He doesn't give a fuck about dying. He just wants to kill his older brother. To murder him. Show him the man he holds in such contempt.

The Scenic comes to a stop in front of a warehouse. An orange lightbulb glows dimly above a metal door. They've got to usher the victims toward their fate, in the belief that one more minute of life is acceptable, because it's better to kill inside than outside. Absurd, blind obedience. Works most of the time, but it's never a given. Enkell gets out of the vehicle and opens Francis's door, keeping him in his sights all the time. Benamer does the same on Raymond's side, but he doesn't move an inch. His brother is already approaching the orange halo at the entrance, followed by the *commissaire central* of the eighteenth arrondissement and his non-standard-issue Glock. Benamer loses his patience.

"Raymond, stop fucking around and get out."

"I can't. It hurts too much."

The situation is in danger of dragging on. They can't afford to delay too long. Enkell's voice is cold.

"Do it there. It's fine, we'll clear it up."

"No—I don't have a silencer. Plus I don't want to have to lug his great big corpse inside afterward."

Benamer moves closer to the hulking Raymond, who appears to be suffering horribly. Even real professionals sometimes slip up. Everything happens very quickly. Meyer the Younger grabs the barrel of the Kabyle *commissaire*'s weapon and in the same movement cracks the man's forehead against the top of the door before taking the gun out of his hand. By the time Enkell's turned around, Raymond is standing opposite him, pistol to pistol.

"Just let me kill my brother and I'll vanish into thin air. I'm not interested in you and your piece of Arab shit."

The two men trace out an elegant curve as they move, never taking their eyes off each other, until Francis finds himself midway between the shooters, facing his brother. The older Meyer is now high as a kite. He addresses his brother in full living-god mode.

"What you are looking for is not here. You're killing me when I'm becoming divine. You're killing me when I want death. Oh how much better to be in my shoes than yours! How long will it take for you to realize? How life is . . ."

Bang, bang, bang. Three shots bring his sermon to a close. One in each knee, and one in the balls. Enkell turns to face Raymond, who's backing slowly away into the darkness.

"Pain will cut through any drug. You can finish him off, I couldn't give two fucks—he'll die knowing what his brother is made of."

For a moment, the *commissaire central* thinks he's hallucinating himself: all that's left of Raymond is a sardonic grin floating in the night.

37

At the Sarah-Bernhardt, Jean has been studying the bubbles in his bottle of Perrier for twelve minutes when Léna makes her entrance with a tall man of about sixty—almost thin, his shoulders slightly hunched. Once the introductions are over, drinks are ordered. Cappuccino for the psychiatrist; rum and coke for the social worker. Dr. Germain checks his watch.

"So, you want information on Ahmed Taroudant. Information that I am not within my rights to give you . . . Léna explained the situation to me, and I trust her inherently. Nevertheless, I need to emphasize two points: firstly, this meeting never happened. We've never seen each other. Is that clear?"

His sky-blue eyes drill into Jean's.

"Perfectly clear, Doctor."

"Secondly, I will tell you only the bare essentials. Just enough to let you see that he is innocent. If I thought for a second that he might be guilty, I definitely wouldn't say a word to the police. I would, quite simply, keep my mouth shut. Psychiatrists—and particularly psychoanalysts—are not in the business of sending people to prison . . ."

"Just out of curiosity, Doctor: is that true? If you thought he was guilty, you wouldn't do anything at all?"

"Just out of courtesy, Lieutenant: what I would do does not concern you in the slightest . . . Now, let us begin. I have known Ahmed Taroudant for five years. He came to me after entering a state of delirium. He was found walking along the *périphérique* without any idea where he was. He no longer knew who he was, and was uttering incomprehensible words. He stayed at Maison Blanche for twenty days. After that, I monitored him at my clinic. You should know that his mother had been a patient for schizophrenia at Maison Blanche since he was a teenager. One could say that he brought it upon himself. I consider his delirious spell normal given what he had experienced. Quite healthy, even—it was definitely either that or ending up schizophrenic himself."

"And his mother?"

"The last time they saw each other, it went . . . It went very badly. I advised Ahmed not to visit her again. It was the only way for him to keep himself on the straight and narrow, psychologically speaking."

"Sorry to push you, Doctor, but what do you mean by 'it went very badly'?"

Germain's eyes are like two poison darts.

"Nothing more than it would appear to mean, Lieutenant."

Hamelot takes the barbed comment without flinching. He waits.

"To avoid any misunderstanding, it was she who behaved aggressively toward her son. Happy with that?"

"We'll make do, Doctor, we'll make do . . . While we're on the subject, how was his behavior toward the other patients? Was he at all aggressive?"

"Ahmed is not the sort of person who provokes others, nor is he one to be pushed around. His stay went more or less smoothly. Only a few passing difficulties with a local acquaintance, I believe. Without it getting out of hand, however."

"A local acquaintance? Who was that? Moktar?"

Dr. Germain's jaw twitches slightly.

"Listen, Lieutenant Hamelot. I've already said too much, and I'm not about to share with you the extent of my knowledge of any one of my patients. I really need to leave now. I have a session beginning in fifteen minutes."

"Doctor, it's extremely important. It relates to an atrocious murder that was very carefully crafted. Crimes like this one are often followed by others. Please answer one final question: the 'local acquaintance' he had trouble with was Moktar, wasn't it?"

Somewhat disarmed, the psychoanalyst looks across to Léna, who nods reassuringly: it will go no further than here.

"Yes, it was him. I really have to go now. Bearing in mind the circumstances, I grant Léna permission to talk to you about this particular case. She would have anyway. Goodbye, Lieutenant."

"Goodbye, Doctor. And thank you."

Fifteen minutes later and Jean has moved on to the Guinness. Léna's sticking to the rum and coke.

"Moktar was in, like, full-on mystical delirium. Think bad trip . . . A real handful! We were all a target for him. He never stopped talking about Anna . . ."

"The girlfriend he'd been banned from seeing?"

"You know the story already, I remember it clearly when you told me. That night we'd had a few too many of those Cameroonian beers at Mireille la Fine's on rue Marcadet?"

Jean can't help but blush at the memory of that night, which he'd completely wiped from his memory. The morning after, dragging himself out of Léna's bed with some difficulty, he hadn't the first idea what had gone on between them. He had a thumping headache, and turned up in the kitchen looking rough and hunting for aspirin, only to find the social worker from Brittany, all freshness and smiles, making breakfast. Why was she feeling the need to bring up that humiliating episode, let alone add salt to the wound?

"You remember, the evening before that morning when you didn't have the guts to ask me what had happened between us."

Jean goes bright red and desperately tries to backpedal.

"Ummmm . . . Oh yeah, that night."

Léna is sparkling now.

"You still don't want to know?"

Jean gathers himself with a smile.

"Léna, we're still in the professional part of the evening. If I've got any questions about that night, I reserve the right to ask them later, when I've finished work for the day. In any case, what I do remember is that you have never wanted to tell me anything at all about Moktar's time at Maison Blanche."

"The professional part of the evening?"

Léna leaves the question mark hanging in the air. And Jean realizes that tonight it won't be necessary for them to drink themselves to oblivion. He thinks back to Rachel teasing him about Léna. How had she known that there was still a connection between the former lovers from Saint-Pol-de-Léon?

"So, Moktar . . ."

"Patient confidentiality. If I start ratting to the police about my patients' behavior . . ."

"To the police?"

"Well done, you're catching on. Look, I like you a lot, Jean, but in our line of work it's vital we stick to the rules. Starting with keeping professional stuff hermetically sealed from our private life."

"What are you playing at, Léna? Your colleague just exempted you from your patient confidentiality. And, more importantly, we're closing in on a gang of killers which is potentially made up of religious fundamentalists *and* crooked policemen. So anything you can tell me about Moktar is incredibly valuable. For everyone. You and me, in our different jobs, we're both doing our part for society, wouldn't you say?"

"I've never thought about it from that angle . . . I wouldn't be prepared to give in on this point for anyone in the police other than you. Let's just say that you've won this time. Our friend Moktar saw the world as being split into two irreconcilable factions: Muslims and everyone else. And when he said Muslims, he meant the real ones, the purists. This was really tough for the female staff at the hospital. We couldn't be close to him, even by accident, let alone stand next to him. Great when you've got to provide care and dole out drugs! In consultations he would give free rein to his aggressive ranting. At that point, Anna really inspired murderous thoughts in him. He'd endlessly repeat the word '*Shaytan, Shaytan*'. Sometimes, when one of us was passing nearby, he'd start reciting verses from the Koran in that tone of his. It freaked us out. After a bit he calmed down, finally noticed that he'd never get out if he kept on spouting off like that. You know how it is: we can't keep everyone locked up forever. Plus he'd never hurt or killed anybody, even though he did smash up his house. So he left, and after that we didn't hear a peep."

"What's his diagnosis?"

Léna has a sip of her drink, takes a deep breath, and looks Jean straight in the eye.

"This goes no further, okay?"

"Léna, a woman is dead, and there may be more to come. I'll keep it to myself and to Rachel. And my chief. There's no way I can avoid telling them this sort of information. But it won't be written down anywhere."

"Rachel . . . Fine, I'll try not to let my jealousy get the better of me. Degenerative paranoid psychosis. There's no cure and it'll only get worse. Whether or not he'd act on it is another issue, for sure. I'm no psychiatrist, but if you describe the murder to me a bit then maybe I can tell you if it stacks up."

"Okay"

Jean describes the scene of Laura's murder. The meat, the orchids, the balcony.

"Hmmm . . . Strange. Sounds more like the work of a perv. My gut reaction is that if—*if*—he killed her, he wasn't responsible for the grisly sideshow. Seems over the top. How'd you say . . . ? It's as if someone knew his profile and attempted to make him a scapegoat."

"At the moment, it seems more likely they're trying to make Ahmed the scapegoat . . ."

"Ahmed! Him? No way! Absolutely not. As Dr. Germain said, he's categorically not the type. Neither a pervert nor an aggressive paranoiac. Just a bit spaced out, in his own world, but not a threat to others. Right, that's enough work—I'm starving: let's go and eat! Also, if I have another drink I'll be over the limit and you'll have to lead me away in handcuffs . . ."

Clicking into flirtatious mode, Léna looks him directly in the eye. He manages to hold her gaze without blushing.

"Over the limit? You're already there after those two rum and cokes. I could always swing by the police station and grab the cuffs if you're happy to wait?"

Later, they will have this conversation:

Jean: *Why that night?*
Léna: *Because you were ready.*
Jean: *How did you know?*
Léna: *Because I'm an observant woman.*

But that happens later. Hours, months, even years later. An eternity later.

38

Bintou, Aïcha, Alpha, and Mourad. Onur's place. Only Moktar, Ruben, and Rébecca are missing to bring back the good old days. 10:45 p.m. A table at the back, far from the tourists. The atmosphere is charged with both love and pain. Brothers and sisters estranged for years without ever asking themselves why. Silence to start with, then tea appears before each of them, set down by the owner who knows them all well. The boys drop in two little sugar cubes, stirring them in. The girls watch them, happy beyond belief. How they'd looked up to their big brothers! Loved them so much. Until they argued and went their separate ways. Moktar, Alpha, and Mourad one way, Ruben the other. The Muslims and the Jew. All the girls know is that it all happened when Moktar went crazy. Their brothers had never offered the tiniest explanation. From that moment on, they simply ignored Rébecca, their ex–best friend's little sister. As if the Aboulafia family in its entirety had ceased to exist from one day to the next. This had really upset them. Then when Ruben displayed the same attitude toward them, they had decided to laugh it off together . . .

The boys know that they are expected to talk. Mourad takes up the challenge, even though he's always found words hard when the beats aren't rolling.

"We fucked up, right . . . But you got to see things from our side, too. In this world, Muslims . . ."

The two girls stare at him in disbelief. Alpha places a hand on his friend's arm to bring him back to the reality of the situation.

"No, no, not that . . . I mean . . . We didn't do anything . . . That's the thing—we didn't do anything . . ."

Mourad's voice falters. As if it's finally dawned on him, right there, his glass of tea nearly drained in front of him. Alpha speaks instead.

"Yeah, that's exactly it: we didn't do anything and that's what's eating us up . . ."

He looks up at the ceiling. Breathes in. Blows out hard.

"Every day I wake up and I think of Laura. She's there when I go to sleep. Through the day she comes back again and again. Her wheelie case, her uniform . . . Every day. And them too: Sam, Moktar, that pussy Haqiqi who didn't even show up . . . And there was this other bizarre guy in the background, this real bruiser, who watched us without saying anything. Every time I think of him I get the creeps . . ."

Bintou, her eyes welling up with tears, takes his hand and squeezes it with all her strength.

"Alpha, you've got to tell us everything. Afterward we'll go to the police together. And then Laura will leave you in peace because you'll have done the right thing."

"The right thing . . ."

Boys Don't Cry. Alpha continues, visibly distressed.

"Nothing will ever be right again. Never. We let it happen. We listened to them and then we left. Like cowards."

Emptiness. Mourad's eyes finally stop staring at his tea and catch
sight of a familiar silhouette entering the kebab house. He shuts
them for half a second as a greeting before carrying on as the new
arrival goes to the counter and greets Onur.

"Haqiqi insisted we went to the meeting. He needed us to sort
out something important. Moktar explained that, as a one-off, we'd
be working with Jews. We thought that was weird, but at the time
we trusted him. He'd often counted on us for little missions, as he
called them: handing out leaflets outside the mosques in Paris or
Évry, burning DVDs, simple stuff that made us feel important, made
us feel we were bringing about the *Ummah*. Might sound stupid, but
we really believed it. And we believed in Moktar. He was our childhood friend, but since his journey to the *bled* he seemed inspired,
like he was walking with God: and by following him, we felt that
we were on the right path too. Moktar explained that there was a
dangerous woman living among us. Laura had looked at him several times. It was Haqiqi who wised him up about it; reminded him
it was those kinds of look that nearly made him lose his way in
his old life. He said that she got kicks from turning on all the true
believers in the neighborhood. That made him think that she had
been sent by *Shaytan* to unsettle our community. At that point, me
and Alpha looked at each other. Sam noticed, and so did the weird
dude, who hadn't come out with a single word but who listened to
everything we said, monitoring our every movement. Moktar was
in full flow and didn't notice anything. Two nights earlier, Haqiqi
had had an amazing, troubling dream which took place in Medina
at the time of the Prophet. Some horny woman was walking down
a street turning on all the men. She went past the group of first
believers—the holy ancestors—who were getting ready to pray. The
sun was setting to their right, in the west. Then she committed a
grave error: she revealed herself to them with her head, arms, and
chest uncovered. But the pure-hearted had raised their hands and
closed their eyes, and uttered the holy words *Allahu Akbar*. The next
second the woman disappeared. Because the sun was setting in the
west, the event happened before the Prophet had instructed them

to turn toward Mecca rather than Jerusalem to pray. For Haqiqi, the meaning was clear: however wacky it might seem, we needed to ask the Jews for help to find out what to do with this impure woman."

"And that's when I turned up."

Surprised at the interruption, the girls swing around to see Ruben standing there in jeans and a T-shirt, his sidelocks half let down, a glass of tea in his hand.

"Right when Sam took the floor to explain that Imam Haqiqi and Rabbi Seror had decided to act together to protect their respective communities from this depraved woman. I know Sam well—he's my uncle. A doofus who thinks he's smart. As for Seror and Haqiqi, they were sure we'd all agree to rein Laura in, our sisters' best friend. She was the one, they thought, who prevented us from keeping you girls under control. They saw us as good little soldiers, and they weren't wrong. But they overestimated the grip they had on us when they tried to get us to kidnap Laura. I'm not sure how, but they'd gotten their hands on her flight schedule, and they asked us to intercept her at midnight between the Métro station and her apartment. Then we had to take her in a van to some warehouse beyond the *périphérique* where Moktar and the other guy would be waiting. It was all supposed to be about scaring her, making her move away from the neighborhood, and making her leave the faithful, and our sisters, in peace. All three of us looked at each other for the first time in four or five years and it was like we'd just woken up from a bad dream. Like in the movies, when the hero is released from the witch's spell. It was when Sam used the words 'the believers': it didn't ring true. All of a sudden we realized that it sounded just as false coming from the mouths of our leaders, the people we'd been following for so many years. We looked at each other and we replied as one that we were refusing to do it; we weren't going to be part of it. Moktar was about to insist, but Sam realized there was no point. Then the other guy—the one who hadn't said a word—came out of the shadows. He smiled at us and threatened us by running his thumb across his throat. Without saying a word. That's the truth. We were scared. If we'd gone to the police when we left Sam's, Laura would still be alive."

Aïcha and Bintou stare at Ruben wide-eyed. Then at Alpha, then at Mourad. They saw the killer. They could have prevented Laura's death. The girls begin to cry. The boys stay quiet as they are forced to face up to themselves. To their passivity. To the unforgivable.

THE CRIME

THEIR CRIME

Several minutes later and the silence becomes unbearable.

"What do we do now?" Alpha asks in a whisper. "Go and see the police?"

Bintou dries her tears with a paper napkin.

"Soon. Before, you've got to talk to us."

With a hesitant motion she goes to squeeze her brother's hand again.

"You've got to tell us about you. How did you get like this? What made you become the way you did?"

"It's a long story. You know a bit about the start: four kids play superheroes in the schoolyard, discover rap at secondary school, become local celebs, and then, a few years later, fall out over standard girl problems."

"Not sure 'standard' is the word."

Ruben finally sits down and continues.

"You remember the romance between Moktar and Anna? When his parents banned him from seeing her, Moktar smashed up the whole house. He ended up in Sainte-Anne; later on, his father decided to send him to the *bled*. Anna was totally devastated. One day, I bumped into her outside the Picard on boulevard Magenta. She was like a sleepwalker. We went for a coffee. She begged me to talk to Moktar when he got back. We saw each other again quite a few times over the summer. I promised to do what I could. When Moktar came back, he had changed inside. There was something completely different about him. A power, an aura. It was fascinating and disturbing. When I spoke to him about Anna, he asked me if I had joined the side of *Shaytan*. Mourad and Alpha were there. They tried to defuse the situation, to laugh it off, but Moktar's words affected them in a way that I didn't realize at the time. Feeling alone and sad, I went to tell Anna that there was no hope. That's the day it happened between me and her. After, it was too heavy for me to bear, so I went to tell Moktar to his face."

He stops, drinks a mouthful of tea. Mourad takes the story from there.

"That day, it was just us at Moktar's. The TV was on: music videos on M6, I think. When Ruben fessed up about what had happened between him and Anna, Moktar went ballistic. He started reciting verses from the Koran that he'd learned in the *bled*, got up and walked straight to Ruben, who pulled back to the front door. Me and Alpha held him off and shouted at Ruben to get the hell out of there, fast. We managed to get Moktar back in his seat, but he was still reciting, chanting. We stayed there until his father got back. The following day, he was admitted to Maison Blanche. We cut ties with Ruben because we were shocked he'd slept with Anna. And we thought it was his fault that Moktar had gone back to hospital. We went to Maison Blanche twice. That was where we really fell under his spell. He was like a holy man, and most of the other patients listened to him. He spoke of the *bled*, of the *marabouts*. He explained how over there people lived in purity, in the truth of Islam. I don't know . . . It was like since his journey he'd found the thing we'd been missing. The magic thing. When he got out, we followed him to Haqiqi's prayer room, where we became completely immersed in their world. They spoke about the time of the Prophet, about the holy ancestors. About the path to follow."

Ruben cuts him off.

"It didn't last with Anna. And I was left abandoned by all. I started thinking about me, myself. What was most important to me: hip-hop or Judaism? Then when my father left and my mother started going along to the Moroccan Hasidic meetings nearby, I threw myself into it too. I became someone else, and I was fine with that. It was the first time I'd felt like my own person. That's what I thought, at least.

Today, all I see when I look back is Laura's corpse. I can't look myself in the mirror anymore."

Aïcha and Bintou are extremely shaken by the stories they've heard. Unable to say a single word, the light-eyed girl tears off a piece of napkin and notes down Rachel's address. Before handing it to Ruben, she writes in the bottom-right corner:

3:30 a.m. All three of you.

39

The cleanup—the worst part. Or the best. Benamer usually likes it. But generally he is not recovering from being knocked out by the very person he was supposed to kill. He hadn't been at all wary of Raymond Meyer. He messed up. He did bad. So many negative thoughts pile up that he forgets the task at hand. Enkell watches him as he continues to sponge down possible traces of the once large splotch of blood on the back window of the Scenic. He gives him a moment to get his act together.

"Aïssa, are you coming? That window of yours is spic and span. We've got to finish off Le Gros's body."

Aïssa Benamer shakes his head, stuffs the sponge into the Leader Price plastic bag along with the other things to dissolve, pulls out a folding hand truck from the trunk, extends it and wheels it the fifteen yards from the car to the corpse, the head of which is now encircled by a deep-red halo. Twelve minutes earlier,

Raymond Meyer's smile had barely disappeared when Frédéric Enkell fired a bullet into the back of Francis's skull. Then he had woken Benamer with two resounding slaps, delegating to him the task of cleaning the blood-stained window. The two of them are now loading their overweight ex-colleague's body onto the hand truck, before fastening it by the neck, chest, and waist, leaving the legs dangling. Nothing more awkward than shifting a corpse. That's why, as a rule of thumb, they try to liquidate them as close as possible to their final destination. The biggest pain is lugging their wheeled cargo up the three outdoor steps. The door opens without any trouble onto a vast, bare room. In the middle, a large dark cylinder topped with a second smaller cylinder, like some sort of arty totem pole. The vat is two yards tall. Ladders run down either side. Between them is a bag from which Enkell pulls two neon-green protective overalls, while Benamer unties Francis Meyer's body.

DISSOLUTION

Getting the body up to the top cylinder is not easy: each of them on one of the ladders, one holding the legs, the other the armpits. Fuck's sake! Then they've got to balance the wobbling body on the rim, one of them holding it while the other hoists himself up to the highest part to unscrew the vat's enormous lid. Ah, fucking overalls!

WHAT THE FUCK AM I SUPPOSED TO DO NOW?

The hole is too narrow to roll in the corpse in one go. Decision time: head first or feet first? The boss opts for the head, which naturally is the part he's holding—he wants to watch. Then everything moves very quickly. Like when you're diving. The vat is remarkably well designed: no splash at all. Almost could have managed it without these damn overalls, thinks the other man. Then there's the sound. The sound that renders the situation extremely real. The sound of disappearance itself.

FSSSHHHHHHHHH

There we go—all done. But there's plenty more work to be getting on with tonight.

40

2:30 a.m. at Rachel's. Aïcha and Bintou are sitting patiently across the table from one another. Malongo coffee and Monoprix cookies at the ready. The laptop is on and they are logged in to Aïcha's Skype account. Silence reigns, and it's starting to get oppressive. Who's going to get the ball rolling?

"We've got something to tell you," Bintou says.

"Go on."

"Our brothers are coming around in a little bit after our chat with Rébecca. Ruben too."

Rachel waits for the follow-up. Bintou breaks off half a cookie and looks up at a colorful print depicting an Indian deity with two goddesses at his side. She takes it in for a moment—its serenity, its gentleness—before returning to the current situation, the horror. She takes a deep breath.

"They didn't do anything. And that will haunt them for the rest of their lives. That night, they saw the murderer. Sam was there with Moktar and another big, creepy guy. Moktar and the barber asked them to kidnap Laura, our brothers refused, then the creepy guy threatened them and they left . . . There you have it; that's how it went. They left, and she was killed. My brother did nothing to prevent the murder. Nor did Aïcha's, nor did Rébecca's. They did nothing . . . Our brothers! . . . Our very own brothers . . ."

Bintou starts sobbing and looks at Lieutenant Kupferstein, searching through her tears for the answer to the question she dares not ask. Rachel provides it with a resigned smile.

"Three years: that's what they're looking at. Failure to report a suspected criminal offense. Three years and a forty-five-thousand dollar fine. Article 434-1 of the *Code pénal*. Of course, if they present themselves at the commissariat on their own accord, and if they help stop the killer, the judge will take that into consideration. I'm going to call Jean to make sure he's there when they arrive. Later on we'll all go to the Bunker together."

2:45 a.m. Just enough time to telephone her colleague before their Skype date with Rébecca. No answer. She doesn't leave a message, hangs up, and calls back. He picks up on the third ring.

"Uhhhhh."

"Jean. Can you be here in half an hour? It's important."

She can hear him murmuring to someone.

"Look, I'm sorry if this is a bad time, but I really need you now. Let's just say things are accelerating. I'll explain. Give my best to Léna."

"I'll be there."

Aïcha stands up and comes around the table to hand Bintou a tissue and stroke her hair; her eyes work their way along the wall and settle on the brightly colored picture that had intrigued her friend a few minutes earlier. The polygamous Indian god. Rachel lets her soak up the image before deciphering it for her.

"It's Murugan, the brother of Ganesh. I bought it in a shop in La Chapelle run by a family from Kerala. I've always dreamed of going to Kerala. Maybe I'll never go; maybe it'll remain one of those unfulfilled desires that you accumulate through life, like when you keep loving a man who doesn't have any idea and never will, but who you can keep, intact, in a sacred part of your heart. A man you can't even imagine making love to. Anyway, for those fantasies you've always got the actors: Irrfan Khan, Tony Leung, Charles Berling . . ."

"Or Javier Bardem . . ."

The words slipped out of Bintou's full lips with a very soft breath.

"Or Javier Bardem, yes . . . Each to their own. They're precious. But it's different with gods or religious icons. In them, desire is abolished. In them, we find peace."

Bintou listens to her intently, and continues to do so despite Rachel's silence. Where did it come from, this astonishing closeness forged with these girls she hadn't even met the day before, and whose brothers have been implicated in this ghastly murder? Like with Ahmed: the trance, the miracle of the encounter. The miracle of this investigation. Beneath the timeless smile of Murugan, surrounded by his beautiful, eternally satisfied wives, radiating a sense of fulfillment that is at once carnal and not carnal, a moment of magical harmony unfolds. Divine fulfillment, thinks Rachel. So simple, so clear that humankind strives not to attain it.

About twelve minutes to go until the call to Rébecca. Something in the air demands that a true word be said. And it springs delicately from Bintou's lips.

Even though I walk through the valley of the shadow of death,
I will fear no evil,
for you are with me;
your rod and your staff,
they comfort me. You prepare a table before me
in the presence of my enemies;
you anoint my head with oil;
my cup overflows. Surely goodness and mercy shall follow me
all the days of my life,
and I shall dwell in the house of the Lord forever.

She stops, closes her eyes for a second.

"When Rébecca started dressing up like an Orthodox Jew, it was to keep her mother and brother happy, but it was also to see what it was all about. She read the Bible. I was curious, so I learned a few passages with her. That psalm moved us. It's sad and beautiful. Unsettling, but at the same time reassuring. What's even stranger is that I've never read the Koran. I think it's a menacing, dangerous book, while the Bible has never scared me. It wasn't the book of my religion, so I didn't risk anything by reading it."

Rachel interrupts, surprised.

"Menacing? Why?"

"I'm going to tell you a secret; something that happened back when I was eight. We were in the suburbs of Paris at my cousin's house, Fanta, who was nine at the time. At one point we locked ourselves in the bathroom. I can't remember how or why, but suddenly she asked me if I'd been cut. I had no idea what she was talking about, so she showed me. And I saw what she was missing; what I still had. I started crying. I'm not sure if I was sad for her or for me, but I wasn't able to stop. It wasn't until we got home that I ended up telling my mother what had happened in the bathroom. Mom consoled me, reassuring me by saying that no one would ever do something like that to me, even though she had herself suffered the same fate, back in the village, when she was a child. Shaking her head sadly, she kept repeating: "We're not in Mauritania now, but still, poor Fanta . . ." When I was older, she told me how the village imam back in Sélibaby, on the north bank of the river, had publicly declared that girls had to remain pure, even in the land of the infidel—especially in the land of the infidel. He was an old, toothless imam with a face harder than a zebu's skull. Unfortunately for Fanta, her mother had obeyed the man of God. I think that all I am comes from that bit of luck—from not being my aunt's daughter. From preserving my body intact. I don't feel superior to Fanta, nor to any girl who's been cut. That's not at all what I mean. I just think that the most profound part of my identity is rooted in the fact that I wasn't. It comes from my mother's desire for me to be different from her. It's strange—this is the first time I've told this to anyone other than Rébecca or Aïcha. The first time I have truly understood how much it has made me who I am."

She looks up at the Indian deity and laughs.

At 3:01 a.m., the Skype ringtone shakes them from their reverie. Aïcha looks inquiringly at Rachel, who nods at her to answer. A blurred face gradually appears on the computer screen. A beautiful young brunette with a fair complexion. She looks worried. There's a window behind her shoulder: night is starting to fall. A seven- or eight-hour time difference, maybe central United States or Canada, Rachel calculates, snapping back into police mode.

"Hey, Aïcha, Bintou, you there? I can't see you . . ."

"Yeah Rébecca, we're here—we don't have a webcam on this laptop but we can see you! How've you been since yesterday?"

"Yeah, okay."

"We're with Lieutenant Kupferstein . . . Rachel, who we mentioned. She's cool, you can tell her everything."

"Hello, Rébecca."

"Hello, Lieutenant."

"Thank you for agreeing to speak to me. It's really important for the investigation, to catch the killer as quickly as possible."

"I'll do all I can to help you . . . Laura's death . . . it broke my heart—literally shattered me. It's thanks to her that I'm here, that I managed to escape the life that had been mapped out for me."

"Tell me everything from the start."

Rébecca recounts her near-miss arranged marriage, how she ran away with her friends' help, Laura's especially. The two strange encounters in New York: first Laura's father, then Dov, her would-be fiancé. About her new life at college, where she's funding her studies by giving French lessons. The life she'd dreamed of were it not for the death of her friend and the fact she had left her family behind. Rachel listens to her story until the end, then asks her to return to

Laura's reaction when she saw her father kissing the young female stranger at Grand Central.

"She went into a state of shock, then got really angry. She told me about the violence, the hatred her parents inspired in her, talking in a way I'd never heard before. She said how she had left home the day of her eighteenth birthday. Her father was on a trip to the Jehovah's Witness headquarters in Brooklyn. Birthdays were never celebrated in the organization; they think such practices are the Devil's work. Laura had waited patiently for that day to reject the absurd restrictions she'd grown up with. She baked herself a nice round chocolate cake with shiny icing, and the words 'Happy Birthday Laura' written in italics. When her mother came back from the Kingdom Hall, she found the table laid for two and the cake topped with eighteen lit candles, and champagne with two flutes. Laura smiled at her from her seat and blew out the candles. Before she'd even taken her next breath, Mathilde Vignola came hurtling and screaming toward the table, grabbed the knife, lifted her arm, and brought it down with all her strength. Laura managed to dodge the attack and got away with a graze to the arm. Completely drained, her mother collapsed onto the sofa, still gripping the kitchen knife. Laura called an ambulance, went with her mother to the psychiatric hospital, filed a report with the police but didn't press charges, happy instead just to leave for Paris without giving an address. When she saw her father kissing that woman, everything came flooding back to the surface, and she decided to get it all out the next time she went to Niort. She wanted to tell her mother everything so that they'd split up. To make them suffer, basically. But obviously not everything panned out as she intended. The last time we spoke on the telephone, two days before she died, she just said: 'The crazy old bitch didn't want to hear any of it. I'm never going back!'"

Rébecca breaks down in tears, eight hours away in the distance. Over there where night has now fallen. Rachel checks her watch. Time to wrap up the conversation.

"Rébecca, thank you so, so much. I'm sorry for making you relive all that."

"No, Rachel, thank *you.*"

The buzzer goes. It's Jean and the brothers. The next phase is starting.

41

Rue Eugène-Jumin. Benamer and Enkell are on autopilot. A couple of telephone calls to pin down their next two victims, both of them at their place of work. Heads or tails? Heads says it's Sam. The street is deserted. The door to the salon is half-open—trusting as ever. The barber is sitting in the Skaï chair used by his clients, smoking one of his cigarillos, facing the mirror in which he sees the two policemen make their entrance.

"You didn't hang around . . ."

Benamer cannot get over the man's stupidity, his blind faith. The same kind their friend the *brocanteur* showed the Meyer brothers. He wants to wipe that smug smile right off Sam's face, that misplaced calm assurance.

"Yes, and as we're tired, we'll do it quickly. Don't worry: we won't make you suffer."

Sam's hand twitches toward the drawer in search of some potential means of defending himself.

"Don't move. Don't turn around. Keep your beak shut. I'll do it very neatly, here in the back of your neck. You won't feel a thing. And I will take comfort from the fact that I am liberating this arrondissement of your inane prattling. It'll feel like I've given something back to society. For as long as I've had to put up with your endless, self-satisfied bullshit, I've promised myself that when I get around to bumping you off, I'd make you a little speech. Just to let you know how much you've pissed me off. Just to let you know that whenever I thought I couldn't bear you any longer, I found a way to tolerate you, to listen to you, to pretend that I found you intelligent—and that was by imagining all the different ways I might kill you. And in the end, it was the last time, at that couscous restaurant, that I thought up this wonderfully simple death—the one you're now due. A bullet in the back of the neck. Just . . . a bullet . . . in the back . . . of the neck. See how fucking tedious it is to have to sit through a spiel that you really, really don't want to hear? Right, I'm done—even I'm getting bored now. I can't even be bothered to tell you how we're going to do Haqiqi once we're finished here."

Enkell is at the entrance, motionless, his Glock leveled at the barber while Benamer screws the silencer onto his Beretta. Pinned to his seat and with fat beads of sweat running down his face, Sam is reeling off a string of incomprehensible words in a low voice. Silencer attached, the *commissaire adjoint* approaches, cocking an ear.

"Goodness me, you're praying—so you really are religious after all."

He lifts the barrel to the back of Sam's neck at a forty-five degree angle. Standing still, he takes a second to listen to the words spouting from the barber's mouth.

Chma, Israel, Adonai Elo-henou, Ado-nai Ehad' Baroukh chem kevod malkouto le'olam vaed

Pop.

Benamer takes off the silencer pensively and turns toward Enkell.

"You find out what a man is like just before he meets his end . . . As it turns out, Sam was a true believer. I'd never have thought it."

"Okay, shall we?"

* * *

It's even quicker with Haqiqi. Benamer has no intention of making even the shortest of speeches. Just wants to finish him off.
Unlike with Sam, the imam realizes right away why the policemen
are there. He barely has time to fill his lungs with air to scream
before he finds himself gripped by the hair and dragged backward,
his throat uncovered and immediately slit by Benamer's Laguiole.
From the door, Enkell draws the service to a close.

"Right then, let's get some sleep. Our business meeting at Charles
de Gaulle is in less than five hours."

42

Rachel's studio apartment has never been so packed. Jean, Bintou, Aïcha, Ruben, Mourad, and Alpha. The boys have relayed
their account of the evening at Sam's to the two lieutenants. They'll
have to do it again at the police station, and once again for the *juge
d'instruction*. Luckily Jean came in a police car. He'll take the boys to
the Bunker, with Rachel following on her scooter. She takes out ten
dollars to pay for a taxi for the girls. Aïcha thinks about refusing, but
tucks the bill into the bag slung around her shoulder. They're about
to set off when Ruben clears his throat.

"There's one more thing I've got to tell you. Or show you, more
like."

He opens his hand and presents the two detectives with a pill, a
beautiful sky-blue in color.

"I've no idea how or why, but I really think this is why Laura was killed."

Jean grabs hold of the pill.

"What is it? Some type of ecstasy?"

"You could say that, but it's super-powerful. A new type of drug. When you take one you feel like you're God Himself."

"And where's it from, this pill? Did you buy it? Are you selling them?"

"Two months ago, Rabbi Seror assigned me a mission: to go to Niort with a few other Hasids to pick up a load of tefillin, Torah scrolls, and mezuzoth blessed by the rebbe in Brooklyn."

Rachel jumps with surprise.

"Niort? Are you sure?"

"Yeah—you couldn't make a place like that up. It did seem strange, but you know, I didn't question the rabbi's instructions. Then when we got to the house where we were meant to pick up the stuff, there was this weird guy there. About sixty, I'd say. Really nervous. Quite blunt, but a good-looking man. I don't know, it felt like something was up. He showed us the boxes that needed shifting. There were others nearby, one of them was open—I could see it contained piles of *Watchtower*, the Jehovah's Witness magazine. I didn't say anything. He just told us which boxes needed to be loaded in the back of the van and which needed to go by the door. When we stopped for a break on the motorway, I was left alone for a while. I opened one of the boxes nearest the back of the van, rummaged around inside and pulled out a plastic bag full of these pills. Since then we've done three more loads. The last batch is in a kosher goods warehouse not far from here, near porte de la Villette. I can take you there."

Jean and Rachel are dumbfounded. All of a sudden Laura's murder seems charged with a totally different meaning. They need to get to the police station as fast as they can, take down the statements, inform Mercator and arrange for a raid on the warehouse.

43

Mohamed and Ahmed have done a lot of talking and a lot of smoking. And now they're studying the Glock. This all came about in peculiarly simple fashion. On his way home from meeting Rachel and Jean at MK2 on the quai de Seine, Ahmed took a detour via Monsieur Paul's. He asked Ahmed how everything had gone since the morning. After hearing the bit about his trip to Sam's, the old bookseller had paused for a while, a worried expression on his face. Then he had dug around in the bottom drawer of his desk and brought out the revolver.

"Take it—might come in handy."

"Hang on, what are you doing with one of those?"

"Oh, I've got a customer to thank for it, a Serb. He left it for me as a deposit. Needn't have bothered: a week later, he got himself shot by another Serb. Some sorry business from over there that caught up with him over here. Anyway, I decided to keep it, telling myself that this gun owed someone a life. And you're the only person I know who needs protection."

"But I don't want to use it, plus I've never fired a gun in my life."

"Of course, and I wouldn't want to push you to do so. I'm not sure why, but I just don't like the thought of you being unarmed against Sam, Moktar, and Co. Take it! It'll sound strange to you coming from an old anarchist like me, but it's got a mystical quality. This weapon . . . I'm not sure how to phrase it . . . It'll do what's required."

Ahmed arrived back at his apartment—armed with the Glock, some cheese ravioli from Franprix, and a new cell phone from the SFR shop—to find Mohamed out for the count on the carpet. He lay down himself and nodded off in a matter of seconds.

When he woke up, his cousin was standing on the balcony, smoking beneath the stars. At 11:00 p.m., Ahmed had—as agreed—called Rachel without really thinking about what he was going to say, and left his cell number on the voicemail belonging to the policewoman of his dreams.

In the dead of night, the two cousins contemplate the Glock and the future. Mohamed had spoken at length, and confided a straightforward secret in Ahmed: he didn't want to go ahead with the marriage arranged by his mother because girls didn't really do it for him. Simple as that. He had confessed to Ahmed that he'd known his uncle's secret for years, and that he had no desire to live a lie in a sham marriage. His mother knew, no doubt about it. She knew her son, but she didn't give a shit at all, as long as he agreed to play the game, to have children. Up to a point, Mohamed could see where she was coming from, but what he couldn't bear was the fact that in the process she had no qualms whatsoever about bringing misery to an innocent young girl he would never love or truly satisfy. The cruelty of it disgusted him. All for status, honor, family, for the continuation of who knows what anyway . . . *Fuck!*

His cousin seemed like a different person to Ahmed. And it delighted him. He never thought he could feel so close to a fake cousin from the *bled*. It reconnected him with that unknown part of himself, with that land of his forebears who maybe weren't as far away as he'd imagined after all. Fate, with all its twists and turns, had just handed him the brother he had so longed for.

4:00 a.m. He can't sleep. The heat is drawing him to the street. Ahmed drags his cousin, his brother, his kin outside for a midnight stroll. He hesitates about taking the gun. Then decides *why not!* But where will he put it? It's so heavy . . . Mohamed is carrying a canvas bag slung over his shoulder. He knows how to shoot; he learned when he was younger from an army officer uncle who'd fought at Amgalla. He takes charge of the weapon. The two young men exit the building, breathe in the summer air and its promise of good fortune.

All quiet on rue Petit. They turn down rue Eugène-Jumin. Ahmed feels carefree, protected by the weapon in Mohamed-the-marksman's bag. The barber shop sign can be seen twenty yards away. He's no longer scared of evil Sam, not now. Something suddenly catches his attention: the door to the prayer room is slightly ajar. Complete darkness, thick with silence. He motions to his cousin to be quiet and keep watch. Mohamed slides his hand into the bag, cocks the pistol, puts his finger on the trigger, and nods at Ahmed, who pushes the prayer-room door open with his elbow and enters the total darkness within. He uses his cell to light up the room: carpet; prayer mats rolled up at the sides; empty shoe lockers, with the exception of one pair of Reeboks. A disquieting detail—an open Koran, the pages creased. The cell goes out so Ahmed presses the button again, shining it on the area around the holy book. A hand, a leg, a throat. Gaping open. A well-groomed beard. Haqiqi. He retreats, letting the door close quietly on itself. He takes a deep breath and, seized by a sudden impulse, marches his cousin, gun still raised, three doors further down. Another door slightly ajar. No point going in—he knows what he'll find. A smile for Monsieur Paul, whose Glock has given him the courage to face the dead.

What about the living?

Back up to the apartment, treading lightly on the steps. Sitting at the table, an empty plate with traces of olive oil and pepper in front of them, Ahmed studies his telephone, hesitates a few seconds, then hits the green button. Rachel answers before he's even had time to say "Hello." This means that she hadn't been able to call him back but had gone to the trouble of saving his number in her list of contacts. This simple fact fills him with joy.

"Ahmed? I couldn't pick up earlier, but that's not why you're calling me so late, is it?"

"No. What does the word 'confidence' mean to you?"

"What do you mean?"

"If I tell you something now and ask you not to repeat it to any-one, does that mean anything? Or does your duty as a policewoman come first?"

"What is this 'something'?"

"Something useful for you, for all of us, for Laura . . ."

"I can confirm that this conversation won't go any further."

"Go to rue Eugène-Jumin. The prayer room and the barber shop. Destinies have been rudely interrupted there. As for me, I've been at home with my cousin all evening. If you want to come by for some tea . . . You never know . . . Fine if it's seven in the morning or five in the afternoon."

44

Rachel hangs up. 5:15 a.m. She rereads Mourad's statement while a few yards away Jean is questioning Ruben, and Kevin has just fin-ished with Alpha. She gestures to her partner, who takes a few sec-onds out from his questioning to come over and join her.

"Taroudant just called me. He told me to go to rue Eugène-Jumin, to the prayer room and the barber shop. 'Destinies have been rudely interrupted there': those were his words."

"And you're thinking of going alone?"

"No, I'm taking Kevin with me."

"Kevin . . ."

"Yes, Kevin. He's done with Alpha, and besides, you have to orga-nize the raid on the warehouse after Ruben's statement."

"That can wait. I'm coming with you. I'm not letting you risk your neck like this!"

"Hey listen, I'm a police officer just like you, aren't I? Badly paid to risk my neck, same as you. It's my lead so I'm going, I'll take a look and secure the area. You and Mercator can make sure you get a warrant as quickly as possible to search the warehouse, and I'll meet you there as soon as I can."

Rachel feels driven by something greater than her, something that makes her a bit harder with her colleague than she might have wanted. She appeases Jean by planting a little kiss on his right cheek.

An hour and a half later, rue Eugène-Jumin is crawling with police. Two murders twenty yards away from each other with the same MO. . . . That means a lot of people are getting involved. Fingerprints, photos, samples, witness reports. Haqiqi and Sam: big names in the neighborhood. Nobody saw a thing. The rotund figure of Mercator is leaning against a wall. He is chewing pensively on the end of a Café Crème cigarillo. Rachel spots him and heads over.

"So, Rachel—what have you found out?"

"Sam: a bullet to the back of the neck at point blank. Haqiqi: throat slit by a pro. Extremely sharp blade; clean incision. Two executions . . . We absolutely must bring in Moktar and Rabbi Seror—they could be next on the list."

"And Meyer? Where is Meyer? Have you seen him the last few hours?"

"Meyer . . . I almost forgot—he intercepted a telephone call that was meant for me and then disappeared, so far as I'm aware . . ."

"So, in fact, no one has seen him since five o'clock yesterday, and he's not answering his cell phone. Seems odd, does it not? Did you know he had a brother?"

No response from Rachel.

"And that the photofit of the strange, disturbing character of which our young friends speak looks particularly like him?"

Again, no response.

"Do as you think best, Rachel. Jean is en route with arrest warrants for Moktar and Seror. He'll take care of that with Kevin while you try to manage the circus here. When you're finished, leave four officers here to guard the crime scenes and let Forensics do their thing. The rest can regroup at the level of the Zénith at the end of boulevard MacDonald. We will not begin the raid until my signal. However long that might take. Right, I'm off—I've got things to do."

Jean has appeared alongside Rachel. He's about to say something, but she holds up her hand to stop him. Mercator rolls away from the wall, flicks his cigarillo into the gutter, and takes three steps before turning around.

"Evil, you know—evil. Do not forget that this is what we are dealing with. Though its faces are many, it is unique."

Jean needs to talk to Rachel and update her on the investigating magistrate. He wants to tell her that he's taken it upon himself to find the three boys a lawyer, and so they ought to get released on bail. Always better if you can turn up free in court. And always better if you don't have to go to prison, especially when you're twenty-five and you've got a pert ass. Rachel processes all the information.

"Right, okay, no problem. Now go and deal with Moktar and Seror. Take Kevin—go on, fast as you can! I'll hold the fort here."

45

Roissy-Charles de Gaulle Airport, Terminal 1.

The Barnes twins didn't check in any luggage at Newark. Just a shoulder bag for James and a regulation-sized wheelie case for Susan. As they come through the automatic glass doors, Susan's cell vibrates in the inside pocket of her coat.

"Yes."

"Hello, Susan, welcome to Paris."

"Hello, Aïssa. You're calling right on time."

"I know. Let's meet in the parking lot. Bay number B 254."

Three minutes later and the introductions are being made. Frédéric Enkell, Aïssa Benamer, James and Susan Barnes. The Parisian policemen are tired, on edge, their clothes crumpled. The American twins immediately realize that something's not right, but they don't let on at all. During the journey into Paris, most of the conversation is between Enkell and James in French. The *commissaire* is acting tough, sticking to the facts—businesslike. He makes it seem as though the cleanup went according to plan. As though Raymond Meyer, for example, were not still at large. Most of all he keeps mum about his plan to take down the twins as soon as Vignola is out of the picture.

"So, there is just one small obstacle to negotiate before we restart our operations in Belgium."

"Yes, Vignola. We're on the case. If I understand correctly from what you told me this morning before we left New York, you have already taken care of the . . . nuisances who witnessed the unfortunate accident that befell his darling daughter?"

"You understand correctly."

"Perfect. So we'll deal with Vignola. You have to realize that he's one of us. This is, in a manner of speaking, an internal affair."

"Yes, I understand entirely, but you don't know the terrain. You're not from around here, and easy to identify. Leave it to us. He's meant to be coming to the hotel this afternoon, is he not?"

"Yes, at 3:00."

"Fine, we'll pick him up before he's even made it to reception. I'll call as soon as it's done, and you can get on the first Thalys train to Antwerp. How does that sound?"

"I'm sorry but I really must insist. My sister is particularly intent to settle this as a family matter. It is, after all, thanks to her that we are all engaged in this joint enterprise that seems destined for a bright future. You could say that she has gone to every effort to ensure its success. And as regards the specific person in question, Susan has even—if I may be so bold as to suggest—put her body on the line. So she has decided to allow herself one final pleasure with the . . . obstacle that you mention. A particularly intricate, theatrical scene, though nothing quite like the savagery his daughter was subjected to; something a little more subtle, as you'll see."

Enkell's face hardens when James Barnes utters the word "savagery." He attempts to pass it off as concentration on his driving as he switches lanes to come off the *périphérique*. After a few hundred yards, he turns left onto avenue de la Porte des Ternes, where he parks just opposite the Notre-Dame-de-la-Compassion church.

"We'll think about your proposal and talk over the phone at midday. We're a stone's throw from the Concorde Lafayette—you can see it from here. Straight ahead, first right. Are you happy to do the last two hundred yards on foot? Safer that way."

"No problem."

"See you later, then."

"See you later."

The Barnes twins get out of the car and slam the doors shut. James turns back to the open window on the *commissaire*'s side.

"Oh, by the way, Monsieur Enkell . . ."

"Yes?"

"No offense, but it's not a 'proposal'. And there's no need to worry—we won't be identified."

Enkell hesitates two seconds too long: the Barnes twins are already marching toward their hotel at a steady pace.

Sitting next to him, Benamer hasn't said a word since leaving Charles de Gaulle. He hands a piece of paper to his superior.

"I made a list to ensure we don't forget anyone. If we're agreed, we can memorize it, destroy it, and get to work."

Done:
  Francis Meyer
  Sam Aboulafia
  Abdelhaq Haqiqi

To do:
  Vincenzo Vignola
  Raymond Meyer
  Mourad Bentaleb
  Alpha Aïdarra
  Moktar Touré
  Ruben Aboulafia
  Haïm Seror
  James and Susan Barnes

Enkell reads it, stays quiet for a moment, then turns to his right-hand man with an air of incredulity. He comes back to the piece of paper and counts:

"One, two, three, four, five, six, seven, eight, nine. With the three we've already done that's a total of twelve. Throw in the *brocanteur* and we've got thirteen. With Laura we're up to fourteen. Do you really think we can bump off fourteen people—eleven of whom live within a one-mile radius—without anyone noticing? What's wrong with you, Aïssa? Did you lose your mind when things went to hell with Raymond? Is that it?"

Benamer has gone mute. The police officer—usually so sure of himself, so domineering—is like a little boy who's been caught peeing his pants by the schoolteacher. Enkell slaps him with the back of his left hand. He needs him: right here, right now. He needs his second-in-command by his side, not some mindless killer.

"Wake up, Aïssa! We'll let the Barneses get on with their twisted crime. Suits us fine if they want to do our job for us. And you know what? Let's hang them out to dry afterward. We're reaching the tipping point, the moment where enough is enough. We reached it yesterday, in fact, when Raymond escaped. It was a sign, and we need to wise up and read it. From now on, we hold fire. They won't find Raymond Meyer, and he'll leave us in peace, I'm sure of it. He has no interest whatsoever in risking another showdown. As for Haqiqi and Sam, they'll be racking their brains to find anything that links them, apart from the fact they live on the same street . . . But it'll never come back to us, because no one else knows that we were in contact with them. No one, do you hear me! Not Moktar, not Ruben, not Mourad, not Alpha! Not even Rabbi Seror! Do you hear me, Aïssa! And you know the funniest thing of all? Young Laura . . . If we hadn't smoked her then none of this would have happened! Nothing at all. She had no idea about the drug ring her father was involved in. She posed no threat whatsoever. We acted on reflex, without thinking. We set off this shit like that, with a click of the fingers, drunk on our own power, on our impunity. So that will do for now! Let's think before we act. It's not our role in life to be angels of death."

"What is it, then?"

Benamer looks his chief in the eyes. A strange light flickers in the depths of his pupils. He fires. With the silencer on, the bullet makes only a measly little pop. Overbearingly simple. The traffic continues alongside the Scenic. No one notices as Benamer struggles to haul Enkell from the driver's seat to the passenger's. The *commissaire adjoint* gets in, starts the car, lets out a cryptic sigh, and slides into first gear. If he takes the *périphérique*, the warehouse on boulevard MacDonald is only a ten-minute drive. Should still be some space in the vat.

46

Mercator and Van Holden are sitting on folding chairs, waiting. The first short and round, threatening and easygoing in equal measure; the other large and red-headed, a touch of the geeky scientist about him. In front of them, the dark, motionless mass of the vat can just be made out. They are pleased with this unraveling of time and their growing certitude of being able to crack the case. Why are they so sure of themselves? How do they know that their prey is ripe for the taking? For the same reasons that they are as senior as they are, even if their ascent has happened without the protection, or even the kindness, of anyone in the police hierarchy. Is it three hours, ten minutes, three days they've been here? They couldn't say. For ammunition, they've brought M&M's, marshmallows, ice tea, and a pair of nine-millimeter automatic pistols. Enough to keep them going a lifetime.

After leaving the crime scene, Mercator went to parc des Buttes-Chaumont, stopping by the little breakfast joint where Van Holden can be found every morning having a coffee and *tartine* before taking his seat behind the director's desk at the IGPN. All Mercator said was that he had a meeting with Enkell and Benamer, and that it would be nice if he came along. So off they then went aboard the no. 75 bus, getting off at boulevard MacDonald. Van Holden had found the address by complete chance two months earlier. Ever since he'd started sifting through administrative documents in the course of his long inquiry into the corrupt policemen of the eighteenth, he'd worked out how to spot a nugget. As was the case here: the simple sale, well below market price, of a warehouse belonging to a butcher on rue du Mont-Cenis who had bizarrely been cleared in a scandal

involving the sale of out-of-date meat after the only witness suddenly withdrew his testimony. The buyer was one Ezzedine Moussa,
a resident of Saint-Chamond. It turned out that he was an old school
pal of Aïssa Benamer's, and had gone on to have a few brushes with
the law . . . Van Holden had mentioned his discovery to Mercator
by the by, and his memory had been jogged when reading Ruben
Aboulafia's statement. The warehouse allegedly belonging to Ezzedine Moussa was next door to Kosher Facilities, the very one where
Ruben had claimed he'd dropped off his consignment of magic pills.
The lock opened easily enough with a master key, and two folding
chairs—chance or destiny?—appeared to be waiting for them, carefully propped up against the wall at the far end. All that was left for
the two comrades was to sit down, their standard-issue Manurhin
revolvers on their knees, and the M&M's, marshmallows, and ice tea
within easy reach.

A key turns in the lock. The door opens. Heavy breathing strained
with effort. A strange noise that is part metallic, part pneumatic.
Benamer is so occupied with hauling his trolley that he doesn't
notice them. It's harder by yourself: the body flops from side to side,
left and right. Then he hears one click, two clicks. His eyes aren't
yet adjusted to the darkness; it takes him a few seconds to identify
his colleagues. An absurd, belated reflex takes over and he lets go
of the trolley, which collapses with a crash, as he moves to grab his
Beretta.

"Wouldn't do that if I were you, Aïssa."

And indeed Benamer does not do that. He feels tired, suddenly,
very tired. He puts up no resistance as they cuff him. In actual fact,
he feels relieved.

From then on it's all go. The end of any investigation is a process of precipitation—in the chemical sense—where all, or nearly
all, of the threads untangle. Kupferstein, Hamelot, Gomes, and half
the arrondissement's uniformed officers arrive at the scene no more
than two minutes after Mercator's call. The Godzwill pills are found
without much trouble, stashed unsubtly inside a fake casing installed

within the foot of the acid vat. The search of the Kosher Facilities unit carried out as a security measure brings up nothing. Back at the Bunker, Aïssa Benamer starts talking immediately, like a sink that has had its plug pulled out. Without any delay, arrest warrants are issued to apprehend the Barnes twins and Raymond Meyer.

The handcuffs are slipped onto Rabbi Seror right at the moment when he is putting on his tefillin for morning prayer. Barely had the Hasid taken his seat in the interrogation room when he—not needing to be asked twice—began providing very detailed information on Rebbe Toledano's Brooklyn organization. First and foremost he reveals the identity of Dov, Rébecca's ex-fiancé, the virtuoso chemist without whom this adventure would never have taken place. Moktar's interrogation is considerably more hazardous. Getting a psychotic to talk is never easy, and this one is a particularly tough nut to crack. Through a mixture of patience and tenacity, Rachel and Jean are just able to make him recount how he and Raymond Meyer, having been denied the support of Mourad, Ruben, and Alpha, had waited for Laura on the landing outside her apartment as she came home from her Los Angeles–Paris flight. Threatening her with a knife, Raymond ordered her to keep quiet and open the door. Then he gagged her and tied her up. Meyer had suggested Moktar take a Godzwill with him. After that, the paranoid beatmaker-cum-Salafist can't remember a thing. Not that that changes much anyway: his psychiatric evaluation will deem that he was not responsible and he'll go back to the hospital for a very, very long time, whatever the role he played in Laura Vignola's drawn-out agony. As for Raymond Meyer, he's nowhere to be found. Same for Vignola, one of the accessories to the murder along with Enkell, Benamer, and the Barnes twins.

Mercator contemplates the blank sheet of paper, his Sheaffer hanging in the air. A moment's hesitation, then he shakes his head with a soft smile, lays down the pen and motions to the three lieutenants to come in. Kupferstein, Hamelot, and Gomes walk up to the desk, preferring to stay standing since their chief is not sitting down. Mercator starts speaking.

"So, this case is over."

Gomes reacts with surprise.

"Over? But Vignola and Raymond Meyer are still at large. And the Barnes twins, and . . ."

"And the Hasids in Brooklyn. I know. We won't catch any of them. Not for the moment, at least. We will, of course, do everything in our power to do so. Release descriptions, international warrants, notify Interpol . . . all that jazz. We'll find one of them, sure: Vignola. My guess is that his body will appear not far from where we are now either tomorrow or the next day. He might even be engaged in killing himself as we speak, but who knows where? The Barneses will vanish into thin air; so will the chemist in Brooklyn. As for Rebbe Toledano's Hasids, we'll never be able to prove anything."

Hamelot and Kupferstein are wearing wry smiles. Gomes looks furious. Mercator continues.

"The evil in all this, Gomes—the evil it was our job to vanquish— was Frédéric Enkell, Aïssa Benamer, and Francis Meyer. They walked among us, you understand? They were the rot, the antithesis of what we ought to be. As for the rest, we have done what we can, which is already not bad. But there's no such thing as absolute victory. There is no end to this fight. It has been going on since time immemorial, and it will continue to go on forever."

He laughs.

"Right! Time for a drink. We've deserved it. Fifteen-year-old Lagavulin. After that, you ought to go away for a few days, Hamelot and Kupferstein. You won't be any use to me if you don't."

47

The Barnes twins, of course, never set foot in the Concorde Lafayette. After Vignola's phone call the day before, just as they were leaving New York, they had changed their plans and booked a room at a small hotel in Saint-Ouen under the name Arthur and Melissa Kacynski, a young couple from Brisbane, Australia. In a public toilet in porte Maillot, they had switched outfits. A ginger wig for Susan; fake Trotsky-style beard and tortoiseshell glasses for James. After taking out Vignola, they'll only need to change their appearance and identity one more time before boarding a night train to Madrid and from there a flight to Guatemala, then across the border to Belize where they're supposed to meet up with Dov. Right now, however, they are in their room at Hôtel d'Aquitaine, busily preparing the details of the crime scene that Susan is so determined to devise. Nothing fundamentally all that original. Just a classic bondage session gone wrong. Her wheelie suitcase is packed: latex costume, handcuffs, whip, mask, gag.

From the moment Susan lets Vignola through the door of room no. 202 at 3:00 p.m. sharp, he is enchanted by what appears before him. The woman who has taken control of his fate is dressed from head to toe in dominatrix gear, an extremely beautiful Venetian mask covering her eyes. The shutters are closed, a dimmed light in the ceiling revealing the scene. A leather strap is dangling midair against the wall at the back.

He already knows everything. It's why he came. To die by her hand. Nothing remotely commonplace: a certain beauty, even. Surprising that it's happening in this room, with its peeling, shabby

wallpaper, in a one-star hotel less than three hundred yards from
marché aux Puces. Once his hands are tied behind his back and the
noose has been placed around his neck, Susan makes her lover swallow a Godzwill pill. Only then does she gag him. She'd read in several
books and on various sites that strangulation heightens the orgasm,
intensifying it. Susan Barnes had always wanted to experience it.
Not herself, but rather via a male, disposable subject. The gag in his
mouth prevents Vincenzo Vignola from articulating the magnitude
of his pleasure achieved by the combination of sex, strangulation,
and the drug. Alas the precaution is necessary, what with the hotel
being poorly soundproofed. But Susan will never forget his eyes.
They look as though they are finally beholding the wonders of the
Kingdom of Jehovah in all its glory.

48

Ahmed and Mohamed have gone to lend Monsieur Paul a hand.
Lifting some crates, bringing others down. The bookseller was
pleased with the way his present had proved itself useful. "Yes, it's
important to know how to confront the dead . . . Sometimes they can
be as formidable as the living." Every five minutes, Ahmed looks at
his cell screen, as if by some chance he'd missed it ringing. Mohamed
and Monsieur Paul catch each other's eye and laugh. Ahmed ignores
them. He's eager to return home and wait for the visit he's expecting.
   When they reach the iron gate to his block of apartments, Ahmed
gets a strange feeling at the back of his neck. He turns around to
discover an enormous, familiar silhouette on the other side of the
road. The embodiment of his fear. The man responsible for five years

of drifting and internal exile. Mohamed realizes right away. He grabs Ahmed's arm as it moves instinctively toward the Glock in his bag.

"Don't be crazy, Ahmed. He's a killer, a murderer. You're a dreamer, a human being."

Raymond Meyer is lost in thought as he looks up at the balcony of Laura's apartment. As if it carried a secret that had until now been beyond his reach. A strange, marvelous thing to which he must bid farewell today. He lowers his head to see two young Arabs staring at him from across the street, one of them almost black and vaguely familiar. They know. They know everything. But they won't do anything because they value their lives. He could cross the road and wipe them out like that, in thirty seconds and six stabs of his knife. The street is full of people. Way too many people. And there's no shortage of police officers in the neighborhood looking for him. It's time to vanish. To go and see if the grass is greener on the other side. So Meyer smiles broadly. He smiles and leans forward. And disappears. Ahmed tells himself that's how it has to be. He did what he could. He'd been there for Laura throughout the inquiry. But he's no superhero; just a man, a dreamer. And evil will continue to exist. The earth will never stop producing Meyers and Lauras. And Ahmeds. And Rachels.

He grabs his telephone with determination and dials the only number he's got.

Four hours later, Rachel is sitting next to him on a Thalys bound for Amsterdam. They still haven't kissed. But for that, there is forever.

Playlist

Pissing in a River Patti Smith

It's Magic Dinah Washington

La femme des uns sous le corps des autres Serge Gainsbourg

Glory Box Portishead

Sidiki Les Ambassadeurs Internationaux

Dil Cheez Bally Sagoo

Religion Public Image Ltd.

Sympathy for the Devil The Rolling Stones

J'ai rencontré l'homme de ma vie Diane Dufresne

Melody Serge Gainsbourg

Ouais ouais Booba

KARIM MISKÉ was born in 1964 in Abidjan to a Mauritanian father and a French mother, and grew up in Paris before leaving to study journalism in Dakar. He now lives in France and is making documentary films on a wide range of subjects including deafness, for which he learned sign language, and the common roots between the Jewish and Islamic religions. *Arab Jazz* is his first novel.

SAM GORDON is a translator of French and Spanish. He has translated a range of short stories; *Arab Jazz* is his first novel-length translation.

About the Type

Typeset in Minion Pro Regular, 11.5/15 pt.

Minion Pro was designed for Adobe Systems by Robert Slimbach in 1990. Inspired by typefaces of the Renaissance, it is both easily readable and extremely functional without compromising its inherent beauty.

Typeset by Scribe Inc., Philadelphia, Pennsylvania.